Bitter Mayhem

Bitter Mayhem

Dakota Destruction Book 1

Millie Copper

Written by Millie Copper

Edited by Ameryn Tucker

Proofread by MDC Proofreading and WMH Cheryl

Cover design by Dauntless Cover Design

Also by Millie Copper

The Havoc in Wyoming Series

When a series of coordinated attacks devastate the United States, the people of Bakerville, Wyoming, must come together to survive. Unfortunately, not everyone has the town's best interest at heart. Some are striving for personal gain during the apocalypse.

The Montana Mayhem Series

A group from Bakerville, Wyoming strikes out on their own while searching for the desires of their heart. Unfortunately, the road will not be easy, and sometimes the heart is hardened and deceitful. When things don't work out as they hoped, will they become stranded in the wilderness? Or will each be able to find their way home?

The Dakota Destruction Series

After a series of coordinated attacks devastate the United States, Katie and Leo sacrifice everything to help their country. But some things aren't as they seem. Is it time to go home and start fresh, or can something good come out of this terrible situation?

Nonfiction Books

Millie has penned seven nonfiction, traditional food focused books, sharing how, with a little creativity, anyone can transition to a real foods diet without overwhelming their food budget. Many of her books also include preparedness and food storage tips.

Find these titles at:
MillieCopper.com

Join My Reader's Club!

Receive a complimentary copy of *Looming Mayhem: A Dakota Destruction Prequel*. As part of my reader's club, you'll be the first to know about new releases and specials. I also share info on books I'm reading, preparedness tips, and more. Please sign up at:

MillieCopper.com/Join

Preface

This story takes place in the beautiful Black Hills of South Dakota. Having visited the Black Hills many times, I've come to love not only the area but the people. In many ways, I'm reminded of my home state of Wyoming. I've included many real locations and landmarks, along with embellishing a few locales and creating fictional towns when necessary to spin this work of fiction.

Chapter 1

Leo puts one hand on my shoulder and the other to his lips in the classic shushing motion. He moves his hand slightly and mouths, "Don't let him see you."

My heart is pounding in my ears. I get ready to take the shot.

Leo shakes his head. "Wait."

After a few seconds, in which time seems to stand still, he gives a single nod, slowly repositions his rifle, and lifts his chin in my direction.

I swallow hard and shift my body as I raise the compound bow. We'd agreed the silent bow was the best choice, allowing us to take out our first target without alerting the others. Leo will use the rifle only if necessary.

"Katie?" He raises his eyebrows as he mouths my name.

I direct my attention to the arrow, already nocked and in place. We're well hidden in the brush, in a swath of shadow produced by the early morning light. With both knees on the ground, I sit back on my heels, making a solid platform at a ninety-degree angle from my target. I lick my lips and resist the urge to clear my throat—a nervous habit.

I twist my torso and draw my bow to reach my nock point, then drop my shoulders slightly. I settle my breathing and focus on my mark.

Leo shifts next to me, his rifle at the ready.

I take in a partial breath, holding it before I let the arrow fly.

I fight the urge to close my eyes, to not watch where the arrow hits—to not watch if the hit is true and life-ending. The arrow covers the distance in the time my thoughts can form. He lifts his neck, then rears back and takes two steps forward before collapsing.

"Bingo," Leo says under his breath.

Out of habit, I pull a second arrow from the quiver and make it ready. I give the bow a slight rub, silently thanking my mom for bequeathing it to me.

"Let's hang tight a minute. Make sure he stays down and see if he has any friends." Leo's voice is low, barely audible.

I lean toward my husband. "Won't his body spook them and be a dead giveaway?"

Leo contorts his face at my unintended pun. His mustache wiggles as he fights to hold back a chuckle.

"You know what I mean."

He drops his hand onto my leg, leans close, and whispers, "You did good, Katie."

A thrill runs through me as his breath tickles my ear. My heart does a crazy little flip as I turn to face him. He drops a solid kiss on my mouth. Even after more than a year of marriage, his kisses still make me tingle. He pulls back and gives me a smile.

Our wedding wasn't what I'd imagined it would be. Though still lovely, we shared our day with two other couples. A triple outdoor wedding at my parents' homestead. With supplies finite, everything is shared—even weddings.

After a few minutes, I look at Leo. "Now?"

He bobs his head. We slowly move from our hidden blind.

Leo motions me to leave the bow and have my pistol ready. He slings his rifle and pulls out his handgun.

We move silently and stop within ten feet of the three-point buck. I bite my lip. As part of the hunting crew, we've done the job we were assigned.

"Perfect shot." Leo gives me a smile. "I'll start the field dressing if you want to retrieve the horses. You think you can?" His green eyes travel to my face.

"Sure. I like the horses. Unlike someone I know." I bump my hip lightly into him.

"Well, at least they listen to you. I'm pretty sure they hate me." He glances back at the deer. "Um, first, shall we give thanks?"

I blink my watery eyes. We may have done our job, helping to provide food for the Guard District, but it's still hard to take a life. I holster my pistol. Leo does the same before reaching for my hands.

"Heavenly Father, we thank you for this bounty. May this deer provide nourishment to many people helping us through these dark times. We pray these things in the name of Your Son, Jesus. Amen."

Dark times.

That's a bit of an understatement. It's been almost fifteen months since the planes were shot out of the sky, beginning the downward spiral and leaving us where we are now—living in an apocalyptic world. While the plane crashes and events in the days that followed weakened us, the nukes changed everything.

The east and west coasts of the United States were essentially destroyed. The middle of the country was spared the ground detonations and subsequent radioactive fallout. Instead, we were hit with a high-altitude nuclear weapon, resulting in an electromagnetic pulse. An EMP.

When the lights went out, we were already in Bakerville at my mom and stepdad's homestead, a place they'd set up specifically in case we ever needed a refuge. At the edge of the wilderness, well away from the big cities and crowds, it seemed like the perfect hideaway. And it was . . . to a point.

Even with their planning and provisions, they couldn't keep us all safe. Keep us all alive. The all too familiar sensation of grief washes over me like the open wound it is.

"This should help with our efforts." When Leo takes in my face, his smile falters. "Katie?"

I wave a hand. "Nothing. Just . . . memories." I lift a shoulder.

He puts a hand on my face. "I understand."

I turn my head slightly and kiss his palm. I let out a breath before pulling away. "You were saying?"

"This is good. You've done well. It's exactly what we need to help prove our worth. We'll get him back in time to do an evening hunt too. No one will be able to say we aren't pulling our weight."

I respond with a slight smile. "I wish I could tell Jake about this. Let him know how the time he spent training me paid off. Let him know how well Mom's bow worked." I drop another kiss on Leo. "I'll be right back with the horses."

My stepdad, Jake, taught me archery last winter. He was training my brothers and nephew, and I'd join them if my work schedule allowed. At first, I was pretty terrible and barely hit the target. Eventually, my arrows stopped having a mind of their own and went where I sent them. I've aimed at many targets before, but today was the first time I'd taken an animal with my bow.

When Leo and I enlisted with the United Volunteers—a federally supported alternative military group tasked with the country's reconstruction efforts—our archery skills were something to be proud of. Bringing my inherited compound bow and quiver of arrows was also appreciated. Our country is trying to get back on its feet, but industry is still lacking, and provisions are in short supply with ammunition being no exception.

Joining the United Volunteers, commonly referred to as the Volunteer Unit or just the Volunteers, wasn't an easy decision for me.

Leo had originally believed he'd be able to return to the Marines since he'd served with them straight out of high school. But when we fled our home in Manhattan, Kansas, in the early days of the attacks, he didn't think to take his discharge documents out of his safe deposit box. Without the proof of previous enlistment, the Marines wouldn't take him. Neither would the Army.

When he said the Volunteers would be happy to take both of us, I agreed. It's only a one-year commitment, and I needed to get away. To leave Bakerville and the constant reminders of my mom. And specifically, how I failed her.

Our assignment is in Rapid City, with South Dakota's Camp Rapid National Guard—well, not Camp Rapid itself, but the Guard District hospital a few blocks away. For now, at least.

When we return from this hunting trip, there's a good chance we'll be sent packing, forced to find a new Volunteer Unit to finish out our commitment.

Eight weeks ago, when we arrived in the Black Hills, the Volunteers were welcomed with open arms. Things were good.

Leo's a medic, working in the hospital and occasionally on patrol with the National Guard or even with the sheriff's department.

I'm a nurse. At least, most people refer to me as a nurse. I don't have any formal training, not like the rest of the nursing staff who went to school. Before everything fell apart, I was getting ready for my senior year of college, majoring in graphic design and art.

Art!

Not medicine. I'd had a few first aid classes and read some of Leo's books when he was studying to become an EMT.

Somehow, when my older sister was shot last summer in the early days of the trouble, I was recruited to join the medical team in Bakerville, Wyoming. I had little book knowledge and zero practical experience. Since then, I've treated many people. Sickness, disease, gunshots, injuries from a bear mauling—you name it.

Not long before we'd arrived, there was a major attack on the nearby town of Black Canyon, resulting in the death of many residents after a fire was deliberately set. When people tried to put it out—people who had fought hard to survive the harsh winter and food shortage—they were assassinated by hidden snipers. The attackers faded into the night, likely moving on to another unsuspecting town, to take what they could and leave death and destruction in their wake.

Our Volunteer Unit was sent here to help prevent those things from happening again. Even though our country isn't officially under martial law—as far as we know, at least—the Army, Marines, Air Force, Navy, and even Coast Guard are acting in a law enforcement capacity with help from the newly formed Volunteer Unit.

This is often alongside the local sheriff or police, but in many cases, the military is it. The local law enforcement is either dead or incapacitated in some way, and the military has stepped in.

This seemed to be the case in South Dakota too. The Volunteer Units are helping to restore order. The town of Rapid City, formerly known as the Gateway to Mount Rushmore and a bustling city of seventy-five thousand, divided the town into districts to help aid in the rebuilding of the nearly destroyed small city.

Each district has a hospital or medical center, along with their own system for providing food and supplies to the people in the district. Specific ration chips and tokens have been adopted for each district. While the original Rapid City residents were hit hard, with a death rate of well over 50 percent, news of the successful reconstruction has spread, bringing in refugees from nearby who are looking for a better way of life.

Ten days ago, there was an incident in the Downtown District. Something happened in the line of people waiting to pick up ration chips. A Volunteer Unit out of Montana was stationed there, tasked with making sure people behaved themselves while collecting weekly rations.

Someone overreacted, and a shootout occurred. Six civilians and two Volunteers were dead when it was over. The Volunteer responsible—a kid really, only eighteen—felt so bad about it that he took his own life.

What exactly happened changes depending on who tells the story, but the bottom line is something went wrong and the Volunteers were blamed.

By order of the governor of South Dakota, the Volunteers are no longer welcome in the state. Even nearby Ellsworth Air Force Base—who'd played a prominent role in rebuilding the area, to the point that Rapid City is now known as one of the leaders in the reconstruction efforts of our country—was given specific orders of what they could and could not do.

The governor is taking the Posse Comitatus Act seriously, telling the feds to back off. Ellsworth must still be doing something since we'll occasionally see or hear an airplane or helicopter, but all policing matters are left to city and county departments, along with the South Dakota National Guard.

When things changed in Rapid City, Leo went to Captain Williams, the doctor in charge of our hospital and a longtime officer in the local Guard Unit. Leo's mission was to convince the captain of our worth, that we had skills. Not only with our medical training but much more. Leo, me, and half a dozen others from the United Volunteers asked to be released from the Volunteers and allowed to join the South Dakota National Guard.

Leo's petition worked . . . to a point. When the rest of the Volunteers left the state, eight of us were allowed to stay under the temporary authority of Camp Rapid while they make a decision.

We're currently in limbo as they decide if we're Guard material. In addition to the military deciding, there's also a representative from the sheriff's department, the medical center where we work, the main hospital in the area, and even an agent from the governor's office voting on the matter.

It seems like a whole lot of hoopla to go through. Part of me wishes we'd gone with the rest of the Volunteers. I'm not even completely sure I want to join the National Guard. The Volunteers made sense for us, but Leo said the Guard will require a three-year commitment. Three years away from my family.

I let out a noisy sigh and shake my head. I'm just not sure it's what I want.

Trig and Ryder, the horses we were loaned for this hunting trip, are pretty much where we left them, their front legs hobbled so they can graze along the edge of a meadow. We were hunting here yesterday and knew this would be a great spot to set up this morning. The horses, well trained by a ranch outside of Rapid City, have done exactly what we'd hoped—stayed put and had a snack.

It takes me several minutes to get the horses unhobbled and ready to go. We left the saddles on since we knew we'd only be away from them for a short time, which helps my efforts.

"All right, boys. Let's go. We'll put those saddlebags to use getting the deer back to camp."

Chapter 2

The crisp scent of pine wafts in the cool morning air and tickles my nose. I relax in the saddle, a goofy smile covering my face.

In many ways, being a part of the hunting party makes me feel more needed than my job at the hospital. While Doc Nettie, who's unofficially become my mentor, often tells me I'm an asset, the things old Dr. Newsome says to me are probably more legit. At least Captain Williams seems to think I'm doing an okay job.

It's easier to believe Newsome, to believe I have no business being there. My shoulders slump as the happiness I was feeling slides away. He's probably right. I don't really know what I'm doing. Maybe my knowledge was enough for the makeshift clinic we had at home, but it's definitely lacking for a real hospital.

Being out here, though, in the forest and away from the stress, is something I could get used to. Camping and spending all day with my husband is certainly wonderful. Leo said they'll be sending out hunting parties from now until the snow makes it too difficult.

I give an involuntary shudder. A winter hunting trip left my sister a widow last year. Her husband and father-in-law went out with a group and somehow became separated. They were never found. The snow can be deadly.

I glance over my shoulder, reassuring myself that Leo is right behind me.

He lifts his chin while giving me a broad smile, which instantly fades when his horse pulls its head up slightly.

I snort out a laugh. "Relax. He knows you're uptight."

"Because I am. It doesn't feel natural to be up here, so far off the ground."

In the days leading up to this hunting trip, we were both given what could only be described as a crash course in horsemanship. I'd been on a few trail rides when I was younger, but Leo's a total newbie.

Even after the cars stopped working, when many people took up riding as our fuel supply dwindled, he wasn't one of them. As part of the community's security team, he spent most of his time on foot patrol or sentry duty. When he had to reach faraway duty stations, he rode his mountain bike. But horses . . . nope. Not once.

When they assigned us to come on this hunting trip—as a way to get us out of town while a decision is made about what exactly to do with us—both Leo and I said we'd be happy to ride our bicycles to the camp and either hike or use them when we went on hunts. Instead, after a half day of lessons, we were given a couple of horses and told, "Good luck." Seems rather fitting.

Leo's horse, Ryder, settles into his slow walk. Leo's shoulders visibly drop. "That was some fine shooting, Katie Burnett. You did well. Great, even."

My cheeks warm at the compliment, and my stomach gives a flutter from the way he says my name—our *shared* last name. "Thanks. I had a good teacher. And I appreciate you letting me take the shot. I'm also glad you were ready in case I missed."

"You didn't even need me. You should be proud. Archery takes some skill." He motions to the canvas tarp behind his saddle, where three of the quarters of the young buck are secured. The final quarter, tenderloin, and backstraps are in my saddlebags. "Maybe, next time, you can shoot from the horse."

"Shoot from the horse? With my bow?"

"Sure." He dips his chin slightly. "Didn't you hear Opal Maher talking about her nephew? He does horseback archery or something like that. She said he's good. Wins competitions, and even met his wife at one. Opal said the wife might be even better at it than her nephew."

"From the back of a horse? While it's moving?" I shake my head. I didn't hear this conversation and don't even know who Opal is. Maybe one of the women at the camp?

He lifts a shoulder. "I guess." Ryder shakes his head, causing Leo to stiffen.

I let out a light chuckle. "Even Ryder thinks it's a terrible idea."

The relaxing rhythm of my horse comes to an abrupt stop. "Hey there, Trig. Let's keep going. It's still a few miles to camp."

Leo's horse lets out a loud breath through his nose. "Whoa, boy." Leo's voice is shaky. "Whoa, Ryder."

I glance over my shoulder in time to see Leo and Ryder doing a sidestep. Leo ducks as a low limb comes close to his head. He's not quick enough. It smacks him in the forehead and knocks his ballcap back, the bill now pointing to the sky.

I open my mouth to ask him if he needs help when Trig does his own sideways prance. I tighten my ankles to his sides and pull back on the reins.

A low, throaty growl sounds from somewhere nearby. My heart beats much too loudly as my eyes frantically look for the source.

My mind has time to register another growl and a yip before Trig finds his feet. The massive horse jumps in the air, spinning in a half circle so we're facing Leo and Ryder.

Leo's eyes are wide as he pulls back on Ryder's reins. His mouth is moving.

Trig's hooves touch the ground, and we're off like a shot. As an afterthought, I pull back on the reins as I hold on for dear life.

Trig navigates the skinny path like we're in a pinball machine, weaving toward the trees along one side before bouncing to the other. The whip of a skinny limb catches me across my torso. I lower my head and squeeze my ankles against the horse again. A loud bang has me move even lower in the saddle.

A gunshot?

I use every limited horsemanship skill that I have to keep him under control. My entire body aches from the effort. I've all but given up, deciding to hold on and pray, when Trig skids to a stop. He's heaving, and his black satin coat is covered in a layer of sweat.

"Okay, good." I pat his neck. "Thanks . . . thanks for stopping." I shimmy out of the saddle, hoping he holds still long enough for me to get my feet on the ground.

My legs are shaking. My stomach is sour.

Trig gives a shudder and lets out a human-sounding sigh, then lifts his head and makes a chuffing sound.

I untuck the lead rope. "I'm going to tie you to this tree." My voice is as shaky as my legs. "You wait for me while I make sure Leo and Ryder are okay. Whatever happened—what was that, anyway? A coyote?"

He chuffs again.

As I loop the lead rope around a fallen tree, I shake my head. I'm sure this isn't right, tying him like this. But Leo may need me, and I can't risk taking Trig back there. I loop it but leave it loose in case he needs to get away. In case the coyote finds him.

"Okay, boy. Just wait for me. I'll be back as quick as I can with Leo and Ryder." I glance at the saddlebag containing the deer quarter. Did the coyote smell it? "You . . . stay safe."

Removing my cap, I rub my arm across my forehead to get the sweat out of my eyes. It comes back streaked in red. Not only sweat, but blood. Grabbing a bandanna from my pocket, I give my face a quick wipe. I check my daypack, part of my daily attire since the lights went out, and tighten the straps.

I'm still working on the straps as I take off running. With the pack secure, I increase my speed, almost sprinting toward my husband.

"Get back!"

I skid to a stop as the yell breaks the silence of the forest. A guttural groan follows, then another yell from Leo to stay back.

I unholster my sidearm, keeping it close to my thigh. I'm gasping for air. I take a few deep breaths to calm my pounding heart, then move forward and round the bend in the trail, creeping slowly and methodically while using the trees as cover.

Leo's on the ground. His back's against a spindly tree, its leaves already changing color with the season. His legs are angled not toward a coyote, but a wolf.

The wolf's head is down as he growls and moves toward my husband. Leo lifts his leg and kicks at the canine, again yelling at it to get away. From where Leo and I are—with the wolf between us—I can't shoot. Why isn't Leo shooting? He isn't even holding his gun. And where's Ryder?

My eyes dart around, looking for a loose branch, as I holster my sidearm. I find a suitable candidate and bend to pick it up, making all sorts of noise in the process. The wolf spins in my direction. No longer needing to be stealthy, I grab the heavy bough and let out a war cry as I advance toward the wolf.

I'm about to swing when I see something shiny on his neck. My movement falters as my brain tries to register what I'm seeing.

A collar.

This isn't a wolf. It's an enormous dog wearing a collar. Someone's pet.

The dog snarls his massive lip and launches himself at me. Operating purely on instinct now, I swing and connect with his shoulder, whirling him sideways.

He stumbles a time or two before getting to his feet and facing me again. Now he's away from Leo and I have a clean shot. I regularly practice drawing . . . but am I fast enough to shoot him before he reaches me?

"Shoot him, Katie." Leo's voice is calm and steady. "Do it now."

I move the branch to my left hand and poke it in the dog's direction, trying to look tough as I keep him at bay. My right hand is on the butt of my gun when his muscles constrict. Time slows as I release the branch and pull the gun from the holster.

He curls his lip again before launching himself into the air. I track his movement with my eyes as my pistol catches up—the front sight finally lining up with his massive chest. The 9-millimeter sounds like a cannon when I pull the trigger. One. Two. Three. Four times. He doesn't even yelp as he folds into himself and lands with a thud.

I take several steps back with my gun still trained on him, watching and waiting.

"Keep your eyes open. He has a friend. At least one." Leo lets out a weak cough followed by a moan.

"Are you hurt?" I step sideways, still watching the dog as I move toward my husband.

"Yeah." He coughs again. "Ryder tossed me."

At his side, I move to a squat. "You watch the dog, and I'll check you over."

I start to holster my gun. "Leave it out. This one won't bother us, but I'm not sure about the other." He moves slightly and winces. "I shot him before Ryder threw me. Fairly sure I got him, but he ran off. We need to be careful. Where's Trig?"

"Tied a few hundred yards up the trail. What hurts?" I place the pistol on a log within easy reach.

"Arms. Ribs. Back. You name it. It all hurts."

I check his left arm first since its closest to me. The wrist is already swelling and has a bulge near the thumb. "Tell me you didn't put your arms out to break your fall."

"Um . . . I might've. It all happened so fast. I shot the other dog. Ryder didn't think much of that, and . . . here I am." His words and breathing are slow and labored.

"Talking is hard?"

"Ribs. Hurt."

"Broken? How about the other arm?"

"Yeah. Higher up. Elbow. Humerus, maybe. Ribs. Both arms. I'm a mess."

A sinking sensation travels from my stomach to my chest. I swallow hard. "Your legs still work fine? I saw you kicking at the dog."

He gives a slight nod. "We need to find Ryder. He has the deer."

"We'll shoot another deer."

"No. They were after the meat. If there's more of them, he could— " Leo coughs and winces.

"What do I do? Get Trig? You can ride him while we find Ryder?"

"No way can I get up on the horse. Get your horse, and we'll . . . I don't know."

"You'll be okay alone?" I look around, trying to find the other dog, the one Leo shot.

"Hurry. Take the piece out of my ankle holster. And grab my 1911. It's lying over there. Put them both next to me."

"How can you shoot with two broken arms?"

"I'll figure it out."

Tears sting my eyes as I stare at my husband. We're in a mess. A big, huge mess. I close my eyes and send up a silent petition to God. *Please, Lord. Please help us.*

Chapter 3

Nervously clearing my throat, I take Leo's Sig P365 out of his ankle holster before retrieving the .45 lead slinger from the edge of the clearing. When I bend over to pick it up, a splatter of blood on the nearby brush catches my eye. "Is this where the dog was?" I point at the mark.

He dips his chin. "Around there."

I check Leo's handgun. My brow creases. I only heard one shot, but it's missing three cartridges. With my pistol still next to Leo, this is now my primary as I check the blood sign. Like Leo, I have a backup on my ankle—an S&W micro compact 9-millimeter with one in the chamber and thirteen in the magazine.

"Be careful," Leo warns.

With a nod, I move toward the splatter. Less than ten yards past the blood sign is the black and brown remains. Where the other dog resembled a wolf, this one is slick haired and only slightly smaller. He's black with brown around his snout and on his legs. My heart lurches as I see his pink collar.

Her pink collar. Fifteen months ago, both dogs were probably beloved family pets. Now they're in the wilderness, feral and doing what they must to survive.

I turn away from her, willing the tears to stay away.

Leo gives me a slow nod. "I hate it too."

Setting my shoulders, I lift my chin and purposefully stride back to my husband. "You shot three times. Want me to reload?"

"I'll be fine."

"I still don't know how you'll use this."

He motions with his chin to his right arm. "Set it next to my hand. It still works, and if I have to, I can move my arm enough to do what's needed."

I respond with a curt nod. "Good thing you've practiced shooting with both hands." I motion to my left-hand dominant husband. When his guns are accessible, I reload my semi-auto and reholster it. I lean in to kiss him. "I'll be right back."

"I'll be waiting."

My pace back to my horse is only slightly slower than the near sprint I used to reach Leo. As I make the final turn, I see Trig looking at me. I slow to a jog. My face is wet from perspiration and tears.

Part of me knows it's the stress of the situation bringing on a physical reaction. While I ran, I went over Leo's injuries in my mind and how we can stabilize him enough to get back to camp. I think the best choice will be for me to go alone and bring back help. A stretcher or maybe the wagon would be good.

A rustle in the trees brings me to a full stop.

The air is almost electric as the hair stands up on the back of my neck. My breathing turns shallow as I scan for the noise. Another, louder noise, helps me pinpoint the location. I move to the foliage along the trail, releasing my pistol from the holster as I go.

Trig lifts his head and tail. Looking toward the noise, he releases a soft snort.

A snort of reply returns as Ryder steps out of the brush. "Ryder! There you are."

The two horses, from the same ranch, share a greeting that's almost like a hug—if horses could hug. I rush to them, giving Ryder a quick check. He seems okay. There's a small cut above his eye, but it doesn't look serious. Not even much blood. He doesn't have any gashes, and the deer is still tucked in place.

I check Trig. He's fine too. Both could use a good grooming. I run my hand under the edge of each saddle pad, checking for any larger pieces of vegetation from the forest that could rub. With Ryder coming out of the woods, I'm surprised he isn't more of a mess.

Holding both lead ropes, I walk back to Leo. With Ryder here, too, things have changed. Leo may not be able to get on the horse, but I now have not one but two first aid kits.

I run through the contents in my mind, categorizing what we can use for his injuries. We each have an emergency splint kit, anti-inflammatories, analgesics, and a couple of muslin cravats, which are something like a scarf. They're useful as a sling, bandage, or even a tourniquet. We also both have a short length of duct tape, along with some twine and several other miscellaneous supplies.

It's not the supplies we'd have at the hospital, but it's not terrible. I can put Leo together enough to get him some real help. The emergency splint—compliments of the National Guard—is a true blessing. While on this hunting trip, Leo and I are the designated medics. Not a good thing when one of the medics is injured. Especially when it's the medic with the most training.

Should I try and set his arms before moving him? I've never done that on my own. In the fifteen months since I started medical training, I've watched breaks being set many times, and even helped on a few. Accidental broken bones are as common now as ever—illness and, as evidenced by the death of my mom, disease too.

Not realizing my mom was so sick is something that haunts me. Maybe, if I'd paid closer attention, if I'd insisted she got treatment sooner, she'd still be alive. I knew she got tired easily, but we were all working so hard to survive. Living without electricity, running water, food from the grocery store, and instant heat wasn't easy. It took the entire community pulling together to supply what we needed.

That hasn't changed.

When we left Bakerville, everyone was toiling from sunup to sundown to raise the food they'd need for winter. Part of me feels disloyal for leaving them. For striking out on my own with Leo. For joining the Volunteers and moving to another state—helping rebuild someplace other than home.

But I couldn't stay there. Everywhere I looked reminded me of my mom. Reminded me how I'd failed her.

As I round a bend in the trail, Leo comes into view. He's leaning against the tree, his chin resting on his chest. "Leo?" My voice cracks.

He slowly lifts his head, grimacing from the motion. "Hey." He blinks a few times. "You found him? Where was he?"

I let out a loud sigh. "He was with Trig. Well, in the forest. I didn't see him at first, but I heard him. About scared the life out of me."

The corners of Leo's mouth lift slightly. "I'm sure."

As I slide out of the saddle, my eyes drift toward the dog I shot. I hate to leave him here like this. He should be buried. A vision of the other dog, the female, pops into my head. The memory of her sprawled on the ground sparks something in my brain. Something . . . odd. I crinkle my forehead. Something wasn't right. An involuntary snort escapes through my nose. None of this is right.

"Everything okay?"

Holding onto Trig's lead rope, I make a loose knot with Ryder's, securing him to Trig's saddle. "No. Definitely not okay. I don't think

I can get you out of here. Maybe I should go on back to camp and get help?"

"I was thinking that too. But since you have Ryder with you, maybe I can make it on my own."

"Thought you said you couldn't get in the saddle?"

He gives a slight shake of his head. "Don't think I can. Not at the moment. Give me half an hour. Maybe then."

My eyebrows shoot up in question.

He winks. "There are painkillers in my kit. Strong ones."

"Really? Where'd you get those?"

"Doc Nettie."

"Nettie? How?"

He scrunches up his face. "Military supplies."

I give a nod. "Good. That's good." I should be happy we have painkillers for Leo. Why am I feeling . . . what? Disappointment? Nettie trusted him with the painkillers but not me? Leo was military, plus he had EMT training back when things were normal. I've had nothing but on-the-job training in the time since the collapse. Nettie says she sees a lot of potential in me. Apparently not enough to trust me with narcotics, but whatever.

After both horses are secured, I unclip Leo's pommel bag. It's a stretch to reach it, but Ryder seems to understand my need and holds still while I retrieve it. The good-sized bag, attached to the saddle horn, has his medical kit on one side and a pocket for a water flask on the other.

My eyes land on the flask. I purse my lips as the image of the female dog comes to mind. I draw in a sharp breath as I realize what's bothering me about her. The view of her stomach. It wasn't tight and smooth but loose and swollen. Bulging in spots. The mammary glands were protruding—filled with milk.

I swallow hard and will the emotions away. Was she pregnant or nursing? Nursing pups that are now orphaned? I shake my head and take the bag to Leo. "Where are the meds?"

Once he's been medicated and has drained about half the canteen, I lean back on my heels. "I'll get my med bag too. I think, with what we have between both kits, we can splint and sling your arms. You'll be more comfortable."

"When these pills do their job, my comfort level will improve."

"Will they hit you too hard? You'll be able to walk out?"

"They'll take the edge off. It's . . . it's pretty bad, Katie."

"Should I try and set your arms?"

"Let's just stabilize them. Use the splint material on the wrist. We don't have enough to do the humerus properly. You'll need to find some twigs. Use them and the twine to make a ladder splint. You know how?"

I close my eyes and envision what he means. Thin twigs lashed together with thin rope to create a splint and hold the bone in place. I give a nod. "Use the cravats as slings?"

"Yup. It'll be . . . fine." He grimaces. "Twenty minutes, half an hour tops, and the pills should be working."

Kneeling next to him, I check his color. He's pale, but not overly so. There's a sheen of sweat on his face. He's shocky. I reach inside the med kit for a mylar emergency blanket, one of several we've hoarded since the beginning of the apocalypse.

"Don't waste it. The cravat is enough. Open it up, like a blanket."

My eyes meet his. "You sure?"

"Yeah. I'm okay. Drape it over me."

I unfold the lightweight muslin and drape it over Leo. I rest the back of my hand against his forehead. "Do you have a fever?"

"No, I don't think so."

"Can I look at the other arm? I didn't even check it before I went for the horses."

"Let's wait until the meds work. Do it all at one time. I think I'm going to rest for a minute." He doesn't even wait for my response before closing his eyes.

I bite my lip and look down at Leo's left wrist. "I'll find the twigs we need. And the other dog. The one you shot. She has pups. I want to check her."

Leo's eyes pop open. "She's pregnant?"

"Maybe. But I think . . . not pregnant. Recently given birth, maybe."

Leo lets out a strangled sigh. "You sure?"

I shake my head. "Not sure. I think."

"S'pose we both know you aren't going to let this go. Be careful. I only saw the two dogs, but that doesn't mean— "

"I know. I'm only going a few yards away. You saw earlier where I found her? I need to look at her to make sure."

"And if it's obvious she has pups?"

I tilt my head. "I don't know. I can't . . . I just don't know."

"Go ahead. Check her out."

"You're sure? I'll be right over there." I motion to the general area where the female is.

"If it's what you think, holler. Let me know what you're doing."

"I shouldn't leave you."

"No reason not to. It's going to take a bit for the meds to work so we can get out of here."

"What if you have a reaction to them?"

"I'll be fine. We both know you won't stop fretting until you have the answers you need."

"If she has pups . . . "

"Go on. We'll deal with it as needed."

I send my husband a grateful smile. One of the things I love about him is how he's always so willing to confront things. To do what's needed. I also love how we work together. We'll deal with it. We're a team.

Chapter 4

I slide into my light backpack. Leo reminds me to be careful, to use my voice to let him know what's happening. Going immediately to the dog, my suspicions are confirmed. She's not pregnant but is definitely nursing.

My eyes sting as I check the tag on her collar. *Cupcake.* Her name is Cupcake, and she lived in Keystone, South Dakota. I close my eyes and focus on my South Dakota geography.

Our base camp for this hunting trip is Pactola Lake, which is about twenty miles west of Rapid City, where we've been living and working for the last couple of months. Keystone is about twenty miles south of Rapid City, close to Mount Rushmore.

I've never been to Mount Rushmore—not before everything fell apart—and it's not likely I'll be able to go any time soon. There's a special unit of the South Dakota National Guard stationed there, protecting the memorial. There's no visiting or gawking at the carvings now. It's off limits to tourists.

Tourists. Are there even tourists in the apocalypse?

A few years ago, a trip like this—riding horses and camping by the lake—would've been my idea of an amazing vacation. I've always been up for an adventure. My mom and Jake used to take us camping. Mostly car camping, but in recent years they started backpacking, and I once went with them on a weekend excursion.

Somehow, it's not quite the same when we're on a multiweek camping trip with the sole purpose of collecting as much food as possible.

While we're deer hunting, others are foraging for wild berries and foods, fishing, hunting waterfowl and other small game—almost anything we can find that's edible and will sustain us through winter.

We've already had more large game success than expected. Leo said we'd probably cut the deer hunt short so we don't affect the herd. Instead, we'll focus on fishing, foraging, and waterfowl.

But now, with Leo injured, things will change. Getting him back to camp is only the first step. From there, we'll need to take him to one of the medical centers in Rapid City. It took us about four hours of riding to get to the camping spot, and the wagon didn't arrive until almost dark. Will they be willing to take Leo back in the wagon? I hope so.

"Katie? You find her?"

I put my hand on the dog's shoulder. "Found her. It's what I thought. She has pups somewhere."

There are several beats of silence. "You'd better see if you can find them. Ten minutes. Be back to me in ten minutes. You have those trail markers?"

"In my pack." I glance around at the area, wondering where to even start looking. Would they have a den somewhere? Would a house pet gone feral know how to survive in the wilderness in the same way a coyote or wolf does? Are they even near here? Could the adult dogs have traveled some distance in search of food?

I look again at the dog—at Cupcake. Her ribs are visible. Tears sting my eyes. I've seen a lot of hungry people in the time since we left Bakerville. Emaciated. Some could barely walk because they were so weak from hunger. Malnourished children, with their bellies bloated from the buildup of stomach acids.

Back home, we were on rations, and everyone lost weight, but no one was skeletal. There was no bloat. Even our dogs and cats were doing okay. We had it good. *Incredibly good.*

Out in the real world, away from the refuge of the community, countless people and their pets have starved to death. I don't know how Cupcake or the other dog ended up here. Were their families camping when everything fell apart? Were they turned loose when the food ran out?

I need to go to the other dog, the one I shot, and check his tag. Find out his name. He and Cupcake also need a proper burial. How can I do that while also needing to get my injured husband cared for?

I stifle a sigh as I stand. There's a narrow game trail a few feet away. It's as good a place as any to search. "You're okay?" I holler to Leo.

"No change yet. Do what you need to do. I'll hang out here and wait."

"Don't go off having any fun without me."

His face distorts as he attempts a grin. "I'll try. See you soon."

"Ten minutes." I glance at my wristwatch, a windup one that belonged to my mom. One of my treasured possessions.

Most of our stuff was left in Wyoming. If it wasn't small enough to wear, tuck in our pockets, or carry in our multiday packs, we didn't have space for it. Bringing the bow and quiver full of arrows that used to belong to my mom were even a challenge. Adding a special sling to my backpack allowed me to carry it, although it is sometimes awkward. Traveling by foot certainly limits a person's options.

Even my paintings, which I forced Leo to pack when we quickly left our home in Kansas, are now at my family's homestead. At least I know they're safe there. Besides, looking at those paintings may stir up memories I don't want. My mom was my biggest fan. She was also so proud—and amazed—at the art I could create. I don't paint now. I don't sketch or draw either. Not only do I not have time, but it's too intertwined with the memories of my mom.

I take a deep breath; my hand moves to the butt of my pistol. Although I know it's nestled properly in the holster, confirming its placement is comforting. Along with the watch, Jake gave me a couple of Mom's concealed carry holsters. The one holding my backup gun belonged to her.

My mom had never even held a gun until she moved from the West Coast to Wyoming. Living in Bakerville, she discovered hunting and shooting sports. She also wanted to be sure she could protect herself when out hunting since Northwest Wyoming is a grizzly bear range. Soon, she realized the importance of having protection all the time and took to carrying concealed whenever she left the house.

She had several handguns and a huge collection of holsters. Jake used to joke she collected holsters like other women collected jewelry. He said it did make gift-giving easy, simply find a new and fancy holster or some kind of special conceal-and-carry clothing.

Not only did she carry concealed, but she was comfortable with her firearm. Regularly going to the range and even doing dry fire practices including practicing her draw. She used to say, "Practice your draw, or don't carry." I've taken those words to heart and know, as terrible as it is, it may have saved my life today.

I carefully make my way along the dense trail. The heavy scent of the forest is even stronger here, but it isn't bringing me the same pleasure it was earlier. It's mid-September, and the cool of the morning has faded. There's plenty of humidity, causing my thick, curly brown hair to spring to life as it tries to escape the bun at the base of my neck.

Wet tendrils stick to my neck and creep around my forehead. I swat at a bug buzzing near my face, one of those tiny biting types that loves the heat.

Last year we went straight from summer to winter—at least it felt like it. It started snowing in early October and didn't stop until April. The ski lodge we were living at received several feet of snow each year, but the owners said last year was more than double their usual.

And we weren't the only ones with above-average snowfall. Just about everyone in Wyoming and South Dakota, plus those who traveled through other parts of the Rocky Mountain states and Midwest, agreed it was a record year. Many people called it nuclear winter, brought on by the ground impacts on the west and east coasts of the United States.

For months we didn't hear anything from anyone about what was happening in other places. We wouldn't have even known about the ground-detonated nukes if people hadn't arrived who'd seen the blasts. It wasn't until February when the amateur radio set up at our mountain home picked up a transmission from the president.

After that, we'd get updates every few weeks as he dripped information regarding our country's devastation. Both coasts have been declared uninhabitable, labeled as the Wastelands, with a concentrated effort to move people out of those areas.

While the EMP did a number on us—wiping out all electricity, phones, and many vehicles—the ground detonations destroyed much land, and the radiation killed millions. Declaring the Wastelands as uninhabitable hasn't set well with everyone. We hear rumors of border skirmishes and worse.

My stepdad, Jake, and his parents have been vocal about their concern over this declaration, and especially what it means for my uncle and his family. They live in Northern California. After the EMP, we kept hoping they'd show up in Bakerville, but they never did. Are they even still alive?

We started hearing rumors of the Wastelands around the end of May. My sister Calley had just had her baby, a little girl they named Mollie Deanne, not long before the first military convoy came through and made camp at what used to be a restaurant on the highway. We lived several miles from there, but news quickly spread about them being in the area.

How could it not? It'd been almost a year since the EMP, and our world had changed drastically. The dozen loud trucks made quite a racket, alerting everyone nearby and activating our radio system. At first, we thought we might be under attack. Not even two months earlier, we'd had a major battle with the nearby town of Prospect. We knew almost anything was possible.

From our battle-ready positions, the news finally reached us about who exactly it was. Then it was a celebration. The convoy willingly provided us with medical supplies, vitamins, and more. When they heard about Calley and baby Mollie, they even produced a couple packages of disposable diapers. Because the baby was so young, Calley didn't go to the festivities, but she cried when we brought the diapers and other things home.

Leo and I first learned about the military recruitment and Volunteer Units from the convoy. While some of the Units were going from town to town in the safe zone, most were helping move people out of the nuclear-affected areas.

When we joined the Volunteer Unit, we thought we'd be sent to one of the aid stations or relocation camps to help with the refugees. Those living on the other side of The Western Wasteland—an arbitrary demarcation line that divides the livable United States and what has been deemed as unlivable.

South Dakota wasn't even on our radar. Now it makes total sense why we were sent here. There's a lot going on in the Black Hills. They've organized well.

Not only are there hospitals and clinics, plus the National Guard, but the county and city police are also organized. The sheriff's department is still functioning well and has added a group they refer to as the Citizen Patrol to help with law and order. With the governor removing all federal military from policing, the local people are necessary.

News about how well they're doing has brought in refugees. This is a double-edged sword. The refugees are often in serious need when they arrive. They're given food, medical treatment, and a place to live, with the understanding staying means they need to join the workforce. Workers are always needed, not only for day-to-day survival but also for the rebuilding efforts. There're already several industries operating post-EMP.

Sanford Underground Research Facility in Lead, about fortyish miles northwest of Rapid City, was undamaged by the EMP, thanks to being an underground facility. While I don't know exactly what they were researching before, something about neutrinos and their place in the universe, it's now repurposed to help rebuild our world. In what way, I'm not entirely sure. It's all being kept quiet, and the place is under heavy guard.

There are other wonderful things happening around us. In Deadwood, a few miles from the research facility in Lead, a couple distilleries have worked together to make hand sanitizer, disinfectants, and other cleaning solutions. They're supplying not only the hospitals in South Dakota but also shipping to neighboring states.

One thing they're not making is booze for entertainment purposes. The president issued an executive order enacting prohibition. He'd made many announcements stating it's a temporary thing to allow areas affected by famine to be able to replenish their food stores without any of the ingredients going to non-nutritious endeavors. He commonly says, "Grains are for eating, not drinking."

There's some disenchantment over the South Dakota governor not coming out against the executive order, but there hasn't been a statement of support for it either. Known as someone who often does the opposite of what the federal government suggests, and is vocal about it, many think the fact nothing is said about prohibition in South Dakota is a subtle hint it's not being followed.

Even so, the distillery is smart enough to not advertise if they're making whiskey or moonshine for anything but medicinal use. Others aren't so smart. I've had people come in the hospital and tell me they'd be glad to get me all the booze I needed. Many have even offered it as payment for their treatment. I gently reminded them that, until the crisis is over, we're treating people for free. Money isn't a thing right now.

A small noise to my right brings me to an abrupt stop as I move my hand to my gun.

I hold perfectly still, not even breathing, while I try to source the sound—not easy with my heart ratcheting up several beats and pounding in my ears. I let out a slow, quiet breath as I scan the area. The main game trail has a much less traveled off-shoot that looks like it leads to an area of fallen trees and piled limbs—what may be an old debris pile from a logging operation.

With my pistol now against my thigh, I cautiously take the secondary trail. I've only gone a few feet when I hear the noise again. It's faint, barely a whimper, but it gives me a target to move toward.

After a few minutes of searching with no results, I move to a fallen log. I holster my weapon and plop down. My ten minutes is up. I need to get back to Leo and figure out how to get him to the camp. If the pills have done their job, maybe he'll be able to move enough to walk. I lean forward and rub my eyes as my head drops.

Please, God. Please help me get Leo back to camp. And then, when we're there, please let there be someone who can help me set his arms and get him to a hospital in Rapid. I can't—

The whimper happens again. I lift my head and focus on the slash pile of debris when the sound returns. With my gun at the ready, I creep toward where the noise originated. As I get closer, it's obvious there's a cave-like hole in the pile. I stay back from it as I remove my flashlight from my utility belt. With the flashlight in my left hand and the pistol in my right, I use my left forearm and the back of my hand to create a stable shooting platform. Taking in a deep breath, my thumb finds the flashlight's on button. I move forward, and the beam of light floods the makeshift cave.

At first, I don't see anything. Moving cautiously forward, the light fills more of the area. I move the beam around the small space. At the back, I see movement and hear a mewling. I focus the flashlight. Finding the pup—or *pups,* it's hard to tell how many—fills me with both relief and sadness, along with concern. What am I going to do with them?

Before holstering my gun, I look around the area. At this point, I think it was only the two dogs, but if I get into their den and another dog suddenly appears, I'll be a sitting duck. After scanning the area and deciding it's clear, I squat down next to the opening and sweep the flashlight again.

There's a mound of puppies in one corner. All small. I reach in and gently pull the nearest one toward me. He barely even squirms. He's so young, his eyes aren't even open. My lip trembles. I hate we made these pups orphans.

A tiny whisp of a mewl sounds from the den. I tuck the first pup under my arm and reach for a second and third. With my arms full of puppies, I sigh. "What am I going to do with you guys?"

One of them lifts his chin and opens his mouth. Sliding out of my backpack, I open it and empty the contents. If I rearrange things, I can carry the pups in it—at least back to Leo. When my gear is sorted and organized, I place the puppies on top. I have the last one in when there's a faint whimper.

I shine the light back into the den, searching all the corners. On the opposite side from where I found the mound of pups is a lone babe.

When I pull him out, I'm surprised at how much smaller he is compared to the others. Where each of the others is around a pound in weight and larger than my hand, this little one fits neatly in my palm and weighs half as much. The runt of the litter.

"What are you doing all alone over there?" I croon while I pull him close to me. He lifts his little mouth and nuzzles my neck. "Aren't you sweet? Let's get back to Leo and . . . and figure things out."

Chapter 5

I double time back to where I left Leo. While at the slash pile, I found several small twigs and sticks, along with some long pieces of bark, to use for a splint. With the tiny dog in one hand and a bundle of skinny limbs in the other, along with three puppies who've suddenly decided to wake up and make some noise in my slightly open backpack, I have an urgency to get back to Leo.

Before stepping out of the brush and onto the wider trail, I stop and scan the area, making sure we're still alone. Leo's where I left him, leaning against the tree. Even from here I can see the easy rise and fall of his chest and an improvement in his color. He looks relaxed.

As I near my husband, the tiny pup makes a noise. Leo raises his head and opens his eyes. "How many?"

I allow the sticks to fall to the ground with a clatter. "Four. This one's the smallest. The other three are in my pack." I sit next to Leo and put the tiny pup on my leg while I slide out of my pack. With all the dogs visible, I give my husband a slight smile. "So . . . I don't know what we do next."

"Get your friends there situated. I don't think my ribs are broken. My breathing's easier now."

"Think you can get on Ryder?"

"No . . . no." He screws up his face. "Definitely not. But we're only a couple miles from camp. I can— " He lets out a shudder. "I'll walk."

I have my doubts about how easy walking will be, but I hold my tongue. "Okay. So splint both arms?"

"Let's start with the wrist. Use the emergency splinting material. Do you know how?"

I lift a shoulder. "I know the basics. I've never actually done it, but Captain Williams talked me through it when he had me pack my emergency kit."

I choose not to remind Leo the emergency kit was packed a couple of months ago, when we first arrived in Rapid City. Even though I'm assigned to the hospital and don't double as a patrol or on-site medic like Leo does, each of the doctors and nurses have a medical bag.

The med bags are little more than fanny packs with basic supplies for an emergency, but we're expected to carry it with us as we travel to and from work or go about our days. Since I wear a small backpack daily, my med bag tucks inside. With things like calling 911 in an emergency a distant memory, the med bag helps me be available at a moment's notice.

Captain Williams also makes a point of giving additional training to our sheriff's department and the Citizen Patrol. He even holds monthly first aid and CPR classes for the public. While he doesn't provide them with a kit on the scale of what we have, he does teach them how to use everyday objects—such as twigs and twine—as makeshift medical supplies.

Teaching is big with Williams; he even talks about a med school, of sorts, he wants to open so he can train more doctors and medical personnel.

"The aluminum inside the padding is flexible. Before you start, think about your objective for splinting."

I tilt my head. "Um . . . to make you more comfortable so we can get you out of here?"

"That'd be good. What else?"

"To prevent the bones from rubbing together, which could cause additional injuries not only to the bones or joints but also to the surrounding soft tissue?"

"Okay. Yes. Start with the wrist. What do you need to immobilize to secure the wrist?"

"The forearm?"

"Right. The long bones above the wrist."

"I should check your circulation and motion first?"

"Circulation, motion, and sensation—CMS. Why?"

"Make sure the blood flow is good so you don't lose your hand. Is it . . . do you think it's okay?"

"Probably, but do the proper checks anyway."

I shift my position and gently take his hand in mine. "Tell me if I'm hurting you."

He grunts as I pinch his middle fingernail to watch for the blanching and return of color. It happens within a second or two, as it should.

"Can you wiggle your fingers?"

He grunts again as he moves them slightly.

"Hurts?"

"Not bad."

I run my finger along his pinky. "Feel that?"

"Yup."

I repeat the motion along his ring finger, followed by the other fingers and thumb. "Okay, so, this is good. Your CMS is good. Um, at least in this arm. Should I do the other arm now?"

"Let's get this wrist splinted first."

"My splint material is three feet long. Should I cut it in half?"

"Bend it. Make the bend fit in the palm of my hand."

"The splint goes on the bottom side, right?"

"Right."

It takes me only a few minutes to work the material. It would've been quicker, but the puppies are making a racket and keep distracting me. I try and talk to them in a soothing voice but quickly realize it's hopeless. They're hungry.

When I finally have the splint material in place, I wrap it with long bandages—also part of my official kit—and tie off the end. "Should we sling it now, or wait until the other arm is set?"

He winces as he makes a slight movement. "Let's do the other arm. I don't think it's going to go quite as smoothly."

I scrunch up my face. "Do a coaptation splint?"

"That's the one. With a long bone fracture, what are you securing?"

"The joint above and below so the arm doesn't move." My brows knit together. "This break could have nerve damage with it? To the radial nerve?"

"Right, but I don't think there is."

"Can you straighten enough so I can see if you have palsy? Or maybe we splint, assuming you do? That might be best with— " I motion to the woods surrounding us " —with where we are."

"Probably best."

"I was thinking I'd use my leggings as the splint fabric. I should be able to wrap and tie them up past the humeral head and secure the legs around your neck."

"Criss-cross. Take one leg under my other armpit. That should work. Use the other aluminum splint on the underside from the armpit. You'll need to use a long stick on the outside to go up high.

And use sticks and twine to splint the wrist to prevent radial nerve damage—as a precaution.”

“Did you see the bark I found? I thought maybe use it on the outside. Wrap the bark over the top of your shoulder?”

“Try it. It might need more security. The bark’s pliable. May help. Use lots of padding so it doesn’t rub.”

This arm takes a lot longer than the other since we’re splinting the humerus as well as the wrist. I’ve used not only the leggings I had in my saddlebag, but also a pair of Leo’s boxers and a T-shirt to add extra padding under the bark and sticks. Good thing we made sure to pack a second set of clothes in case we ended up stranded.

The day is heating up. Both Leo and I are sweating by the time I’m done. The pups must have decided they weren’t getting food anytime soon. They settled into a restless sleep with one waking every few minutes, going back to sleep, and then another waking.

With both of Leo’s wrists splinted—the left because it’s obviously broken and the right to secure against nerve damage from the probably broken right humerus—and the elbow and shoulder above and below the long bone fracture secured, I use the cravats from our packs as slings. I secure both arms tight to Leo’s torso. He groans as I finish tying everything in place.

“Too tight?”

“It needs to be tight. Can you get me a drink?” Leo asks, looking sheepish and helpless.

“Yes. And food.” I glance at Trig and Ryder; they seem fine and are snacking on the vegetation within reach. “The horses need water, too, and I need to figure out something for the puppies.”

I get Leo a quick drink of water before moving to the horses. We have a collapsible canvas bucket but not a lot of water. I give them each what is probably not enough but will have to do until we reach a stream. I remember one from when we rode in. I don’t think it’s far from here. I move Ryder and Trig to a new section so they can forage for more food.

The pups need milk. We don’t have any. Instead, I chew up some jerky and thin it out with water. I try to get them to lick it, but they don’t understand what I’m offering them.

“Use one of the vinyl gloves as a bottle. Make a slit in a finger,” Leo suggests.

It seems to work well enough. Their whining stops after each are fed. It also takes forever. By the time everyone's fed, it's well after noon. I undo the elastic holding my hair in place and shake it loose. The damp tendrils around my face stick to my skin.

"Careful. You'll never get that mane contained." Leo gives me a wink.

He knows full well the difficulties I have with keeping my long, naturally curly—and unruly—hair under control. I've thought many times about cutting it off and taking it as short as possible. Without running water, it's hard to wash, and my hair is rarely clean.

"We have biscuits in our pack."

"That'll do."

I help him eat one and give him more of our rapidly dwindling water, along with another pill. There are two tablets remaining to get him back to Rapid City. While I'm glad he has these, I wish there were more. But we do have a few pieces of willow bark Leo can chew to help with the pain. "Does anyone else at camp have narcotics?"

"I'm the primary medic. You're secondary. I can't imagine anyone else was given any. The only one who may have something is Bowski."

An image of Bowski pops into my head. Tall, even a few inches taller than Leo's six-foot-four, and beefy—a rarity fifteen months into the apocalypse. It's obvious he's lost some weight, but he doesn't have the gaunt, underfed look of so many these days. He's part of the labor crews, not anything medical related.

Leo gives a slight shake of his head. "Don't ask." He leans back against the tree. "Give me five minutes to catch my breath. *Five minutes.* I'll be ready. What's your plan for the puppies?"

We both glance at the four babies, cuddled together in a nest of duff I pushed into a bed. I reach out a finger to caress the back of the tiny one. "I figured I'd empty the backpack and put everything in my saddlebags. If I leave the pack open, it should be fine. I'll turn it around and wear it on my chest."

"They'll stay warm enough?"

I shrug. "It's pretty warm now. Plus, they'll snuggle together."

"Okay. Good. The horses?"

"Tie them together. I'll lead Trig. Ryder will follow. Before we go— " I glance at the puppies.

"You want to take care of the parents?"

"There's not much I can do for them, but . . . yes. Something."

"I can't help you. Sorry."

"Keep an eye on the babies for me?"

He responds with a dip of his chin. "Make sure I can see you, okay?"

"I should be saying that to you." I touch his face. "You're sure you're okay while I do this?"

"I know you need to."

It takes me many minutes to move the large dog, the one I thought was a wolf, next to the female. I check his collar. His address is Piedmont, a small town off I-90 between Rapid City and Sturgis. His name is Archie.

When they're side by side, I return to the slash pile and find large slabs of bark, larger limbs, and other things to cover them. When I'm done, it resembles a smaller mound of debris. It's not great, but it's better than nothing.

I kneel next to the makeshift tomb. "I'm sorry this happened. We didn't want to hurt you. I know you were simply trying to find food for yourselves. For your babies. I'll do my best to take care of them." I stay a few more minutes as I get my emotions under control.

Death is such a part of our lives now. Working in the hospital, I see it almost daily. It still bothers me when a man, woman, or—the worst—a child dies. The deaths of Cupcake and Archie are almost as bad. Knowing I'm responsible for one death, and Leo the other, compounds the sadness. Was there another way?

"Katie? Ready to go?"

I rub my wrist against my right eye, then my left. "On my way." I kiss my fingers, then place the kiss on the tomb. I've seen enough death. More than enough.

Chapter 6

Getting Leo to his feet is a slow process. Once he's upright, he leans against the tree for many minutes. I put a hand to his forehead. He's warm but not excessively. Of course, without a thermometer, I can't say for sure that he doesn't have an elevated temperature.

"You sure about this? I could go ahead and get some help, maybe make a stretcher." I move my hand to his fingertips, again checking his capillary refill response and the rest of his CMS.

"Can't imagine a stretcher would feel much better."

"You want to keep holding up this tree while I get the horses?"

With Ryder's lead attached to Trig's saddle, I walk Trig back to Leo. The horses stand stalk still while I get the puppies situated in the backpack and wear it forward facing. "I was thinking, maybe we could use the horses as a brace. When you get tired, you can lean against them—like you did with the tree."

"Might work. As long as nothing spooks them. That's how I went splat in the first place, you know." He gives me a small smile.

Our pace is slow. Not only slow steps but we stop whenever Leo needs. After about half an hour, in which I estimate we've gone less than a quarter mile, I ask if he wants to rest. "Better not. My entire body aches. If I sit down, I might not want to get back up."

"How about some water?"

I help him drink and offer him a few small pieces of jerky. With both arms messed up, I'm hand feeding him. Then I fix another batch of jerky broth for the puppies and soak it in one of our lidded containers.

I awkwardly feed one pup at a time while we walk. Leo *tsks* at my multitasking, worried about something going wrong while I'm holding a puppy in one hand, the vinyl glove bottle in the other, and having Trig's lead rope tucked under my arm. He's right about it not being the best situation, but I do it anyway.

It's late afternoon before Pactola Lake comes into view. The man-made reservoir was the source of water for Rapid City before the attacks and EMP. When the bridges were detonated on day two of the country-wide assaults, a National Guard unit was sent to secure Pactola Dam.

The thought was, if bridges could be attacked, so could dams. An attack on the earthen dam would've caused a massive flood. Rapid City had experienced such a flood in the early '70s when several days of rain caused a dam closer to town to give way.

There's still a concern about the dams being a target. The National Guard keeps a contingent living at and patrolling Pactola and other dams to deter sabotage. The sergeant in charge was notified of our arrival via radio, but we still had to each show a token provided by Camp Rapid confirming we were part of the hunting group.

Just last week, an older lady I was treating at the hospital was reminiscing about the flood and how scary it was. She was in junior high, and even knew someone who died, when debris carried by floodwaters clogged the spillway of Canyon Lake Dam and resulted in a failure. The dam failure wasn't the only issue. Almost all the creeks and rivers were swelled to flood stage. Over two hundred people died and several thousand were injured during the flood event.

She says the flood changed many things within Rapid City and the surrounding communities. Houses and businesses were removed from most of the flood plains, and greenway parks were put in. She released an exaggerated sigh. "Not that it would matter much. Something happens to Pactola Dam or even another big rain like the one in '72, and we'd be in a world of hurt. Especially now. There's no way to have an early warning system."

Undoubtedly, she's correct. The Black Hills are amazing and gorgeous. But I can certainly see how the steep declines and number of rivers and creeks could cause flooding. Those rivers and creeks have been a blessing to the people, though, giving them access to the water they needed when the power went out. They've been able to not only take water directly from the waterways but also drill many shallow wells and install handpumps. We get water at the hospital and our house from one of the new wells.

The Black Hills themselves are home to wildlife, flora, and fauna, providing much needed food. The wilderness, combined with intense management of domestic livestock, food crops, and gardens, have left the people of the Black Hills regions doing better than many other places. In some ways, they're thriving much like my Bakerville home. Of course, some of the choices made . . .

I shake my head as I glance down at the puppies riding easily in the pack on my chest. "I'll keep you safe," I whisper.

"What's that?" Leo asks, sounding weak and exhausted.

I lift my shoulders and arch my back. "Um, nothing. I think we're getting close. We're starting downhill. You want to rest a minute?"

"I'm okay. Let's get there. Before I pass out."

My eyes go wide as I shoot him a look.

He gives me a wan smile. "Kidding. Although, I can't wait to sit down. In fact, let's get me another pill. Best not advertise we have these when we get back to camp."

"I check my watch. It's a little early to take another but not terribly so. There are only two remaining. You want them both?"

"Only one. We'll need to save the other for the ride out in the morning."

"We need to get you out of here tonight."

"Won't happen tonight. Too close to sunset."

"We can get in a few hours of travel time before dark."

He lifts his chin. "Doubtful. We'll need to find Blake—who probably went out on an evening hunt—he'll give the orders as to what needs to happen."

I scoff. "I thought you were in charge of all things medical."

He smirks. "Not sure it counts when I'm the person in need of medical attention."

"Then I should make the decision. I'm the other medic, right?" Even as I say the words, I know what the answer will be.

Bruce Blake is brother-in-law to Dr. Eugene Newsome. Dr. Newsome doesn't view me as anything other than a nuisance. He certainly doesn't consider me a valuable part of the medical team the way he does Leo. I'm not sure what I did to cause his intense dislike, but he does seem to go out of his way to make it clear there's no place for me in his hospital. If it weren't for Doc Nettie and Captain Williams, I'd be out on my ear.

Bruce Blake seems to share Newsome's opinion of my abilities. When Leo and I were assigned to this team, Blake went as far as saying I could stay home and relax, put my feet up and take a few weeks off.

He even called me "the little woman." Leo and I laughed about it later, but we both know it bothered me.

I may not have the years of medical training the other nurses have, or the military experience Leo has, but in the time since my sister was shot, I've seen plenty. My training isn't only on the job either. My teachers, which consisted of a doctor—before his premature death—two nurse practitioners, a chiropractor, and a veterinarian, loaned me books and gave me tests.

In Bakerville, I was a valuable part of the team. Here, sometimes I feel like little more than a candy striper. Of course, before, my confidence level was different too. There was a time I thought I truly knew what I was doing, knew I was making a difference. Saving lives.

Then my mom died. Now part of me wonders if I should even be working in the hospital. What if I make a mistake and cost someone else their life?

Dr. Newsome might be right. I don't have the skills or knowledge needed to be part of his team. Especially with things returning to normal. I might have been needed before, when our world was a mess. But with the rebuilding efforts in full swing, maybe there isn't a need for a pretend nurse who has little training.

When we arrived here with the Volunteer Unit, I was immediately assigned to the hospital as my MOS—Military Operational Specialty—or job as I think of it. The Volunteers aren't considered a part of the "real" military like Marines or Army, but we still operate under many of the same parameters and activities, even sharing some of the popular acronyms.

Leo's a Health Care Specialist, commonly called a combat medic. I mean, I guess when you get right down to it, I'm also a Health Care Specialist, but we're definitely not the same.

Just like Blake calling me the little woman, others think of me in the same manner. I'm only part of the Volunteers because of my husband. I certainly didn't get in by my own merits. Not that it's a super high bar to qualify, but Leo was able to get us special permission to stay together. Truth is, if it weren't for Leo—and my mom's death—no way would I have even thought of enlisting. I was happy to stay in Bakerville.

The first person who sees us is a woman with a long gray braid tending the smoker. She stands and pushes the brim of her wide hat off her face. Even from here, I can see the tan line across her forehead, indicating long days in the hot sun. I watch as the question of what is happening registers. I'm about to call out to her when recognition dawns and she sounds the alarm of "injured man" for the entire camp to hear.

As Leo expected, it's chaotic. Also, as he expected, Blake and the bulk of the camp are out on an evening hunt.

There's a barrage of questions from the people in camp. Leo leans against Trig. "Okay, Katie. Now I'll let you help me to the ground."

"In our tent?"

"I don't think I can. It's too small. Just pull my sleeping bag out here."

"The bugs will eat you alive."

"Get one of the scarves we have. Use it as a mosquito net."

One of the little pups lets out a squeal before I can respond.

"What was that?" The first lady who saw us asks, her hand already on her sidearm.

I motion to the backpack. "Puppies."

Her brows furrow. "Puppies? Here?"

Leo dips his chin. "It's a long story. Katie? The bed?"

I leave the puppies in our tent and quickly pull out not only Leo's sleeping bag but mine too. While I'm in the tent, someone brings over a light sheet. Soon, Leo's settled on the two bags and covered with a sheet, a thin magenta scarf wrapped around his head and neck to cover as much exposed skin as possible. His boots are off, but everything else is left in place, including both slings. I've barely finished covering him when he begins to snore.

Chapter 7

With Leo napping, I turn my attention to those gathered around us. "Can we give him some room?"

"Let's move over to the fire," the woman with the gray braid commands in a mild southern accent. "Bring the puppies. You've got a story to tell."

I follow the woman and a few others to the fire. I've taken the puppies out of the backpack and am carrying them in my arms. They're all hungry and squirming, making it difficult to hold on to them.

The woman who first saw us takes the largest pup from me. "Looks like your husband is quite the mess."

I give a nod as I struggle to remember her name. Jewel? No, but something similar. "Both arms are broken. We thought maybe a couple of ribs, but Leo thinks they're only bruised. Pretty much all of him is bruised."

"Not like Ryder to toss him. He's a gentle one. These puppies have somethin' to do with it?" Opal. Her name's Opal Maher. She and her son are from the ranch who offered the horses to use for the hunting trip. The same woman Leo was talking about earlier who has a relative that does archery from horseback. Maybe if Leo would have shot the quiet bow instead of the noisy gun, he wouldn't be in the predicament he's in.

"The parents. Well, the mom for sure. We think . . . " I bite my lip and will away the tears as two of the other women take the squirming babes. I keep the tiniest one. "We were attacked. I didn't entirely know what was happening. Trig took off right as it started. By the time I got back to Leo, he was on the ground and a big dog was attacking him. I thought it was a wolf. I . . . I had to . . ." I stare at the fire.

"You shot her?" one of the women who took a pup asks. Her voice drips with disgust.

Opal pierces the woman with a look. "Now, you know once those dogs have gone wild, they might as well be wolves. They'll kill given the chance. Remember what happened over in Deadwood?"

"That was a child. She's an adult. You know what happened before. She could've— "

"I didn't have a choice." My voice is squeaky. "He was after Leo. He turned on me. I shot when he jumped."

Opal repositions her puppy so she can rest a hand on my forearm. "You keep sayin' he, honey. You didn't shoot the mom?"

I shake my head. "Leo did. He had to. *We* had to. There was no choice. We feel terrible about it. I found the puppies, and . . ."

"Why'd you bring them back here?" the woman who didn't take a dog asks. "You know they'll just take our food— "

Opal huffs. "No! What happened in Black Canyon was wrong, and everyone knows it."

"Really? You think Blake believes it's wrong?" The two women lock eyes. Finally, the one not holding a dog backs down with a flip of her wrist. "Whatever."

"What kinda dogs are they?" one of the men asks.

I tell him I don't know before describing what the mom looked like.

"She sounds like a Rotty—a Rottweiler. And the dad?"

"Well, I guess the wolf-looking dog was the dad. I don't know for sure."

"Maybe a German shepherd?"

I lift a shoulder while Opal shakes her head. "They're not that big. Not unless they're a mix. Saw some good-sized shepherd mastiff mixes before. But they don't look much like a wolf. Maybe a husky or malamute?"

"I don't know. Sorry."

One of the ladies gives me a dirty look. "What'd you do with them?"

My description of my attempts to bury the dogs is met with another dirty look from her.

One of the men mutters, "A waste of time."

The lady who didn't take one of the dogs mutters something I'm not sure I hear correctly but sounds like, "Should've left the pups right there."

When Opal's puppy lets out a loud squeal, she rubs it's back. "This one's hungry. Did you let them nurse?"

"Let them nurse? What do you mean?"

She moves her head, causing her braid to swing. "On the mom, after you found them?"

One of the women makes a face and shakes her head, emitting a quiet, "*Eww.*"

I swallow back my own response. "Uh, I didn't think of that. The mom was, you know, dead."

"Just thinking they may have gotten a last bit of nourishment. These are difficult times. So what *have* you fed them?"

After I tell her about my chewed up jerky mixture, she nods. "We've got broth goin' from the scraps. That'll do for now. We'll need to find you somethin' better for a bottle. Your glove won't hold up. And don't forget, you'll need to help them with their business."

I blink my eyes several times and give Opal a blank look. "Their business?"

"Mm-hmm. You know. Ya gotta help 'em poo."

One of the men snorts out a laugh. "Why you think their mamas are always licking them?"

I shake my head. "I never thought about it. I've never had a dog with puppies."

Opal gives me a kind smile. "You'll use a bit of cloth, dear. Wet it and give 'em a gentle rub right under their tails. I'll help ya so ya know." She turns to the other women and motions to the deer quarters, which were removed from our saddlebags. "Why don't you work on the deer? Get it hanging so it'll cool. I 'spect we'll take it back fresh."

With the puppies fed, their business ends rubbed, and the sun dropping low, the first of the hunters return. I'm sitting next to Leo now, all four pups resting in a nest I made them.

Opal brought over a mason jar of warm water wrapped in a towel. She said they'll need something to help keep them warm through the night. She also said she'd take care of letting everyone know what happened and would send Blake over once he arrived. She'll try and keep the others away enough not to disturb Leo.

It's easy to see Bruce Blake when he saunters into camp. Even his horse has an air of perceived nobility, holding his head high and walking with purpose. Not that Blake looks comfortable in the saddle. He's rigid and holding the reins, one in each hand. My guess is the horse is holding his head out of self-preservation to keep the bit from digging into the side of his mouth. Blake is even less of a horseman than Leo, but don't try and tell him that.

Someone runs over to him, talking wildly with his hands and pointing in our direction.

I busy myself with checking Leo, counting his breaths and pulse before resting the back of my hand on his forehead. Does he seem warm? He'd already kicked off the sheet. Opal suggested a small smudge fire nearby to help with the bugs; it lets off lots of smoke but little heat. I unbutton the top of his shirt and feel his chest. He's warm but not excessively so.

"Well there, little lady, heard your man has himself a heap of trouble." Blake pushes back the front of his new looking cowboy hat as he squats on his heels.

"We need to get him back to town."

"Guess we do. Seems Opal took it upon herself to get the wagon emptied out. She'll drive you at first light. Not a bad idea to take the meat and fish we have back now anyway. We've harvested more than any of us expected. Do we need to get someone over here to look at him? Pinkard was in the Army. He knows some combat medicine."

Leo opens one eye. "Katie's done what's needed." His voice is gruff and croaky.

I reach for the water jug. "Drink?"

"Well, all right then. If the little lady did what she could, we'll just get you back to town so Eugene can fix you up proper."

As I help Leo with the water, our eyes meet. He gives a slight raise of one brow and something resembling an eye roll. I bite back a grin.

"Guess I'll let you get some rest. Opal said to tell you there's stew if you're up for it." Blake gets to his feet, then points at the sleeping dogs. "What's your plan for them?"

"I'll take them back with us tomorrow."

"Too few dogs around. Lost too many in the early days before people got organized. Lots were turned out, probably like the ones who attacked you. Others . . . " Blake shakes his head. "It's a shame. Some were so worried the humans would starve, they couldn't fathom sharing our food with pets. I never had a dog, but I'll tell you, I wouldn't mind having one now."

My eyes dart to Leo, who looks as bewildered as I feel. The way Blake is talking, he makes it sound like he's innocent of what happened in Black Canyon. That's not the story I heard. Doc Nettie said Eugene Newsome *and* Bruce Blake—both residents of Black Canyon before it was attacked and essentially destroyed—were in the group who said there wasn't enough food to share. They, along with several others, wrote up rules about pets.

Rules that make me sick when I think about it. Rules some people agree with even now, after the mandate was rescinded when the news got out to other parts of the state. Even the governor became involved, sending a messenger by horse to stop the atrocity.

The damage was already done. There were few dogs, cats, fish, or any other pets remaining. Some believe the attack on the town was in retribution for the loss of the pets and what happened to the people who disobeyed the edict.

When we arrived in the spring, the Black Canyon incident was spoken of in hushed and cryptic tones. Doc Nettie, who was stranded in Rapid City while doing a medical internship, was the first to tell me about the carnage. "I understand needing to save the food for the people, but what they did . . . it makes me sick every time I think about it," she had said with a shake of her head.

It makes me sick too. When I first suspected I may have killed a dog that was nursing pups, I was mainly concerned about finding them. When I did find them, I didn't give much thought to what had happened last year, the way Black Canyon slaughtered the pets. A few survived the carnage, their owners hiding them or something similar.

Doc Nettie said that, too, was bad. One man hid his service dog and was turned in by a neighbor. They made an example out of him. A meeting was called at Black Canyon's high school. Once everyone was gathered, they killed the dog while the owner watched. To ensure the message was received, the man was executed.

Their plan backfired, though. The support for the decree dwindled after the execution and news of what was happening in Black Canyon spread. I've been told, to this day, Newsome and Blake insist they made the right call. According to them, countless lives were saved by the reduction of nonhumans without a purpose.

No way is Blake taking one of these pups. Absolutely no way.

"Hey, Leo. You're looking a little rugged."

Blake's eyes narrow as he swings his head in the direction of the new voice. "Kasubowski. Why you here?"

"Heard Burnett took a tumble. Thought I'd check on him."

"He says they got it under control. Be taking them out at daylight. You're welcome to go along with them if you wish."

Ritchie Kasubowski—or Bowski, as most people call him—fakes a hurt look and puts his massive hands on his chest. "Leave? Why would I want to do that? I'd miss your charming personality."

Blake grunts before redirecting his attention to Leo. "Well, if you and your little lady are all set, I'll let you be. Might see you in the morning before you go, might not. Plan to get to my spot early, bring down the big one I caught a glimpse of this morning. He was at least a five by six. Massive rack."

Bowski strokes his beard. "You know, the small ones eat just as good."

Another grunt plus several mutters accompany Blake as he stomps off. He's several feet away before he looks back over his shoulder. "Herd management. It's herd management." He gives Bowski a hard look, then spins around and continues his stomp toward his tent.

"That dude." Bowski shakes his head. "Whoever thought it was a good idea to have him leading this expedition had a screw loose."

I tilt my head and lift a shoulder.

"Right. Eugene Newsome. With him now on the district council, all sorts of flunkies are given more power than they deserve. Heard he even— " Bowski slams his mouth shut as his eyes go wide.

I raise my eyebrows. "Heard what?"

"Probably nothing." He waves a hand. "More scuttlebutt. You know how the rumors travel."

He's right about rumors, but my guess is he knows plenty.

"So, Leo." Bowski kneels down. "Bet you're hurting plenty bad." He reaches across Leo's chest, and his hand drops something close to me. He produces a small silver flask in the other hand and sets it at Leo's side. "Go easy. One or the other. Not both. You're a nurse. You know." He gives me a nod and pops to his feet. "See you in the morning."

I watch as Bowski meets up with another man. Both men have large handguns strapped to their legs and rifles slung across their backs. The second man, of average height, almost seems miniature compared to the overly tall Kasubowski. I met the second man earlier. Brock or something like that. He was on the gruff side, barely looking at me when we were introduced.

Both men now look in our direction. Bowski lifts his chin at me. The other man is completely emotionless. His hard eyes narrow before quickly dismissing me and turning back to Bowski.

I lean close to Leo. "Who's that guy again? The one talking to Bowski?"

Leo responds with a snore.

Chapter 8

Blake was right about us not seeing him this morning when we left, only not for the reason he'd said last night.

Bruce Blake, leader of the hunting expedition, was still in bed when we left. Bowski, though, true to his word, was at our camp when we started to stir. He helped me get Leo up and moved to the wagon. He and the other guy, the one with the hard eyes, helped get Leo to the latrine last night. The man, who reminded me his name was actually Bryson, even delivered a fresh hot water bottle incubator for the puppies.

I didn't know Bowski before this trip. I'd heard rumors about him, but I'd never spoken to him. If it weren't for his height and overall stature, I'm not sure I could pick him out of a crowd. I still haven't had a real conversation with him, but his willingness to help and the fact he doesn't call me *little lady* puts him well ahead of Blake in my opinion of him.

His friend Bryson, though not the warm and fuzzy sort, was truly helpful. Younger than Bowski but probably a few years older than Leo, the shorter man had zero trouble supporting Leo's weight as he helped him maneuver.

The medication Bowski slipped us was five opioid pain relievers, which were more than enough to get Leo through the night and will help with the return trip to Rapid. The bootlegged booze is a backup. Leo took a whiff of it and declared it "strong stuff" that would probably make him puke.

Resting my hand on his forehead, I check my husband's temperature. He was warm last night, but it never amounted to anything. This morning, as we ride in the back of the wagon, his skin's a little chilly, likely from the cool morning.

Even with the dropping temperatures and a week and a half left of hunting camp, the people were extremely generous. When we arrived at the wagon this morning, a plush bed was already made for Leo. Opal went around camp and asked for donations to make his ride as comfortable as possible. There were a couple of mattress pads, another sleeping bag, several blankets, and even a few pillows.

Leo talked me through checking his splints this morning to make sure they were the proper tautness. I did a circulation test, and everything seemed to be fine there too. We discussed whether he still needed the secondary splint on his right wrist—the side with the broken humerus—but decided to leave it in place. He said he didn't think he had any nerve damage, but it probably wouldn't hurt to treat it prophylactically.

Thanks to Bowski's gift, Leo is sleeping somewhat soundly as the wagon bounces along. I pull the sheet up around him tighter as a puppy lets out a whimper. Several camp people offered to keep them so I could tend to Leo without worrying about them, but I brought them with me.

Mainly because of Opal. She said she thought it best for me to keep them for now since we didn't know the true intentions of everyone in camp. It does make sense, especially considering Bruce Blake and his history. Sure, he may have *said* he's thought about getting a dog, but I can't forget what he actually *did*.

"Need to stop?" Opal calls from her perch at the front of the wagon. Her youngest son, somewhere around Leo's age, is sitting next to her, acting as security.

"We can keep going. I can feed them while we travel." Opal made sure I had more broth for the road, but I don't know if the broth is enough for them. I can't help but think, at this young age, without milk, they won't have the nutrition they need to grow.

My sincere hope is, when we get back to town, there'll be someone to take the puppies and raise them. If not in the Guard District of Rapid City, maybe in one of the other districts or nearby Sturgis, Spearfish, or one of the other multitudes of small towns without brutality toward their animals.

Thankfully, the troubles going into this winter aren't as pronounced as they were last winter. Part of me understands Dr. Newsome wanting to preserve what food was available for the people. His plans had serious results, though. Not only did it bring Black Canyon under scrutiny, but the lack of cats and dogs also resulted in an increase of mice and rats over the winter.

My guess is Newsome didn't remember his history. During the World War II 900-day Siege of Leningrad, almost all the cats, dogs, horses, rats, birds, and more "disappeared." Even the famous Pavlov's

Dogs are said to have been eaten during the siege. The increase in rats was helpful at first—more food for the starving people—but in the end, the rats caused mass devastation. As the siege was ending, cats were shipped in to help get the rat population under control.

What I need is to find a veterinarian who can help me with the food. When I told Doc Nettie about the veterinarian we had on our medical team in Bakerville, she said they had a few local vets in the early days of setting up the hospital. One died, and one left in the early spring. She knows there's at least one working out of the main hospital and probably others in various districts.

Once Leo's stabilized, maybe I can find help for the pups. Milk might be a challenge. We get goat's or cow's milk as part of our weekly allotted rations, but not much, and not nearly enough to feed four hungry puppies.

Although nothing like what happened in Black Canyon happened in Rapid City, there are still far fewer domestic animals than before. In the Midwest and Rocky Mountain states, well over half of the population has died since the electromagnetic pulse . . . some estimates say even more, maybe 80 or 90 percent. In many cases, people's pets died right along with them.

Or, sometimes, the pets were turned loose—possibly what happened to Cupcake and Archie—and they became feral. The world we have now isn't the same as the world before with cute little dogs carried in purses and pampered cats.

There's talk of an initiative to rebuild the dog and cat population. Maybe I can find help from them? Especially if they can see these dogs can have a purpose.

Opal said they use dogs on their ranch, always have and continue to do so. They help with the herds and act as part of their sentry team. Although she does say they're a lot more careful with their dogs, by making sure they have eyes on them all the time and bringing them in at night. But she thinks it's more likely a hungry person would take a calf than a dog.

With the wagon traveling at about the same speed as a slow stroll to keep the bumpiness down, it's nearly sunset before we reach the makeshift hospital Leo and I work out of in the Guard District. We talked about going to a different clinic, one not as far, but decided nearer our home, with people we know, would be best.

Opal brings the wagon to a stop and hands the reins to her son. "I'll go in and get some help."

Leo, now propped into a sitting position, shakes his head. "I can walk."

"Sure you can. But why? Don't they have stretchers or some such thing?"

I rest my hand on Leo's leg. "Gurneys. Thank you, Opal."

Leo grunts before settling back. Within a few minutes Doc Nettie and one of our medics come out with a gurney. Leo makes another noise of disgust. "My legs work fine."

As they get Leo situated on the gurney, Opal pulls me aside. "How about I keep the puppies for you? You focus on your man tonight. I'll see you in the morning."

A wave of nervousness rushes through me, but she pats my arm. "Don't you worry none. My son and I— " She shakes her head. "You know how I feel about what happened. He feels the same way. My entire family had plenty of sad days when we heard about the atrocities. 'Sides, ya don't really want to take them in the hospital, do you? Wha'f Newsome shows up?"

"Where will you stay tonight? You won't go to your ranch?"

"Not tonight. Too far. I have a friend we can stay with. She's of the same mind as I am. It'll be fine. I'll check in on you tomorrow, before we head back to camp."

"I don't know if they'll keep Leo overnight. We don't usually for a broken arm. Do you know where we live?" I give her easy directions to our house, which is only a couple blocks away.

She pulls me into a hug. "God bless you, Katie. You and your husband. It'll be a rocky road, but he'll be fine. Thanks to you. You'll see."

As Opal walks back to the wagon, I scurry off after the gurney. Doc Nettie has them head straight for one of our treatment rooms. Leo's gently moved onto an exam bed.

Nettie asks Jacquie, the nurse on duty, to check his vitals, then she turns to me. "I knew sending you two off to hunt and fish was a bad idea." She gives me a wink to let me know she's kidding.

After the vitals check, Nettie does her part. She starts with the broken wrist, removing the emergency splint before the exam. "Without an x-ray, I can only assume it's broken." She makes a few tutting noises. "I can't imagine it's *not* broken. Before, it possibly would've even been surgically repaired and held together with a plate and screws."

Leo nods. "And now?"

"Now we put it back as best we can and hope for the best. The splinting was done well." Her eyes meet mine, and she gives me a slight nod. "We'll cast it, and Leo will be taking it easy for a couple months."

My husband makes a face and rolls his eyes.

"Let's reposition you slightly so I can check your ribs. You had trouble breathing at first, but it's okay now?" Nettie spends many minutes checking the ribs on his left side and listening to his lungs. "This side is clear. Let's unwrap the other arm and see what we have there."

I watch as Leo tightens his jaw while the lower makeshift twig and twine splint is removed. Nettie checks the wrist for dropsy, a sign of possible nerve damage.

"Everything looks good," Nettie says, then moves on to the splint on his upper arm. After she removes the emergency splint and bark, she has the nurse cut the sleeve off. "Good thinking leaving the shirt in place to provide a barrier between the splint materials and his skin."

"Leo's idea." I motion toward my husband.

Once the material is gone, Nettie spends several minutes looking over the arm. "There's a small friction rub on the shoulder where the padding slipped, even put a hole in the shirt. Looks a little angry. We'll get it cleaned up."

I move to where I can see what she's looking at. Angry is an understatement. It's nasty. Much like a bed sore. How did I mess up the padding enough to cause such a wound in so little time? I clear my throat. "Will you plaster cast both arms?"

"That's probably best. I sent someone after Dr. Newsome. He'll be the final decision on how these breaks are treated."

I close my eyes and exhale through my nose. I'll admit, I was happy Newsome wasn't the one here when we arrived. I know Doc Nettie, only a medical student before our world fell apart, doesn't make major treatment decisions without Newsome's or Captain Williams's say-so, but I was hoping Williams would be the one she called.

"Well, well, well." Newsome strides into the room, as if my thinking of him conjured him up. "When I heard the Burnetts were here, I was surprised to hear it was Leo injured. Thought for sure it'd be you." He points a bony, wrinkled finger in my direction.

I wither under his bitter gaze. His eyes narrow as he gives a slow shake of his head, his mussed-up, thinning strands rubbing across his wide forehead. The man looks like a wreck, in need of a shave and in general disarray. He's still wearing his parka and boots but has tucked his stocking cap into his pocket, the bright orange pom-pom hanging halfway out.

When he looks toward Leo, his demeanor changes—*softens*. "Let's see what we have and get you fixed up. Can't have one of our best people out on sick leave."

I give Leo a brief smile, then turn my attention to Newsome. "Indeed. Thanks for your help, Doctor."

Chapter 9

"I'll take over Leo's treatment. Your shift is almost over anyway. You and Jacquie can run along and do your paperwork," Newsome says, then turns to medic Jesse Talbot. "You can assist with the casting."

Jesse and Doc Nettie share a look I can't quite decipher before she turns to Newsome. "As you wish, Doctor. Will you have Leo stay the night?"

Newsome mutters something before agreeing Leo should stay. After Nettie and Jacquie leave the room, Newsome gives Jesse orders on how to set things up and then excuses himself to go to the bathroom.

When he returns, it's obvious he washed up a bit. His sparse hair is combed, and he's now wearing his hospital attire. He even brushed his teeth, his breath giving off a minty yet medicinal smell, likely from some kind of homemade tooth powder.

Nettie slips back in the room. "I'd like to stay and observe, if you don't mind."

Newsome waves a hand at her. "Probably smart. You'll learn something important."

He starts with the broken humerus on Leo's right arm. Newsome tuts several times over the abrasion on the shoulder before piercing me with one of his looks.

"Obviously, your training didn't provide you with the necessary knowledge to know there should always be plenty of padding under a splint. Especially if you're using items found in the woods. Have you any idea what kind of bacterium or fungi you may have introduced to your husband's bloodstream? While I should commend you on doing a fair enough job—he'll probably have at least partial use of both hands and arms without nerve damage—you may have cost the man his life. Nerve damage is nothing compared to sepsis."

His stare lingers on me another minute while I wither under his gaze.

He gives me one final dirty look before turning to Nettie. "Do you know the treatment for sepsis?" His tone isn't much kinder than the way he spoke to me.

Nettie licks her lips. "Ideally, we should draw blood and do a culture first—if we suspect sepsis."

"Ideally, yes." Newsome motions with his hands for her to go on.

"Antibiotics should be given as quickly as possible once sepsis is recognized."

Leo clears his throat. "I don't think I have an infection. No fever. And other than my arms being broken and an overall ache, I don't feel bad." He moves his chin toward the shoulder with the wound. "This doesn't look like much."

"Well, *Mr. Burnett,* that may be so, but I've seen plenty of dirty wounds, even ones that don't look nearly as bad as yours, turn into a firestorm in a matter of hours." He turns back to Nettie. "Give him an injection before we cast the wrist. We'll also send him home with a course of oral antibiotics. Give him the real stuff, not that magic potion garbage the so-called herbalist makes out of algae."

While we do have some prescription antibiotics, much of our medicine these days is crafted by an herbalist who helps at the hospital. She has both a garden and greenhouse for growing medicinal herbs and plants, plus she does a considerable amount of wildcrafting to find naturally occurring medicinal plants.

The *magic potion garbage* Newsome's referring to is a tincture made from a lichen in the Usnea family. It's used as an antibacterial and antibiotic with excellent results.

Newsome turns back to Leo, his voice kind. "How's your pain level? You use the meds in your kit?"

Leo dips his chin. "I did." He doesn't mention the meds Bowski gave him, or the flask still tucked in the bottom of my pack.

"The last one?"

Leo looks to me.

"Around sixteen hundred," I respond with a nod.

"We'll give you ketorolac IM. That'll help with the pain."

The casting of the humerus is kept low enough so the wound at the top of Leo's shoulder isn't included. Newsome grumbles about the sore. "I would've preferred the cast go over the cap of the shoulder."

After the casting is finished, Nettie reluctantly leaves for home.

~~~~~
~~~~~

"Good mornin'," a cheerful voice calls out. "Figured they'd keep you, so I checked here first." Opal waves from the doorway.

"Doc Nettie said I can leave as soon as I'm dressed." Leo eases to the edge of the bed. "I'm ready to get out of here."

Opal throws back her head and gives a hearty laugh. "Oh, yes. You've been here for *soooo* long. But I get it. Restin' at home is much better than a hospital. Can I give ya a ride?"

"Do you have— " I tilt my head and bug out my eyes. "Are they in the wagon?"

"Yup. Shawn's with 'em. We found a little wooden crate for them. They're fine. We may have spoiled 'em a bit last night, holding 'em and all. My friend even had a doll bottle, and she shared some of her milk allotment with them. She sent the bottle with me so you can have it."

My brow furrows. "Milk for her child?"

"Not enough it'll affect the girl. My friend knows better than that."

The use of rations and ration chips is strictly monitored. Even though many families and neighbors band together for their food, it's frowned upon. I can't imagine the hoopla if anyone knew she'd shared with the puppies.

It's not only food being controlled, but goods too. If you need a new pair of shoes before you're scheduled for them, you have to go through the process to get a ration chip or token for them. Either that or through the black market, which is how I suspect Bowski came by the pain pills and booze for Leo.

The black market is notoriously well known, but it's a mystery to me as to how it actually operates. Where do they find the goods in today's world? As Volunteers, we didn't have a need to get bootlegged items. Our supplies, like shoes and boots, were readily given to us. We still use ration chips for food, but we also get additional items to increase our calories when needed—like when Leo is sent out on patrol.

Other situations also go outside the bounds of ration chips. The hunting group we were with was allowed to take food with them from their weekly rations, but instead relied on wild game and fish. Leo and I weren't at all disappointed when told we'd be part of the hunting group. Fresh venison and fish, along with camping, sounded good to us.

Two broken arms and four puppies were not part of the deal.

There's a light rapping on the door frame, then Doc Nettie strides in. "Ready to go?" Arnetta Wolff, who we call Doc Nettie, looks fabulous. Not at all like she worked late last night and got up early this morning. Her dark hair is pulled into a tight smooth bun. Her blue eyes are crisp and alert. She even has a tinge of pink to her cheeks. Though short, at only four-foot-eleven, she seems to fill the doorway. Nettie has a manner about her that's much larger than her physical stature.

"More than." Leo's vigorous nod causes him to wince.

"Let me take a quick look at you." She checks his nail beds and has him wiggle his fingers, listens to his lungs, asks about his pain level, and several other things while Opal and I stand by. As Nettie puts her stethoscope in the pocket of her lab coat, she glances over at me. "You hear the news?"

I lift my shoulders. "What news?"

"The special council held their meeting yesterday afternoon."

Leo crinkles his forehead. "I thought it wasn't happening until Saturday."

"Don't know. Things changed, I guess. I'm actually surprised Newsome didn't say anything about it last night. I only know because we received a delivery of supplies from Lieutenant David Paul with the National Guard. He told me."

The beat of my heart increases. "And?"

"And . . . congratulations to you both! Everyone was accepted."

I let out a loud breath. I should be happy, but what I actually feel is something else. Disappointment? I paste on a smile. "Really? That's . . . that's great."

Leo lets out a whoop. If his arms weren't in slings, I'm sure he'd be pumping them. "All right." He looks at me and nods. His happiness fades when he sees my face. "Katie?"

I widen my fake smile. "It's good news. Definitely good news." Denial would have meant we'd need to hook up with a Volunteer Unit in Wyoming and be given a new assignment to finish out the year we committed to before going home to Bakerville. As National Guard, we'll commit to three years. Three years until I see my family. With the way things are, it's not like we can hop in a car for a weekend visit.

At least something resembling mail service is happening. We were first able to send letters in late summer. A few weeks ago, Nettie got a letter from Kansas, and I've heard of others receiving mail. I've sent a couple of letters home but have yet to receive a response. I shouldn't be surprised. Bakerville is off the beaten path, nestled at the base of the mountains.

Nettie says she grew up in a tiny town, too, not much larger than Bakerville. Extremely tight-lipped about her past, I was surprised when she volunteered the information. I asked her more about living in Kansas, since I went to school in Manhattan and Leo grew up in a small town in Southern Kansas near the Oklahoma and Missouri state lines. Nettie promptly changed the subject.

I'm trying to be patient, but I'd love to hear from home. How are my sisters and brother? My nieces and nephews? Jake? Is he coming out of his grief from losing my mom? My eyes well, the way they do whenever thoughts of my mom pop into my head.

"You're sure, Katie?" Leo's mouth is tight.

"For sure." I force the happiness into my voice. "I'm surprised, though. I thought for sure Dr. Newsome would vote no. At least for me."

"Well . . . " Nettie tilts her head. "The decision was a majority but not unanimous."

"Of course it wasn't." I shake my head like it's on a swivel. "Do you know, will we still be assigned here? Or will they move us?"

"I don't know. I hope you'll stay here. We need you."

"Here, I think." Leo smiles again. "Captain Williams wants to keep us. Lieutenant Paul said it was likely too." He meets my gaze with a nod.

Lieutenant David Paul is someone Leo met when going out on patrol as a medic. Now they even do PT together. I'd call them friends, but Leo says since he's only a sergeant and Paul is a lieutenant, they keep respect of rank.

"We'll have basic training and still need to have shifts here, and . . . well, it's going to be a busy several weeks. Months even." Leo's grin falters. "For you, anyway. I'm not sure what they'll do with me."

"They'll give you time to heal." Nettie gives a firm nod. "David heard about your fall. You were still asleep, or he would've come in to talk. He said he'll be by your place soon. He has an idea of your treatment plan and limitations."

I almost laugh at her use of the word limitations. With both arms broken and in casts, Leo's *limitations* are massive. He can't even use the toilet by himself. I'm not sure how I'll be able to do basic training, hospital shifts, and care for him.

And I almost forgot about the puppies. Right now, they need round-the-clock care and, like my husband, can't use the bathroom by themselves either. I'm going to have my hands full. Soon, the dogs will have their eyes open and will be bouncing everywhere.

Things could get a little crazy.

Chapter 10

"Thank you for your help, Opal. We'll put the box in the living room for now." Opal gently puts the box of puppies on the floor next to the couch while I help Leo to the recliner. "You want to put the chair back?"

"No. Might not be able to get it back upright." Leo's face is pinched. "Just let me rest."

"Need me to stick around?" Opal waves her arm, encompassing our space.

We live in a recently remodeled older home, only a few blocks from the medical center. The owners were away when the attacks started. It's a cute place, with an open-concept living area and two bedrooms. Perfect for the two of us. It's also the largest home we've had since our wedding. For most of our time together, we lived in a motor home we shared with another couple. This is pretty amazing.

"I think we're okay," I tell Opal with a thankful smile. "You still need to get back to camp, right?"

"Yup. Will be a quicker trip back than it was comin' down yesterday."

"Thanks so much for your help." Leo squeezes his eyes and carefully adjusts himself in the recliner. "Please thank your son for me also."

"Ya bet. We'll check in on you when we get back. My guess is we won't stay out as long as we planned. We've already brought back more food than they expected. A good hunting trip for sure."

Opal hands me a jar of broth and a leg bone. "To make broth for the puppies."

"No, I can't."

"It won't be missed. I'll check on you when I'm back in town. We'll be praying." Opal wraps me in a hug and leaves.

There's little waste with the deer and fish. The livers, hearts, and other offal were cooked and eaten at camp. Broth was made from the smallest scraps to add to meals while we were there, while larger bones were wrapped in fabric and brought home.

Smoking and dehydrating were also done in camp, but the deer we harvested along with another fresh kill were brought back raw to be handed out with this week's rations.

Ration chips are strictly monitored, but individuals and communities are encouraged to garden to add to their diet. Our next-door neighbors, the Harringtons, have an amazing garden, producing an insane amount of produce on a normal-sized lot.

They focused their growing efforts on root vegetables—potatoes, carrots, turnips, and beets. Even with the season winding down, they're only now beginning to harvest. They went in with a few other families who focused on other things so they can all trade.

Leo and I didn't get into town early enough to become involved in a co-op. We have our ration chips and stick to ourselves for food. We arrived too late for much of a garden, but we did get a little lettuce and some radishes, and I'm attempting an indoor winter garden. Mrs. Harrington has been tending to my seedlings during the time we were with the hunting group.

Fellowship during meals is probably one of the things I miss the most, the talking and sharing of things that happened during the day—both good and bad. I also miss church services and Bible studies.

Since moving to Rapid City, Leo and I haven't found a church service we go to regularly. There are a few we've visited, but either our work schedules are a problem, or something just wasn't right. We've been discussing how we truly need to find a home church, how we both miss being with other believers on a regular basis.

Leo shifts in his chair. "Can you get me some water?"

After helping him drink, he leans his head back again. "I don't know how you're going to do it, Katie. I'll be completely useless for weeks, months maybe. Everything will fall on you—gathering water, food, all the cooking, and work too. Not to mention starting basic training." He shakes his head. "The timing couldn't be worse."

I move to the couch. "Funny how that works, isn't it? I mean, really, is there a suitable time to break both arms?"

"Did you hear Newsome muttering when Nettie told him why I fell off the horse? About the pups?"

"It's not surprising, considering his previous actions. I know he's a good doctor, but I don't think much of him." A knock at the door interrupts the less-than-kind comment I was about to give. I lift my shoulders and heft myself off the couch. My entire body aches from the events of yesterday and sleeping in a hospital room chair last night.

"Caution, Katie." Leo repositions himself to sit on the edge of the chair.

I tilt my head at him. "You think a robber is going to knock on the door?"

He gives me a stern look. "You forget about the rash of break-ins?"

I resist rolling my eyes. In the past few weeks, there has been an increase of burglaries. Usually, it's when people are at work, but there was a break-in near the town of Sturgis that resulted in a man's death.

Leo was concerned we might be robbed while we were with the hunting group. I reminded him we had nothing to steal. Furniture isn't a high-demand item. We took our food and anything important—like my watch and our weapons—to camp. Anything else special to us was left in Bakerville with the people we love.

I peer out the window, then glance back to my husband. "Lieutenant Paul," I mouth, then scurry to the front door. While the house is an open concept, the entryway is closed off from the living room—a feature I find to be annoying. I'd prefer to see the door from the rest of the space.

"Hello, Lieutenant. Nice to see you."

"Private Burnett. I heard about the troubles."

"Yes, please, come in." I step back from the door as he removes his cap and steps inside.

While I don't care for Bruce Blake calling me little lady, I'm also not overly fond of being called Private Burnett. I guess, though, I'd better get used to it since I'll soon be an official part of the South Dakota Army National Guard, and there will be no getting out of it.

At least with the Volunteer Unit, most people realize it's a laxer situation than the regular military. Captain Williams refers to me as private, but Nettie was more than happy to call me Katie when I asked.

"Lieutenant." Leo's practically sitting at attention in the recliner.

The lieutenant cringes and shakes his head. "I shouldn't be surprised about your condition. I've always thought you were a bit of an overachiever."

"Yes, sir. I guess that's about the size of it."

"Stopped by the hospital first. Heard you're out of commission for at least three months."

Leo's face falls. "I was only expecting six weeks or so, sir."

"Yeah, well . . . " The lieutenant lifts a hand. "And with the condition you're in, I'd say the private here— " he clears his throat " —your wife, will have her hands full. I spoke with the general after we found out about your fall. He suggested we put your enlistment on hold. Both of your enlistments."

Leo and I share a quick look before I turn back to our guest. "Would you like to have a seat?" I motion to a chair, and he gives me a nod. "Can I put on the kettle for tea?"

He waves me off. "None for me, thanks."

I take my spot on the couch. "Is there any issue with us delaying? I mean, we're still officially part of the Volunteer Unit and were told we could only stay until the decision was made about what to do with us."

"When the rest of the unit left, the general assumed responsibility for you until the decision was made. That won't change. You'll still be on the official Volunteer roster, such as it is, under the command of Captain Williams."

I do like the prospect of staying at the hospital. Even if Newsome drives me crazy, I enjoy working with Williams and Nettie. "So, our three years will start after Leo's healed?"

Lieutenant Paul raises his hands, then looks toward Leo.

Leo visibly swallows. "Uh, Katie, it's an eight-year enlistment."

My stomach churns. Leo and I talked about this. "You said three years."

"I misunderstood."

Paul clears his throat. "The total enlistment time is eight years. In the past, three was a possibility, four more likely. The rest of the eight-year commitment would be on IRR, Individual Ready Reserve. Kind of like being on call at the hospital. You could be called up if needed, like if war broke out. And, uh, IRR is still a possibility if the reconstruction efforts go the way some are promising. But . . . " He lifts his hands. "Currently IRR is suspended. We're telling our new recruits to expect the full eight years. In many ways, we're at war."

I understand about IRR. Leo did IRR the last half of his time in the Marines—four active and four IRR, for a total of eight. I look to my husband, who is studiously avoiding my gaze. "When did you learn about this?"

"There's nothing certain." He still doesn't meet my eyes.

"I, uh . . . I should've had this conversation with you." Paul leans forward in his chair. "We certainly do anticipate the reconstruction efforts to be successful. Things may come together, and we'll reinstate IRR. You may not need to be active the entire time. There's a chance." He bobs his head.

"I just— " I don't like the high-pitched tone to my voice. I clear my throat. "I didn't expect to be away from my family longer than a year. When Leo said three, I accepted it, but . . . "

"It's not too late to change your mind. Discuss it. We'll leave you at your current status until Leo's healed. You have until you take your oath to change your mind."

Leo's mouth goes into a tight line. "Thank you, sir."

I stare at the floor as I fight down the combination of anger and bewilderment. Leo knew about it being eight years. He knew, and not only did he not tell me, he lied to me.

"One other thing."

I force my gaze up. "Sir?"

"Both of you went to college?"

Leo nods. "Yes, sir. I graduated with a Bachelor of Science in Business Administration only weeks before the attacks. Katie would've graduated in December with her degree."

Paul turns to me. "Nursing?"

"I was an art major. Didn't Leo tell you? The Bakerville doctor and nurses trained me."

"Yes, yes, I remember now. I heard such good things about you from Nettie—Dr. Wolff—I'd forgotten your history."

I attempt a smile. "Doc Nettie is very kind. The two of you are friends?"

His neck turns crimson. "Uh, yes. We, uh . . . yes." He clears his throat again. "Anyway, do you have any paperwork showing your degree or credits?"

"Nothing." Leo shakes his head. "Like my discharge papers, they're in a safe deposit box back in Manhattan. I don't know why I didn't think of bringing those things."

"We should have," I agree.

"Too bad. Proof of your credits could move you from enlisted personnel to commissioned officers." Paul's eyebrows wiggle slightly as he talks. "It could change things."

"So instead of private and sergeant we'd be lieutenants?" I ask.

"Well . . ." Paul looks to Leo.

"I'll be a private too. They won't acknowledge my rank in the Volunteers, and without proof of my prior military service . . . it's like it doesn't exist. I'll be starting fresh, just like you."

My eyes go wide. "What kind of proof would you need?"

"Copy of your degree or proof of ninety credits."

My parents were sent copies of all my records. If the mail starts working, could Jake send me proof of my credits? Is there some way we could get a copy of Leo's credits?

"Never thought I was cut out to be an officer anyway." Leo's cheerful expression doesn't make it to his eyes. In fact, his eyes are barely open. He needs to rest.

Lieutenant Paul must notice it too. "I've taken up enough of your time. I wanted to make sure you both know we're looking forward to having you— " he looks at me " —should you decide the National Guard is for you. We'll work with you on the timeline. You'll definitely have your hands full for a while."

After the lieutenant leaves, I check on the puppies. They were completely quiet while he was here. I don't think he even realized we had them.

"Sorry, Katie. I should've explained it better."

I don't look at him. "Did you purposely mislead me?"

He lets out a sigh. "Purposely? I didn't . . . " Another sigh. "I guess I did."

I sink to the floor next to the box. "Why? Did you think I couldn't— " My voice cracks.

"I don't know."

"So now what? We're pretty much stuck, aren't we? Our unit is gone, everyone else is going to join the Guard."

"I'm sure, once I'm able, we can go back to Wyoming, find another Volunteer Unit and finish out our year . . . if that's what you want." His voice has an angry snap to it.

"It might be. I don't know. I would've liked to have had *all* the information before agreeing to stay here." I let out a rattly breath.

He lets out his own noisy exhale. "I need to rest. We'll talk later."

I bite back the response forming on my lips. None of this should be a surprise to me. I should've been told the truth from the beginning.

As Leo begins to snore, I turn my attention to the puppies. The smallest one doesn't even notice as my tears begin to fall on his tiny head.

Chapter 11

I've been back to work a week now, on my second set of three-twelves. At least this time I'm on days; when I first went back, my shifts were the overnights. Captain Williams thought it might work better since Leo would be sleeping. It didn't. Neither Leo nor the puppies slept much while I was gone.

Day shifts haven't been great either. At least I'll be on my last one tomorrow, followed by two days off before another set of shifts. I'm hopeful Leo and the puppies will all be doing better before I'm on nights again.

Dr. Williams and Nettie act happy I'm back, like I was missed. Today I'm working with one of the traveling docs, Chastity Morrow. The traveling doctors rotate throughout the district medical centers to provide extra time off for our regular doctors. While usually an MD or DO, Chastity is a physician assistant—or as she told me, a physician associate, the name her profession was in the process of adopting prior to the EMP.

Today is Tuesday, which means it's automatically a busy day at the hospital. One day a week, we operate more as a doctor's office or clinic and less as a hospital. We even bring in extra nurses' aides from the care facilities to help with the patient load. Clinic days are usually hopping, and today is no exception.

It's late morning and I'm working in the stockroom, gathering things to refill the patient rooms. As normal for clinic days, we've had a lot of minor issues. There's a break in the action as the early morning rush has cleared out.

If our day goes the same as most Tuesdays, we'll get busy again around 1500 hours. That's one of the shift changes for several of the work crews. With the clinic set up as first come, first serve, people try to come in around their regular work duties.

A rustle at the half-opened door catches my attention. Newsome slides in and shuts the door hard. I stand up straight, my hand instinctively traveling to the butt of my handgun.

With a smirk, he leans against a wall and crosses his arms. "Heard you brought some mongrels back from the woods. You'd have been smart to dispose of them like you did the parents. Our lives are still too precarious to be housing pets. I have a friend who's found a beneficial use for dogs, cats too. I could make the arrangements. Get them off your hands."

My jaw drops.

"Don't act so surprised. Don't you know your history? Lewis and Clark ate plenty of dog during their travels. It's still a staple in some Asian and African countries, even before the lights went out. You think people aren't doing what they need to do to survive?"

I shake my head and look back at the supply shelves.

He scoffs a few times before opening the door. "Do what you want. Think what you want of me. I sleep easy knowing I did what was best for the people in my town. People who were starving. If it weren't for me, making the hard decisions, our dead would've doubled."

"Didn't it? Double, I mean, when the attack happened? Or is it simply a rumor your town was singled out because of what you did?"

He narrows his eyes and moves closer to me. "Don't believe everything you hear, Private Burnett. You don't know much about what's happening."

He stomps out of the room and mutters several things about my intelligence, or lack thereof.

I bite my lip, turn back to my work, and replay the incident in my head. There are so many things I wish I would've said to that man. So, so many.

"Hey, you okay?" Chastity Morrow asks from the doorway. "I heard him bothering you."

"Sure. It's nothing new." I'm sure the quiver in my voice is less than convincing.

"Really? Nettie told me about how he makes a point of seeking you out to reprimand you. Even when whatever happened wasn't your fault."

I fake a smile. "He's a good doctor."

She lets out a snort of laughter. "I'm beginning to think he may have issues with women. I've seen how condescending he is with everyone. Especially Nettie and me. It's like he goes out of his way to find fault in everything we do."

I let out a legit laugh and bob my head in agreement. When he showed up at the medical center about an hour ago, he said something completely patronizing to Chastity while we were between patients.

She ignored him; he got snappy. She turned and gave him a zinger right back while reminding him she is the doc on duty for the day and if his services were needed, she'd send for him. He huffed off to the breakroom.

He treats Nettie the same way he tried with Chastity, but Nettie is much more diplomatic in her responses. She still puts him in his place, but not quite as overtly as Chastity did.

Chastity motions to the hallway. "Let's get a cup of tea. Things are quiet, and we should take advantage of it."

We're on our way to the breakroom when Newsome steps out of the bathroom, brushing the door jamb with his shoulder on the way out. "Thick as thieves, I see. I guess you girls got to stick together."

"Break time, Dr. Newsome." Chastity makes a point of keeping her voice even. "You're welcome to join us for a cup of tea."

I attempt to hide my surprise at her invitation.

Newsome looks completely shocked. "Why, I . . . uh, thank you, but no." His steps falter slightly as he makes his way toward us. "I have the radio if you need me."

Chastity stops moving when we reach the breakroom door and motions me to go in. I move inside but continue to watch as Newsome approaches. He's altered his course, going to the other side of the hall.

"Doctor." Chastity raises a hand. When he stops, she steps close to him and whispers something. His face turns pink. When she says something else, the color deepens.

He makes a few sputtering noises.

Chastity raises her voice. "You need to get this under control." He opens his mouth to respond, but she lifts a hand and shakes her head. "I know the truth. Seek help."

His red face turns from embarrassed to angry. He narrows his eyes and gives her a biting look. "Good day, *Miss* Chastity." He stomps off, then trips over the toe of his shoe. He stumbles but recovers.

Chastity continues to stand in the hallway, watching until the bell above the door sounds. When she turns toward the break room, I move away from the doorway. I shouldn't have been watching the altercation, and I feel a little badly about spying.

"Did you hear?"

I raise a shoulder. "He's difficult somedays. But he does seem to be a good doctor. Most of the patients like him."

"Humph. Maybe when he's sober. I hope we don't have an emergency. We can't call him back."

My brows furrow. "Sober? He's been drinking?"

"Oh yeah. You didn't notice his eyes? The way he spoke? Smells?"

"Um . . . he usually looks and speaks like that. I wasn't near enough to smell him."

"He didn't the last time I was here. Does Captain Williams— " She waves a hand. "Never mind. You grab the thermos. I have some dried apples. Want some?"

I want to ask more about Newsome. She said he was different last time she was here. I wonder when that was. Newsome's been the same since Leo and I arrived.

The front bell sounds, and I slide my chair back. "I'll go check."

As I reach the doorway, I hear the janitor say, "Have a seat. The nurse will be right out."

I look to Chastity. "I guess break time's over."

~~~~~

"Really, it was one thing after another. Everything minor. I'll tell you, though, the man that came in with a sliver was something." I grin at Leo and put a bowl of greens on the table, forcing a light and airy tone as I share about my day. "Chastity and I were having a break when he arrived. The sliver was several inches long and deep."

Leo grunts a response.

"At least there wasn't anything big. No shootings or stabbings, nothing like that. Sometimes, I just don't understand why people are so ugly to each other. Don't they realize we'd be better off if we all worked together?"

Leo doesn't even acknowledge me.

I bite back a sigh and motion to the salad bowl. "It was nice of Captain Williams's wife to send us salad. Smart of her to make the dressing out of elk tallow. My mom used to make a spinach salad with a hot bacon dressing that was similar. Did she say if we need to warm it up?"
~~~~~

Leo lifts a shoulder while keeping his eyes on his plate. "Nope."

I fix him with a stare. When he doesn't respond, I choose to let it go. "Well, I'm sure it'll be delicious. Maybe our garden pots will give us lettuce for salad soon." I glance at my pathetic attempt at an indoor garden.

I'm trying a winter garden with pots of lettuce and tomatoes that I move outside during the day and bring in at night. We're hopeful they'll get enough sunlight from our east-facing window to grow most of the winter. Maybe a shelving unit in front of the window would help to give my sad seedlings better light.

"Oh! I got so excited about the salad, I almost forgot the bread." I give him another smile, which he doesn't see before I turn back to the kitchen.

It's been almost three weeks since Leo fell off the horse. The first week or so, he was as helpless as the puppies. He was also in considerable pain—not only in his arms, but his entire body had taken a beating. He ached all over.

Nettie gave him three narcotic tablets to get him through the first few days, along with a handful of over-the-counter anti-inflammatory pills. They barely touched the pain. When herbalist Stella heard about his fall, she brought several items from her medicinal garden to help with pain, including wild lettuce tea tincture.

Williams and Nettie have added Leo to their house-call patients. In addition to our hospital, which is set up for only emergency and short-term patients, there are several houses between here and there used as long-term care facilities.

These are usually operated by a husband-and-wife team who live on site, along with twenty-four-hour staff that mainly consists of nurses' aides. These are the same aides we utilize for our clinic day. If Dr. Newsome had his way, I'd be working out of one of these places instead of the hospital. It was Captain Williams who said my skills are needed where I am.

Even though Newsome does house calls to the care facilities, he hasn't stopped by to see Leo. It's either Williams or Nettie who pops in every other day to see how Leo's healing.

They're especially paying attention to the ulcer on his shoulder, which isn't doing as well as any of us would like. Leo did a full course of antibiotics, but a few days later, it was obvious he was infected. He's now on his second round of orals, plus a topical antibiotic applied twice daily.

Even Stella stopped by recently to look at the ulcer. She insisted she had the perfect remedy to wipe out the infection but would consult with Williams before making any changes.

As I return to the table with a slice of buttered bread for each of us, Leo is already eating. His right arm, with the broken humerus, now works well enough to eat the simple slices of meat without utensils. The first week and a half or so, I spoon fed him and assisted him in all his daily needs. Leo didn't need a trained medical professional, he needed me—his wife.

I glance at the puppies laying calmly on a blanket, a mound of four keeping each other warm. Their eyes are now open, and they need less care than they did in those early days. They're able to regulate their own body temperatures now and don't need the supplemental heat. They're even lapping at gruel instead of using the baby doll bottle.

Leo finishes his supper in nearly record time, not talking or even looking at me. He doesn't even tell me goodnight when he announces he's going to bed. With my meal half finished, I stare at his back as he walks away.

Chapter 12

I sit up straight in bed. Was that the puppies? With their eyes open and as much as they move around, we had to find a deeper crate for them. The noise sounds again, this time jolting me to my feet. It's not the puppies. It's not even from inside the house.

"It's next door." Leo swings his legs off the edge of the bed.

I slide my feet into my trainers and quickly tie the laces. I learned long ago, when a middle of the night emergency occurred, to sleep in lounge clothes and not pajamas or nightgowns. Leaving the house at a moment's notice is common during the apocalypse. "What do you think is happening? What do we do?"

There's a scream and a gunshot followed by the shattering of glass. The family next door is multigenerational. The Harringtons welcomed their son, daughter-in-law, and two young grandchildren in the early days of the disaster from their home in nearby Spearfish. They said it made sense for them to all be together during this time. They've been great neighbors. *Quiet neighbors.* The men are part of the Citizen Patrol, a group of citizens who have been deputized by the Pennington County Sheriff's Department.

I'm buckling my utility belt when another scream jolts me into action. "What do we do?"

"Cause a diversion and hope it's enough."

"Enough for what?"

"To stop whatever is happening so we can evaluate."

I motion to his arms, both in plaster casts, a sling on the right one to help hold it tight against his body as he sleeps. "You're in no condition— "

He moves as he talks. "I'll be the diversion. I'm going to yell from the front door. You go out the back, through the yard and into the alleyway. Stay in the shadows. If you see anyone leaving, try and get as many details about them as you can, but let them go."

"Let them go?"

"You're one person. Don't do anything stupid." He pierces me with a hard look, completely devoid of love. "I mean it, Katie. Stay hidden. I'll give you one minute, then I'm going to raise a ruckus. Stay hidden and let them go."

With my heart pounding, I grab my parka. I fumble with the back door lock before slipping out. I'm barely out the back gate when Leo's voice booms through the neighborhood. "What in the blazes is going on?"

Moving quickly to a large tree across from the alley, I get into position. Another, shakier male voice calls out, "Yeah. What're you doing over there, Harrington?"

This is followed by others yelling similar things. I'm sure they all think the same thing Leo and I do—it's another burglary. They've been happening with increased regularity throughout the city.

There was even a robbery a few days ago several streets over, in broad daylight. The family was away at work and came home to find their house stripped of anything usable. Their neighbors said they never saw a thing—of course, most of them were either at work or sleeping because they have night jobs, so it's not a surprise there were no witnesses.

"They're gone! We need help please. We need help!" The voice is young and female. Kirstie Harrington is around my age. It sounds like her.

The back gate on the Harringtons' fence slowly opens. A man's head pops out.

Hugging the shadows, with my pistol at the ready, I hold completely still, not even daring to breathe.

"Let's go. Let's move," a gruff voice from behind orders.

"I am," the first man hisses. "What the—why'd you shoot him?"

"Shut up, you imbecile. It was an accident. Now move."

As the first man steps out, the illumination from the moon and the stars gives enough light for me to see his long orangish-red beard poking out under a ski mask. He's medium build and carrying a bulging black duffle bag. The second man, taller than our six-foot-high fence by several inches, with broad shoulders and a scruff of brown beard poking out from his ski mask, shoves the red-bearded man from behind. He's hefting a second duffle bag.

As they stand there, looking up and down the alley, the tall man makes a disgusting noise before spitting out a wad of phlegm. My stomach churns at the sight. They look both directions before heading away from me and slipping between two houses about fifty feet to the east.

I consider following them—at a distance. But Kirstie's second cry for help has me running back to our house to grab my medical kit. I call out for my husband, but he doesn't answer. His medical kit isn't hanging on the hook by the door; he's already gone. I grab my kit and rush out, the storm door banging behind me.

There's a small group of people gathered in the front yard. The neighbor across the street is in a nightgown, a light robe, and slippers, her hair caught up in a scarf. She calls to me as I bound off the porch. "Your husband's already in their house! He said he needs you."

I give a curt nod as I dash from my yard. Inside, Leo, Oscar Harrington, and another man from the neighborhood are kneeling beside someone. I take a quick look around the room. Kirstie is on the sofa, openly weeping, with her children by her side. Mrs. Harrington is sitting on a chair, holding her head.

Leo snaps his head in my direction. "Mr. Harrington was shot. We've sent someone after the handcart. Check Mrs. Harrington." His green eyes convey more than his words. It doesn't get much worse than a gunshot in today's world. Even simple injuries, which may once have had a likelihood of survival, are now fatal. We don't have the supplies to treat everything as needed.

Oscar, Kirstie's husband, meets my gaze, his eyes moist with unshed tears. "My mom was hit on the head."

I give him a curt nod. "I'll see to her." I kneel next to her chair, my movement causing her to lift her head, which results in a wince. I rest my hand on her forearm. "Mrs. Harrington? It's me . . . Katie Burnett."

"Mm-hmm. Is my husband okay?"

My gaze travels to her spouse on the floor. While I didn't get a good view of him before, I now see plenty. Oscar and another man are trying to stop the bleeding, with Leo instructing them. "They're taking good care of him."

"But is he . . . is he still alive?"

The other neighbor lifts his chin. "We're doing what we can, ma'am."

Oscar looks up. "Let Leo's wife check you out, Mom. We'll take care of Dad."

A sound between a gulp and a cry escapes Mrs. Harrington. "Please. Please save him." She sinks into her chair and returns her hands to her head. Her voice is low. "My head . . . hurts."

"You were hit?"

"Mmm."

"With an object?"

"The gun. Here." She moves her hand to a spot above her right ear. "It hurts, but I'm . . . I'm fine."

My lips pull tight. "Let me check your pulse and vitals." I reach for her wrist and look at the face of my watch. Her pulse is fast—to be expected with everything happening.

I open my kit to retrieve a manual blood pressure cuff and stethoscope. "How old are you?"

"Fifty-two."

Barely older than my mom when she died. "Let me get your blood pressure."

She gives a meager nod. "He needs to go to the main hospital—the big one."

I glance to Leo, who's looking at Mr. Harrington while whispering to Oscar and the other man. "He'll need to go to our hospital to get stabilized at least. We're waiting for the handcart."

The handcart is our end-of-the-world version of an ambulance. It's a two-wheeled wagon moved by human power instead of horses, modeled after the handcarts used by Mormon pioneers during the 1800s.

Ours are longer, allowing for a stretcher to be placed on the cart. Each medical clinic has at least one, along with access to a horse and wagon, and even a few biodiesel-powered vehicles. The handcart is the first choice since they don't require any sort of fuel and are much quicker than setting up the horses.

"Which doctor is there?"

"Which doctor? At the hospital?"

"We don't like that Newsome fella. He can't be trusted."

I didn't work today and am off tomorrow. I visualize the handwritten calendar on a dry erase board in the breakroom. "I think Captain Williams is on tonight. Nettie Wolff is his backup. She lives practically next door."

"Okay. Fine," Mrs. Harrington says, then starts to cry. "Why'd he do it? I told him to let them go, let them take what they wanted. But the stubborn fool— " She chokes out a sob. "Why would he do that? He should've just let them go."

I rub her arm while she collects herself. It's several minutes before I'm able to finish with her vitals. The handcart appears while I'm listening to her lungs.

"Can I go with him?"

"Yes, of course. We'll want to have the doctor check you too."

She waves her hand. "I'm fine. It's barely a bump. Doesn't even hurt much now."

"Can you walk? Or we can have the handcart return for you." We've talked about adding a second handcart. I'm going to mention it again.

"I'll walk." She turns to Kirstie. "Will you and the children stay here?"

Her daughter-in-law doesn't meet her eyes when she responds with a nod. The little boy asks if his papa will be okay. Kirstie pulls him close and kisses the top of his head before whispering something I don't hear.

Mrs. Harrington raises her voice, sounding stronger than she has since I've arrived. "Kirstie, this isn't your fault. Now buck up and snap out of it."

"But, Mom— " Kirstie slams her mouth shut. Her gaze drifts to Mr. Harrington. "Do you need me to go with you? To be with you?"

Mrs. Harrington looks to her husband as Leo gives instructions to move the man onto the board stretcher. As they lift him, he lets out a low groan. "Careful," Leo cautions. "The bullet's still lodged. We don't want it moving around."

Kirstie whimpers and buries her head as she pulls her children close. Her tears start again. Mrs. Harrington scoffs and shakes her head. The little boy whispers, loud enough for me to hear. "Aren't you the lady with the puppies?"

I give him a slight smile. "I am."

"Are they at your house? Alone?"

Swallowing the lump in my throat, I dip my chin. "For now. I hope they're sleeping."

"We could stay with them—yeah, Mommy? Could we take care of her puppies?"

"That is a good idea," Mrs. Harrington declares. "Can they take care of them for you?"

The little girl's eyes go wide. "Me, Nana? Me!"

"With your help, of course."

I close my eyes briefly and let out a sigh of relief. Not only because the dogs won't be left alone—not the easiest thing now that they can climb out of their crate and get into all sorts of mischief—but because Mrs. Harrington is talking and seems fine. When I first saw her, I worried it would be like the man we treated not long ago.

He fell while working on his house, hit his head so hard he never regained consciousness. After several days in the hospital, he was moved to one of the care facilities where he slowly withered away until he passed in his sleep.

"Yes, that'd be a huge help," I answer. "The front door is unlocked. They're in the bedroom, the room off the living room. Will you bring them over here?"

Kirstie looks to her mother-in-law before giving a vacant nod. "Will they need food?"

I shake my head. "They're only fed three times a day now. They'll be fine until I return."

Mrs. Harrington clears her throat. "They're leaving with my husband. Will you walk with me?"

I search her face. There's a strange look in her eyes. Maybe she isn't doing as well as I'd thought.

She waves a hand. "I'm fine. Truly. Just a little woozy."

"We should have the handcart return for you."

"No, no. Let's go with them now." She sends her daughter-in-law a pointed look as she stands.

In many ways, Mrs. Harrington reminds me of my mom. Not in appearance—not at all. My mom was shorter than me, where Mrs. Harrington is several inches taller.

Her long black hair is knitted with wiry gray strands. My mom kept her hair short. Even after the EMP, she and one of her friends trimmed each other's hair to keep it tight and manageable. Jake used to joke Mom's hair was shorter than his. Tears sting my eyes as I remember my mom's laughter as she'd run her hand through her newly shorn locks, promising Jake she'd give him the best haircut ever.

Mrs. Harrington, who insists I call her Crystal, walks next to the handcart. She tells her husband how he'll be just fine and they'll fix him right up. We've barely made it fifty yards before she lets out a low moan and slows her steps. "Fast, aren't they?"

"They really are." I keep pace next to her. "That's good for your husband. The sooner he gets there, the better."

"Yes. Yes, of course. I— " She puts a hand to her head. "I'm not feeling too great."

"Your head? Is it hurting?"

"Bad. The headache—oh!" She turns her head and vomits.

I hold her long hair back as she bends at the waist. Head injury plus vomiting is not good.

I cup my hands around my mouth. "Leo! Leo! Send the handcart back for Mrs. Harrington."

He stops and raises a hand. "What?"

"Send the cart back. She can't make the walk. She needs a doctor."

"I'm fine. Truly. I can walk." Crystal Harrington's protest is weak. "I . . . " She sways as her eyes close.

I balance her weight, helping her to the pavement. "Leo! I need help! Mrs. Harrington needs help!"

Chapter 13

Crystal is lying on the pavement. Eyes closed. Breathing shallow.

Two men from the neighborhood, likely part of the gathered crowd who were walking alongside the handcart, come running up to us. One of them leans down. "She doesn't look too good. Don't think we should wait for the cart to return. I'll carry her."

I suck in my upper lip as I run through the troubles that could result from her being carried instead of waiting for the cart to return. She doesn't have a neck or back injury. Getting her to the hospital quickly is probably the best course of action. "She may vomit."

He makes a face. "Fine. That's fine." It takes a little effort and help from me and the other man to get her positioned in his arms.

She moans a few times and moves a hand to her head. "I don't . . . I'm sorry about this." Her voice is a whisper.

"No worries, ma'am. We'll get you there, and they'll fix you right up."

"They're still helping my husband?"

"The cart didn't stop. Burnett sent us back to help you."

"That's . . . good." She lets out a sigh.

Our walk to the clinic is fast. The man moves easily, even with Crystal in his arms. The friend asks once if he needs to pass her off to him, but the carrier declines and asks him to run ahead to make sure they're ready for us.

When we reach the hospital, he's there with tonight's medic, a new man who's been brought in to replace Leo while he heals, waiting at the edge of the parking lot with a gurney. "Thought this might make things easier." The medic motions to the wheeled bed.

"Thanks, yeah." The man carrying Crystal is super gentle as he places her on the gurney. "They'll get you taken care of now. You just relax." She doesn't stir as he speaks to her. He shakes his head before turning to me. "Think they'll need us inside?"

"Nah, man." The night medic is already adjusting the brake and ready to move. "Thanks for getting her here. They've already called in a couple more docs, and with Private Burnett here, we'll be fine."

I help push the gurney inside, holding the door once we reach it. Doc Nettie is coming out of an exam room, likely having been called in as soon as the handcart was dispatched. All of us are housed within walking distance of the hospital. We have walkie-talkie type things for when we're on call, ones with a better range than the basic type. With limited staff, it's important for extra help to be easily accessible.

Each twelve-hour shift only has a single doctor, nurse, medic, and janitor on staff. There are also people who do the cooking, laundry, and a whole host of other miscellaneous things needed to keep our hospital functioning, but they don't work on site. All the extra stuff is done elsewhere and brought in.

"What do we have?" Nettie asks as she starts her exam on Mrs. Harrington.

"Fifty-two-year-old female hit on the head with a gun about— " I look at my watch and try to remember when we heard the first scream " —thirty-five minutes ago. She was talking and coherent. Vitals were within normal range. We started walking here, following her husband. She seemed fine until she vomited and collapsed. She's woken up and spoken a few times but has mainly been out since she went down."

"Wash up, Katie. I'll need you."

"Mrs. Harrington?" Nettie looks at me for name confirmation.

"Crystal Harrington." I hold my dripping hands up, shaking them dry. We keep a cooler full of warm water next to the sink. There are cloth towels for drying, but mostly we drip dry, followed by a liberal dose of homemade hand sanitizer processed by a distillery in Deadwood.

"All right, then, Mrs. Harrington." Nettie vigorously rubs her arm. "Can you open your eyes for me?"

Crystal doesn't exactly open her eyes but does stir, even pulling her arm away from Nettie.

"Good. Good. Katie, start an IV."

As I put an IV in Crystal's hand, Nettie spends many minutes with her examination. She pulls her lips tight and shakes her head. "I think it may be an epidural hematoma."

"A brain bleed?"

"Bleeding within the skull. This injury is sometimes referred to as talk and die syndrome. It fits with what you described, but usually there's a longer period of lucidness, so . . . " She gives a slight lift of her shoulders.

"Talk and die syndrome, huh?" Newsome sniffs as he walks into the exam room. "And Private Burnett failed to accurately diagnose the injury. Sounds about right for a novice who has no business treating patients."

"Dr. Newsome. I didn't realize you were called in for this situation." Nettie gives him a slight nod.

"Of course I was. You think Williams can manage this on his own?" He flares his nostrils. "With only the help of a med student and a candy striper?"

Nettie ignores the jab at us. "This is Crystal Harrington, Katie's next-door neighbor. She and her husband were attacked by intruders."

Newsome waves a hand and directs his gaze to me.

I clear my throat. "Her husband was shot."

"You think I don't know exactly what has happened?" Newsome snaps, then points at me. "I heard about how you let this gravely injured woman walk alongside the handcart. You signed her death warrant."

I lift my chin and stretch my eyes in an attempt to keep the tears at bay. "Can you help her?"

He scoffs. "A sure sight better than the two of you."

He points at me again. "You have no business being here. I was agreeable to you working here in a nursing assistant position—doing the bathing and getting people to the bathrooms, dumping the bed pans. But you've been given far too much latitude. You may have impressed Dr. Williams and General Truss, along with a few others who don't know any better, but I'm putting my foot down. We will not have lay people thinking they know what they're doing and killing people."

"Who's been killed?" Crystal Harrington's eyes pop open. "Is my husband— "

I reach for her hand. "They're still working on him. Captain Williams is taking care of him." I don't like the way my voice sounds. Crackly. Weak. Pathetic. I give her an encouraging look. "Dr. Newsome's here. He'll take care of you."

"Newsome!" A look of panic crosses her face. "No. Not him. He's a— "

"What's the problem, dear?" Newsome steps closer to her.

"You . . . you . . . " She scrunches up her eyes and lets out a moan. "Ahh. My head." Her eyes flutter closed. "Please. Not. Him."

Newsome shrugs. "She's delirious. Common with this sort of injury. We'll need to do our best to keep her comfortable."

Nettie blinks several times. "Are we going to operate?"

"A craniotomy? Under these conditions? Are you mad?"

Moments ago, he said I'd signed her death warrant by allowing her to walk. Now he wants to let her die.

"What if . . . " Nettie takes a step toward Crystal. "What if we tried aspirating? I think it's still small enough it should work."

He narrows his eyes before chuffing out a noise. "Doubtful."

"But it may?"

"There's no way to know how severe the injury is. Not without x-rays and proper testing. She may have a midline shift and herniation. She'd need a craniotomy."

"But it may not be that severe."

He waves a hand. "I won't have you wasting resources."

"I won't, Doctor. Lidocaine . . . everything else is reusable. Katie can assist me."

"Humph. I'll be sure to alert Hugo to start working on another coffin. Maybe he'll do a double deep for her and her husband."

"Did they lose him?"

"That fool Williams is in there still trying to bring the man back. He's another one wasting resources. But he doesn't listen any better than you do." Newsome spins on his heel. "I'm going home and back to bed. You do what you do. It won't work anyway."

As soon his footsteps fade down the hall, Nettie tells me what to gather. As I'm organizing the tray, I ask if Newsome is right.

"About Mrs. Harrington, or her husband?"

"Both. Can they be saved?"

"We're going to try our best for her. I'm not sure about the mister. And no matter what Newsome said, Dr. Williams will not be wasteful of our supplies. He knows better than Newsome what we have and don't have, plus what we can restock."

"Does she have it? The midline shift?"

Nettie puts on a thoughtful face. "There's no way to be entirely sure without imaging, but . . . " Her sigh is loud. "She does have clinical signs her cerebral tissue may have moved. Any time there's a traumatic brain injury, it can happen."

"Will this work?"

"I don't know. But it's our only option. Does she know Dr. Newsome?"

I lift my shoulders. "She didn't want us to bring her husband here. She specifically asked who would be on call. I told her Captain Williams was on tonight and you were the backup. That seemed to alleviate some of her concerns."

"Did you remind her I'm only a medical student and not a doctor?" She points to the scissors I laid out. "Clip the hair before using the razor blade to shave it close. Be gentle."

I trim the hair close to her scalp. "I think after over a year of doctoring, few people remember you aren't a full MD." I grab a safety razor to continue prepping the area.

"Newsome remembers. And he loves to remind me of it." She leans in to see what I'm doing. "Gentle there. Use a light touch."

I lift my gaze to confirm I'm doing it as I should.

"Good. That's good." Nettie nods. "Exactly how Newsome reminds you every chance he gets. He was hard on Chastity while she was here too. Some days . . . I don't know how much longer I can put up with his pompousness."

"At least Captain Williams is different. And Chastity and the other visiting docs treat you like one of them, right? What about Dr. Winchester?" Dr. Winchester, a neurosurgeon, works out of the main hospital but is in charge of all the satellite clinics.

She looks up from the tray. "Dr. Winchester is the reason I'm here. I was doing a short rotation with her—just following her around really— when everything fell apart. I went from shadow to doctor almost overnight. When they set up the district hospitals, she trusted my skills enough to put me here with Captain Williams. At first, Williams and I had one of the veterinarians helping, but he left in the spring. Newsome didn't show up until— " she clears her throat " — later."

"Until the town he lived in was attacked."

"Right. Okay. Looks like we have what we need. Why don't you grab Ryan? We may need the help of a medic. If he's not available, have the janitor help us. I'm going to give Mrs. Harrington a shot to help her relax."

My eyes go wide.

"I know, I told Newsome only lidocaine. But after the ordeal of tonight, she needs more. But we may need help in here to secure her if she comes around. And let Williams know what we're doing. We're going to need his help as soon as he's available."

Ryan, the medic who is replacing Leo, assists us with holding Mrs. Harrington still. It isn't needed, though. The medication keeps her pretty much out of it. Nettie's movements are slow and precise.

Nettie talks through what she's doing as she works. I know it's mainly for my benefit and education, though I don't think I'll even need this knowledge. If Newsome gets his way, I'll be relegated to dumping bedpans and nothing more. If I even get to keep working at the hospital.

My back is already aching when Captain Williams pops his head in, his face still masked but his hands without gloves. "How's it going? Heard you've got a brain bleed?"

Nettie dips her chin. "Her husband?"

"No. Sorry."

I close my eyes and let out a quiet breath. It was obvious at the house he was unlikely to survive, but since they'd been working on him for so long, I thought maybe.

Nettie gives a stern nod. "I've gone as far as I'm comfortable. Can you finish?"

After scrubbing and putting on a new mask and gown, Williams looks over the minor surgery site. "Looks clean."

It takes longer than I think it should for Captain Williams to use the drill and put in tiny burr holes. Captain Williams declares several times how much easier it would be with the proper equipment and an actual neurosurgeon.

"But you've done this before, at least." Nettie's eyebrows raise above her mask.

"And it didn't work, remember?" Captain Williams works in silence for several beats. "Tell me, Private Burnett, what do you think for antibiotics?"

I clear my throat. "Um, yes. It doesn't seem to be overly invasive, but maybe the lichen tincture? Will there be an open wound when you're finished?"

"Not much, no. Sometimes a drain is left in, but not this time. Nettie will close."

"Maybe something topical?"

"Let's give her twenty-four hours. We'll know more within that time if this is even going to work. The damage could've been too extensive."

It's only a few more minutes until Williams is finished. We clean the area and put a small bandage into place.

Nettie lets out a sigh. "Let's get her in a room, make her comfortable. The sedative will be wearing off soon. Find her son. He should be with her when she wakes."

I take a long look at Crystal. She looks so weak, so helpless.

My mind takes me back to my mom, to those final days of her life. She, too, was weak and helpless but would always muster a smile when one of us went into her room. We were with her as much as possible, surrounding her with love. That's the way it should be for Crystal too.

Chapter 14

"Can I get you anything?" The smile I give Crystal is genuine. I'm amazed by how well she's doing.

Nettie's plan to try the less-invasive aspiration as opposed to the only other option—a craniotomy—seems to have been a success. Especially considering we aren't set up for a craniotomy, and as Newsome said, it could be a waste of resources and open her up to infection and other complications.

Kirstie and her children are here for a visit. Her young son leans closer to his grandma. "I can take care of you while I'm here, Nana."

"I know you can." Crystal gives him a squeeze. "But I'd rather have you right where you are. I've missed your hugs. And hugs from your mom, dad, and sister too."

"And Papa?"

Kirstie makes a hushing sound before whispering her son's name.

Crystal's eyes fill with tears. "Most definitely your papa's hugs. I'll miss him forever."

"Me too. Why did he have to die?"

I step out of the room to give the grieving family space. It's only been two days since the middle of the night break-in. After I finished helping to stabilize Crystal, I was interviewed for what seemed like hours by a deputy sheriff. I gave the best description I could from the moonlight glimpse I got of the killers.

Kirstie also saw the men when Mr. Harrington shined a flashlight toward them. I'm told my summary of what they looked like—one with a red beard and the other very tall—matches Kirstie's impressions. Sadly, since they were wearing ski masks when Kirstie saw them, and the lack of lighting when I saw them, our descriptions are vague.

Even with our limited information, the search for those responsible has been ramped up. There'd been several robberies before this, but only one resulted in the loss of life before Mr. Harrington. Of course, most of those incidents happened when people were gone to work or on a temporary out of town job, like the hunting trip we were sent on. As far as I know, there was never a middle of the night break-in.

Crystal's son, Oscar, did mention both he and his dad were scheduled to be on shift that night with the Citizen Patrol. Because of a few new hires—people who've recently finished the training program—the schedule was reworked, and they both got a couple of days off.

Could the robbers have known? Did they think attacking a home in the middle of the night with two women and two children would result in zero opposition? And if they did know Oscar and Mr. Harrington were supposed to be working, how'd they get their information?

I look toward the front door as the entrance bell jingles. "Hey, there," the friendly voice calls.

"Oh, hi, Mr . . . uh, Kasubowski." I stumble over his name as I step toward him.

"Just Bowski's fine. The name's a bit of a mouthful, so . . ." Ritchie Kasubowski lifts a shoulder. "I saw Oscar. He said his mom is still here. Okay for me to visit?"

My forehead crinkles. When I'd given my description of the assailants, I'd mentioned Bowski. I used his height as an example, saying the one killer seemed as tall or taller than my six-foot-four husband but not as tall as Bowski, at six-eight. Now, as I see him again—live and in person—I wonder if maybe the killer was as tall.

There aren't a lot of tall people in this world. Usually, Leo stands well above a crowd. In one of my college courses, I remember a discussion about the average male in the United States standing at five-nine. Worldwide, some countries have a taller average, but many have an even shorter one.

Bowski is definitely well-above average—so was the killer, standing a good head above his red-bearded friend and taller than the fence surrounding the yard. I'm sure it wasn't Bowski. The height may be close, but the body structure seems wrong. The tall man had broad shoulders, but he didn't seem as beefy as Bowski.

I give him a tight smile. "I didn't know you knew the Harringtons."

He nods. "Most of my life. Oscar and I went to school together before he moved to Spearfish and married Kirstie."

"Give a knock on the door. Her daughter-in-law and grandchildren are in with her."

"Is there a limit on the number of visitors at one time?"

"Oh, no. Nothing like that. They were— " I lift a shoulder. "It's a sad time with the loss of Mr. Harrington."

He gives a grave nod. "It is. I helped bury him. I'm glad they're waiting to hold the memorial service until Crystal's up for it. They were married a long time."

"You know them also?"

"Sure." He waves a hand. "Everyone knew Mr. Harrington. He was my third-grade teacher. Principal by the time my daughter started at the elementary school."

"Oh? I didn't even know he was a teacher. Or that you have a daughter."

His smile fades for an instant before he plops it back into place. "He was. Good guy. Crystal was a volunteer at the school. I knew them both."

It doesn't escape me that he doesn't address having a daughter. Is she among those lost since the attacks? Does he have a wife too? Or did he have one?

"They're right in there." I motion toward the room.

"Um, will she . . . " He runs a hand across the back of his neck. "Oscar said she's okay. Only a little confused. She should recover?"

"Are you asking if she'll recognize you?"

"I guess I am."

"I think so. She doesn't seem to have issues with knowing who people are. But I can't make any promises."

"And she'll recover? Be good as new?"

I slowly lift my shoulders. "You should ask Oscar or one of the family members. I can't discuss this with you."

He snorts out a laugh. "Even in the apocalypse, you're keeping patient privacy."

"Well . . . yes. It's not for me to share with you."

"Fair enough." He dips his chin as he steps toward Crystal's room. He takes a deep breath. His back stiffens as he forms a smile. "Knock. Knock. You up for a visitor?"

"Ritchie!" Crystal exclaims, sounding full of happiness. "Oscar said you were back in town. Please, come in."

I shake my head. Back in town? The hunting crew we were on with Bowski ended up being gone for a total of thirteen days. They've been back for almost two weeks, with a second crew going out the day after they returned. Was Bowski on the second crew?

Of course, I don't know the man or what his work assignments are like. Some people don't have stable work and are moved from assignment to assignment for whatever reason. Sometimes it's because they can't do the job they were given. Other times it's because a new crew was created.

Because of the way we became a part of this town, as the Volunteer Unit, we've never really been included in the other assignments. Both Leo and I were medics with the unit assigned to work at this hospital, located only blocks from the National Guard headquarters.

After the terrible incident, when having the Volunteers in the ration line resulted in the deaths of so many, the governor rescinded orders allowing federal troops. Since the United Volunteers, are considered part of the feds we were forced to leave. That's when the scrambling began. Those of us who wanted to stay worked hard to prove our worth.

The other six we were with on the Volunteer Unit are now all officially part of the South Dakota Army National Guard. They've been sworn in and everything. Leo and I went to the small ceremony. I could tell it wasn't easy for my husband to watch the others take their oaths while he sat by with two broken arms.

Nothing is easy for Leo these days.

I bite my lip to keep the tears at bay. My husband is struggling. He's anxious most of the time, pacing our small house, ordered to not wander outside alone because of his balance being slightly off from the double casts. The humerus does seem to be healing well, and thankfully, there's no issue of nerve damage in the lower arm.

The sore on his shoulder is still an issue. It's ulcerated and has been a struggle to keep from becoming infected. We rebandage it twice per day, and both Captain Williams and Nettie check on it each time they make a house call.

The calls are under the guise of caring for the wound, but I know part of it is checking his mental health.

Lieutenant Paul is also becoming a regular fixture at our place. Paul recruited members of a men's prayer group he's a part of—both military and civilian—to help Leo and me with our day-to-day needs. Someone comes around each day to make sure we have enough firewood and water in the house. We're often brought surplus vegetables, too, along with the occasional cooked dish or loaf of bread. I'm assured we're not taking food from anyone else nor are we violating the ration chip requirements.

I'm grateful for the help and that Paul recognizes the issues Leo is facing from his injuries. But I also worry it'll end up being a stigma for the future. Taking care of the quickly growing puppies at least gives him something to do, but I know he misses the busy life we had.

Even before the apocalypse, Leo wasn't one to sit idly by. We met during the summer between his junior and senior years at K-State in Manhattan, Kansas. I was officially going into my third year but taking summer courses so I could graduate a semester early, along with working as a server at an upscale restaurant and doing a paid internship at a local ad agency. I was ready to be done with college and get on with my life.

I was majoring in art, which, when I think about it, almost gives me a chuckle considering what I'm doing now. Dr. Newsome isn't entirely wrong about me not being a good fit as a nurse. There's a big difference between saving lives and drawing pictures.

Not only is Leo struggling from the injury, but we're also struggling as a couple. Our marriage is in a rough place. Other than the puppies, we seem to have little in common. When I first went back to work, I'd try to tell him about my day. I've stopped doing so after he made it clear he wasn't interested in hearing about the glamorous and exciting life I'm having while he's stuck at home.

Considering I was talking about how I'd had to clean up the bathroom after someone missed the toilet, I didn't think it was glamorous or exciting, but I guess he did have a point.

Other than the night of Mr. Harrington's murder, we've barely spoken in a week. I know it's because he's injured and irritated at me for being able to work while he's stuck at home healing. I've become increasingly mad at him for not giving me all the information about our commitment to the National Guard.

Part of me is so mad about being misled; I want to say forget it and finish up my year in a Volunteer Unit. Yes, the Black Hills area is lovely, and we're impressed with the reconstruction efforts, excited to be a part of bringing back our country. But is it worth eight years of my life? I never wanted to be in the military when our world was somewhat normal. Why would I want to be in it now?

Of course, the Volunteers was loosely considered part of the military too. That felt okay to me. A one-year commitment to help people—help our country—get back on their feet. That I could manage. It also seemed a suitable way to help with the grief I was having over the loss of my mom. Getting away from the homestead, where everything reminded me of her—and how I failed her—seemed smart at the time. Now . . . I'm not so sure.

"Help! We need help!" The door of the hospital is flung open, with the bell ringing wildly as a scraggly man in his early twenties runs in. "My wife . . . she's . . . help us!"

Hearing the commotion, the medic on shift, Jesse Talbot, comes running from the back with a gurney. "What's the trouble?"

"Lizzy. Something's not right."

I hustle toward the man. "Where is she?"

"Outside. I brought her in a wagon." He turns and runs back out the door.

"Dr. Newsome?" I ask Jesse.

"Went home to get some lunch. Afterward, he'll do rounds at the care facilities. I'll try to radio him." He grabs the handheld walkie-talkie off his belt.

I keep moving toward the door as he puts out a call to Newsome. He's still moving as we reach the exit. The bright sunshine of the October day causes me to blink. I stand by the door for several seconds and wait for my eyes to adjust. As my vision becomes clear, my gaze travels toward the woman.

She's in a child-sized black plastic wagon, sitting on her bottom but leaning forward. Tears stream down her face as she bites her bottom lip so hard there's a trickle of blood running down her chin. Her swollen belly, awkwardly perched on her skinny frame, fills the wagon.

As I step closer, I notice the blood on her chin is minor compared to the blood pooling in the bottom of the wagon. I stifle a cry. The amount of blood is *much* too much. She's bleeding out.

Chapter 15

Kneeling next to the wagon, I rest my hand on her back. "I'm Katie. Your name's Lizzy?"

"Eliza— " she squeezes her eyes tight " —beth. Only Patrick calls me Lizzy."

"Elizabeth?" I look to the man for confirmation.

He gives a nod as he reaches for her hand. "They're gonna help you, honey."

"Our baby?"

"Him too." He lifts his gaze to me. "What do we do?"

Within a couple of minutes, Jesse and the husband, Patrick, have Elizabeth on the gurney and moved into an exam room. Once she's settled on the table, I use a pair of scissors to cut off her pants before placing heavy towels to capture the blood. I cover her with a crisp white sheet.

Jesse keys the radio and calls for Newsome again. He waits only seconds before calling for Captain Williams, who's on backup and should be listening to the same radio channel. There's static over the airwaves but no response.

"I'll help you get her situated and then try from the base unit. Maybe . . . " Jesse shakes his head. "Maybe that'll reach him. I've left messages at each of the care facilities. No one has seen Newsome yet."

I try to keep the horror from my face as the stark white shows a spot of crimson. This amount of blood . . . I swallow hard before giving Elizabeth a smile. "I'm going to start an IV to help balance your fluids."

Jesse clears his throat and gives me a slight shake of his head. He's right. Newsome will freak if I do anything without his orders. But if we can't reach him, what choice is there? Just let her die?

I glance at her too-pale face and colorless lips as I run through treatment options in my mind. I've read about premature labor. I quickly take her blood pressure. Too low. Her pulse is fast and thready. "When's the baby due?"

"Two months."

"Two and a *half* months," Elizabeth corrects her husband. I'm working out the math in my head when she quietly adds, "Twenty-six weeks. I saw the midwife two days ago. She said things looked fine."

Too soon. Much too soon. "Which midwife?"

A shadow crosses her face.

I rest my hand on her stomach. "Are you having contractions?"

"I don't . . . maybe. There's a pain in my back."

Her belly is hard. "Is this your first?"

She gives a barely there gesture with her head.

Patrick's movement is much more vigorous. "Our first."

I've got everything set up for the IV. I've done these many times, both here in Rapid and at home in Bakerville. Never without a doctor's orders . . . but, really, what choice is there?

Jesse's still trying the radio, with no answer. He excuses himself to try and call from the base unit at the nurse's station. It's true the base has a greater reach, but usually, the walkie works fine to reach the doctors when they're on call. It even reaches my house when it's me or Leo taking calls.

"Hurry," I call to Jesse's back as he marches out the door.

While he's gone, I put together emergency supplies and pull over our newborn kit—a bassinet on wheels with blankets, a suction bulb, and several small washcloths. With things set for the baby, I then make sure we have what we need for Elizabeth's postpartum care.

She's softly crying while her husband hugs her around the shoulders, whispering, "You're going to be fine, honey. And our baby will be okay. The nurse seems to know what she's doing. The doctor will arrive soon, and all will be well."

Jesse's back in minutes. He lets out a combination grunt and sigh. "I'll start the IV." I look to him and shake my head. He lifts a hand. "Perhaps Patrick here can run to Dr. Newsome's home? His walkie may be on the blink."

Jesse gives Patrick the address and directions to Newsome's home. He says if he can't get Newsome, to try Nettie because she's only a couple of doors down. Even though Williams is the backup doctor, he lives in the opposite direction. It'd be too much to task the distraught man with another address and location.

As soon as he's gone, Jesse moves to wash his hands. I slide over next to him. "I can start the IV."

"Newsome will have your head if you do. He's looking for a reason to get rid of you. Let's not give him one."

"He won't be happy with you either."

Jesse lifts a shoulder as he scrubs. "He doesn't have it in for me."

I can't argue. Eugene Newsome seems to like Jesse as much, or maybe more, than he does Leo. The other medics too.

Bowski sticks his head in the door. "Heard the commotion." His eyes travel to Elizabeth, who is softly moaning. His eyes go wide as he takes in the scene.

I motion with my chin for him to leave. "We need privacy."

"Yeah. And it sounds like you also need a doctor. I know you sent the man for Newsome or Nettie. How about I go after Williams? I know where he lives. And that cute little brown-haired nurse. Need her too?"

I clear my throat. "Jacquie Haley? Please, yes. Thank you. Good idea for both." At the very least, we need more than Jesse and me. What if there's another emergency or Crystal Harrington needs something?

Leo's always said the hospital ran too tight with only a single nurse, medic, and doctor on shift—especially considering the doctor also has to make rounds at the care centers. And right now, we don't even have a doctor here. Where is Newsome?

Jesse gets the IV going like a pro while I check Elizabeth. The bleeding doesn't seem to have decreased any. We need a tocolytic—a medicine to stop the labor. When my sisters Sarah and Calley were pregnant, I studied the signs and treatments of preterm labor. But . . . will a tocolytic even help at this point? Not to mention, our supplies of meds used to stop labor are limited. Maybe Stella has an herbal potion?

Elizabeth lets out a low, guttural groan. Her eyes pop open. "Ahhh." She clutches at her stomach. "She's . . . she's . . . coming."

I move to the foot of the gurney and lift the sheet. As I do, there's a new gush of blood and other liquids. Elizabeth screams as I reach forward to grab the tiny baby easily sliding out. She's small and covered in blood with a blue tinge where I can see skin. She's not crying. Not breathing.

"Move her to mom's stomach." Jesse whips off the sheet. "Rub her chest. See if— " He looks at the baby and shakes his head. "Try."

"It's a girl?" Elizabeth asks in a tiny voice. "I knew . . . Patrick thought it'd be a boy, but I knew. I like the name— " she lets out a sigh " —Tracy. Her name is Tracy." Elizabeth's head falls to the side.

Jesse makes his own strained noise as he grabs for the bag valve mask. "She's out! Not breathing! Where's Newsome?"

With the baby still connected to the umbilical cord, I use one of the soft washcloths to wipe her nose and mouth along with the bulb to clear the passageways. I gently rub her chest to try to stimulate her.

"Anything?" Jesse's gaze is piercing me.

"No. I think . . . I'm going to start CPR."

He purses his lips and shakes his head. "Not sure it'll help."

"I have to try."

He puts a hand alongside Elizabeth's neck. "I've lost the pulse. Cut the cord and move the baby to the cradle so I can work on the mom. She may have a chance—if we can get a doctor here and get the bleeding stopped."

With the baby in the bassinet, I locate the breastbone. I've had training in infant and child CPR but not newborn. She's not only a newborn, but a preemie.

Using two fingers and what I hope is the appropriate amount of pressure, I count out thirty rapid compressions, attempting to mimic somewhere between one hundred and two hundred heartbeats per minute. After the thirty, I tilt her head and open her tiny mouth, giving two breaths before returning to compressions.

Jesse's working on Elizabeth, also doing compressions and using the Ambu bag to give the breaths.

I've finished my second round of breaths and am back on compressions when Dr. Williams comes rushing in, with Bowski on his heels.

"What do we have?" Williams asks as he steps to my side.

"Elizabeth. I don't know her last name or age. Her husband brought her by wagon— "

"Saw the blood." He leans over and shakes his head. "You can stop. There's . . . the baby's gone."

My shoulders sag as he moves to Elizabeth. I clear my throat and continue my report. "She arrived about— " I glance at my watch " —

fifteen minutes ago. The baby was born about four minutes ago. Mother lost consciousness and stopped breathing. Jesse bagged her. Her heart stopped shortly afterward."

With my tears streaming, I wrap the baby in a blanket. Even though small, she's perfect. After placing her in the cradle, I move near Elizabeth. "What can I do?"

Dr. Williams shakes his head. "Nothing. Stop all measures. Burnett, call the time."

After audibly calling the time with an unprofessional squeak to my voice, I move to the clipboard. I write in her first name and the time of death on the single sheet of paper. "What should I give as the baby's TOD?"

"Fetal death in womb."

I work to control my emotions as I write *Baby Girl* and *Tracy* in parenthesis. I wasted my efforts trying to revive her. Why didn't I realize there was no hope?

Bowski gives me a brief nod. As he's looking at me, his eyes drift over my shoulder.

I turn to meet the stern face of Dr. Newsome. "What's the meaning of this?"

Dr. Williams spins around. "This? This is what happens when the doctor on duty leaves the hospital and can't be found. The woman's dead. Had you been here, she may have had a chance."

"Humph. Had there been a *real* nurse here, she'd probably be fine. Whatever happened, you can be confident it's Private Burnett's doing. I've said repeatedly she has no business here."

Jesse stands practically at attention. "Katie did everything right. All she could."

"Like put an IV in?" Newsome motions to the hanging bag. "Start treatment? She took liberties— "

"I started the IV."

Newsome snorts again.

Dr. Williams grabs a fresh sheet and drapes it over Elizabeth. "Wipe the baby's face. Clean her up and put her with her mother, please." His voice is full of compassion. Sadness. Even anger.

My legs are like lead as I move to comply. I wet a cloth and gently clean the tiny face before moving her beside mom. Once the baby is in place, Williams moves the sheet up over Elizabeth's face, covering both of them. "Dr. Newsome, shall we step outside? Private Burnett, can you please put the room to right? Where's the husband?"

"He, uh . . . he went to find Dr. Newsome."

"No one came to find me." Newsome makes a wild gesture with his arm.

The urgent ding of the front door causes all of us to look toward the hallway. "I found the other doc!" Elizabeth's husband Patrick skids into the room. "But that Newsome character wasn't anywhere."

He looks to me before his gaze finds Jesse's. His eyes quickly travel over both doctors before landing on the sheet-covered body of his wife. He makes a gurgling sound. "No. Not my Lizzy." He rushes to her side. "Can I— "

I move next to him. "I'm so sorry. We did . . . we did all we could. You can see them, say goodbye."

"Them? Our baby was born?"

I give a slight nod. "I'm sorry. She didn't make it either."

Dr. Nettie steps into the room, her quick glance around tells me she understands the situation. "Here." She slides a chair over by Patrick. "Sit. Jesse, can you lower the gurney please?"

Once the gurney is lowered, Nettie gives me a nod. "Go ahead, Katie. I'll stay with Patrick." Nettie offers him a pinched smile. "You can say your goodbyes."

I start tidying the room. Nettie clears her throat. When I glance at her, she mouths *later*.

Newsome lets out a grunt. "To the office, Burnett. Talbot, you too."

I try not to hang my head as I walk out of the room and into the hallway, trailing behind Williams and Newsome.

Bowski's leaning against the wall. As Newsome walks near, he stands to his full, imposing height. "Where were you?"

Without stopping, Newsome screws up his face. "I don't answer to you."

Williams spins around. "You do answer to me. You were on duty today. Bowski said he heard Jesse say you'd gone home for lunch. But no one could raise you on the radio. The husband went to your home. Where were you?"

"I will not be interrogated in a hallway in front of inferiors. Of bigger concern, why are Burnett and Talbot practicing medicine when they have no business doing so?"

"Why?" Bowski steps forward, towering over Newsome. "Because you were not here. The woman was dying. Are you a complete idiot?"

Newsome lifts his chin and steps into Bowski's space. "Get out of here. You have no business even being in this hospital. Go before I call the Patrollers."

"Call them. In fact, you won't need to. I'll be heading there and reporting a murder."

"Exactly! Her!" Newsome points at me.

I lift my hands in a surrender position as Bowski leans forward and takes a noisy sniff. "I don't think so. I smell the booze on you. That's what you were doing? Off drinking?"

Williams doesn't even try and be covert as he, too, sniffs Newsome, who quickly takes several steps back.

"I . . . I simply will not stand for this." Newsome turns and strides away. As he reaches the door, he whirls around and lifts his finger in my direction. "If it wasn't Burnett's fault, which I suspect it was, it was probably the crazy woman who thinks she's a midwife and natural healer. You know the one. I told you she needed to be shut down and prosecuted. Either way, this is on you."

He turns quickly and loses his balance slightly before recovering. He opens the door hard, causing the bell above it to sway even after he's gone.

Chapter 16

The sun is close to setting when I walk out of the building at the end of my twelve-hour shift. The cooler temperatures have me embracing the October weather, but with the shorter days, I'm missing summer. Sunset is around 1830 hours, giving me about half an hour to jog before going home.

And I need the jog.

Because of our MOS and rations, we're only supposed to do physical training a max of three days a week. Today isn't a PT day since it was a workday.

Running was something I started over a decade ago, and I still love it. Leo and I used to jog together, chatting and laughing until it was time to pick up the pace. I've found running to be the perfect way to release the stuff rattling around in my head. When my feet are hitting the ground, it's all gone. It comes back later but seems to be easier to deal with, somehow changed by the motion—pounded out of me, maybe, and reintroduced as something manageable.

Before Leo fell, I'd have hustled home to him, to his arms, where I could cry about the awful day I'd had. He'd hold me and murmur all the right words. But now . . . I don't know how he'll react. With the way he's been, he may say something awful about how people die, and I'd feel even worse than I do now.

I reach for the flashlight secured in the inside pocket of my light jacket. It's a special kind Jake gave me before we left. It's a little on the bulky side, but I've made sure to keep it with me daily.

In the early days of the collapse, my sister Sarah was attacked right at sunset and one of our friends was kidnapped. Sarah said she was so thankful her husband had insisted she carry a flashlight on her—it helped her get home and get help. Of course, back then, we had powerful small flashlights with a supply of batteries. This flashlight is still powerful yet doesn't need batteries. It works by squeezing it a few times.

After making sure my flashlight is where it belongs, my hand drifts to my hip. The pistol is also in position, snug and tight in a belly band like it was all day at work. The old days of hospitals being gun-free zones are long gone. I'm not even sure there's a gun-free zone anywhere these days.

In the early days of the attacks, I was surprised when Leo started carrying a pistol on his hip. Not that I had a problem with firearms. I'd lived half of my life in Wyoming, where the joke was there were more guns than people. I'm not sure it wasn't true.

Here in Rapid City, it's rare to see someone without a gun on their hip or slung across their back. Ammunition is doled out by ration chips, except in the case of organized hunting parties or by the Citizen Patrol or other law enforcement. Even so, it's restricted.

Our hunting group was made up of many archers, like Leo and me. There are several bowyers and fletchers in the Black Hills—people who make bows and arrows. There's even a lady in nearby Keystone who calls herself an arbalista, a crossbow maker.

I take a deep breath and begin a slow, easy jog, taking Sheridan Lake Road toward Canyon Lake Drive. It doesn't matter I'm not dressed in what would've been considered running clothes in the past. The National Guard is always jogging around wearing their full gear. *Utes and boots.* That's what Leo calls their attire.

Having left my hospital uniform—blue scrubs with the Volunteer Unit insignia and a yellow private stripe—in my locker at work, I'm now in my homemade Volunteer Uniform. Black pants, a black button-up shirt with a layer underneath, a jacket over the top, and lace-up boots are a close facsimile.

My long-sleeved button-up shirt even has a single orange ribbon handsewn around the arm to signify my rank of private, though I'll admit my jacket isn't uniform quality. Since we joined the Volunteers in the summer months, we didn't worry about cold weather wear as part of the uniform, being assured we'd be given what was needed when it was time.

Now, with Leo and me as the only two members of the Volunteers in the area, matching others isn't a concern. Staying warm is our priority. Leo and I brought as much winter gear with us as we could carry, which wasn't much.

I'm wearing a lighter daypack instead of a fully loaded backpack, and I'm not carrying a carbine as the National Guard does when jogging. Even so, I imagine I still fit the utes and boots characterization. We trained in full gear during an abbreviated basic training with the Volunteer Unit. Undoubtedly, if I go through with joining the Guard, it'll be more full-gear training.

Accelerating once I cross over Canyon Lake Drive, I decide to do some speed play, sometimes called a fartlek workout. It's a great way to keep my focus on my exercise and not drift back to the events of the day. The blood. Elizabeth and her baby dying. The awful way Eugene Newsome accused me of being a murderer.

I clamp my brain shut and drastically pick up my pace.

After what I estimate is about thirty seconds, I drop to a jog to recover my breath. I'll do a pyramid fartlek. I give myself about thirty seconds at the jog before I'm back to a near sprint for another thirty seconds, then repeat the jog. I change the times to a minute fast and a minute slow. I take it up a notch, doing two rounds at two minutes of each before going back to one minute.

I'm sweating and finding it harder to recover on the slow time. I glance to the setting sun and decide there's enough time to do one more round of my pyramid. I end up doing two additional rounds.

By the time I've completed my brutal workout, I'm farther from home than I should be, and it's darker than I expected. A breeze chills my sweat-soaked skin. Tightening the collar of my jacket, I turn left at the next street to loop around. I stick with a brisk walk for the nearly thirty minutes it takes to reach my house.

With my key in the lock, the door suddenly pops open. Leo, who's become adept at doing many things without the full use of his arms—including opening doors, preparing meals, and tending to his daily personal needs—is there with a scowl.

"Where were you?" He looks over my slightly disheveled and sweaty appearance. "You went for a run? At night?" He croaks out the last word. "Katie! How stupid are you?"

I bite the inside of my lip as the anger surges through me. My nostrils flare. "Are you going to let me in?"

He steps to the side, and I flounce past him.

"Why did you go for a run? It's not a PT day. You don't have the calories to spare. And you knew I'd be waiting for you."

I keep moving, not stopping until I find Geronimo, the smallest pup from the litter. We've agreed we'll find the other pups homes as soon as we think they're ready, but I'm keeping Geronimo—or as I call him, Gerry.

"Are you going to answer me? You think I like being stuck here alone all day? No one to talk to but these dogs? I was waiting for you."

With Gerry in my arms as he licks my chin, a tear slides down my cheek. Gerry notices it and takes care of whisking it away with his tongue. "Could you not nag at me tonight, Leo? I've had— "

"Nag at you? Is that what you *think* I'm doing? Wanting to spend time with my wife is nagging?" He plops into the chair. "Excuse me for being concerned about your wellbeing. You should've been home an hour ago."

I greet the other dogs clamoring at my ankles for attention. "Please, Leo. Just let me tell you what happened."

"Fine. Sure. Whatever. You get to go out and work. You take off and do who knows what while I'm stuck here taking care of *dogs*." The way he spits out dogs instantly reminds me of Eugene Newsome.

I take a deep breath. Leo's face is a mask of anger and something else. Hurt, maybe? My heart clenches as my own anger subsides. I attempt a small smile.

He narrows his eyes. "Don't. Don't think you can charm your way out of this. Things have to change. If they don't— "

A knock at the door interrupts the rest of his sentence. He shoots me a dirty look, then heaves himself out of the chair. "Don't bother getting up. I'll do it. Just like I do everything else around here."

I sink to the floor, giving commands to the puppies to prevent them from running toward the door. I know it was inconsiderate of me to not come straight home. Wrong, even. But this—the way Leo is acting—it's so not like him. While we've had arguments, like any married couple, he's never been cruel. And what was he planning to say? If things don't change, then . . . then what?

"Lieutenant. Uh, good to see you. I wasn't expecting you." Leo's greeting carries from the door. I don't even bother trying to crane my neck to see the front door. It's not visible from here anyway, and maybe the lieutenant will say what he needs to say and leave. I'm not at all interested in entertaining tonight.

What I'd love is to take a hot bath and forget about everything for a bit. A hot bath won't happen. It's too much water to haul and heat. I'll have to settle for a sponge bath, like every day.

"Leo, do you know Deputy Shaw from the sheriff's department?"

"Deputy Shaw. We've crossed paths, but I don't think we've been properly introduced." I can imagine Leo giving the man a respectful nod.

"Is your wife home?" the deputy asks.

I straighten my back at the question.

"She is . . . " Leo's response is wary.

"May we come in?"

The lieutenant and deputy precede Leo from the entryway into the living room.

I take in a breath and paste on a smile. "Lieutenant Paul."

He introduces Deputy Shaw as I motion for them to take seats. Instead of sitting, Leo stands practically at attention. "Can we get either of you a glass of water?"

When he says *we*, he means me. While he seems to be able to get his own beverages and food while I'm at work, when I'm home, he's back to being an invalid.

The deputy waves a hand. "We wanted to ask Private Burnett a few questions about today's events."

Leo's eyes dart toward me. "Katie?"

That . . . that Newsome! I thought he was bluffing. He seriously called the cops on me? Accusing me of murder? My heart pounds in my ears as my mouth goes dry. I lift my hands. "I . . . I don't think . . . I did all I knew to do."

"That's what Captain Williams said. Both he and Jesse Talbot said you performed your duties as you should, and then some. Your performance isn't at question here."

Leo moves to the couch next to me. "What happened today?" His voice is soft and kind—the old Leo, the one I fell in love with and married.

Tears fill my eyes as I swallow hard. Looking back at the puppies, I shake my head. "I tried to tell you. We— " I clear my throat. "We had a death. A mom and baby."

Leo lets out a sigh.

The deputy leans forward in his chair. "You, Talbot, and Newsome were on duty when the woman arrived?"

"Y-yes. But, um . . . you probably know this already, but Newsome had gone home for lunch. He wasn't there and we couldn't— " I shake my head. "Jesse tried him on the radio. He didn't answer. We thought maybe he went to do rounds at the care centers, but they hadn't seen him. We couldn't raise Williams either. The woman's husband, Patrick, went after Newsome. Bowski volunteered to go after Dr. Williams. He was backup today."

"Did you hear Jesse Talbot call for each of them?"

"I did. I heard the radios click, and he made the calls. There was only static." I scrunch up my forehead.

"Do you remember something?"

"No, no. I'm trying . . . it was a difficult time. After trying on the handheld, Jesse left the room to use the base radio, hoping he'd have better results. Elizabeth was in distress, and we were doing all we could. I realize now we should've also tried the backup nurse." I don't add the rest of what I'd been thinking—she's a real RN with years of experience.

"Pretty much the same thing Talbot said. Newsome did show up later, though?"

"Yes."

"And what did he say about why you couldn't reach him?"

I shake my head. "He didn't say much. Other than he doesn't answer to us." I try and keep the anger out of my voice but know I fail.

"Did you witness the altercation between Ritchie Kasubowski and Dr. Newsome?"

"Altercation? I wouldn't call it an altercation. It wasn't even much of an argument. Bowski was mad no one could find Newsome and that the radio wasn't working. As far as I know, Newsome strolled in on his own. No one actually found him and told him there was an emergency."

"Had Dr. Newsome been drinking?"

I lift a shoulder. "I didn't get close to him today. Bowski said he could smell it, but I don't know."

"Have you known Dr. Newsome to drink on duty before."

"Known? I've never seen him drink."

The deputy and lieutenant both look to Leo. Leo scrunches his forehead. "I've never seen him drink either. But, uh, we've had our suspicions. He's often smelled of booze."

"You've both smelled it?"

I give a shrug and turn my attention back to the puppies. Gerry is on his back, begging me to rub him. Two are sleeping by my leg, and the other one is nosing his way over to the deputy.

Deputy Shaw puts his hand down to let the puppy sniff him. "You're a cute one, aren't you?" He gives the pup—one we call Tank since he's the largest—a pat on the back. "What happened after Kasubowski accused him of being drunk?"

"Newsome left."

"Did you see Dr. Newsome again?"

"No. Captain Williams finished Newsome's shift."

"What time did your shift end?"

"Eighteen hundred."

"And you came straight home?"

"No, I went for a run." I lift my gaze to meet Leo's. "I needed to clear my head."

"What time did you get home?"

"Not long before you arrived here. Maybe ten minutes? If that."

Leo nods. "That's about right."

Deputy Shaw looks toward the window. The curtain is still open. "Do you often run in the dark?" He looks back at me. "In street clothes?"

I'm sure the wet ring around my collar is evidence that, yes, I honestly was running. "It wasn't dark when I started. I just— " I let out a sigh. "I lost track of time."

"And you never saw Dr. Newsome again after he left the hospital earlier in the afternoon? What time was that?"

"Around fourteen hundred. He arrived a few minutes after we called Elizabeth's time of death. He wasn't there long. I never saw him again."

"You don't know where he went when he left?"

"Excuse me, Deputy." Leo leans forward. "Is Dr. Newsome missing?"

"Not missing. He's dead. Murdered."

Chapter 17

Shaw asks several more times about my being out running—in street clothes, in the dark—dropping hints he thinks I may have had something to do with the death of Eugene Newsome, or that I was doing something other than running.

"I can understand you needing to exercise after the day you've had," Lieutenant Paul says. "And I'm sure you've seen my men running in fatigues and full gear. Plus, the Volunteers would run in gear, too, so it's not exactly a foreign concept." He gives me a smile, which helps me breathe easier. Shaw may think I'm a murderer, but not the lieutenant.

Leo is noticeably quiet during this whole conversation. He asks the occasional question but doesn't offer up much in the way of my defense. I guess he can't since he was here, and I wasn't. It's not like he's my alibi.

Tank, the largest puppy, curls up next to Shaw's feet while he questions me. After about half an hour, I guess the deputy decides he has what he needs. He leans over and scratches Tank behind the ears. The dog bounds to his feet and begs to be picked up. Shaw happily obliges. "What're you doing with the dogs?"

"Oh, we, uh . . . we found them— "

He lifts a hand. "Heard that story." He looks toward Leo. "You still have, what, four weeks in the casts?"

Leo tilts his head. "Hopefully less. Nettie was here this morning." I shoot a look at Leo, but he ignores my gaze. "I'm getting some of the grip back in my right hand." He motions to the arm with the broken humerus. "They're going to have me go to Monument Hospital to see an orthopedist. Captain Williams thinks it's a good idea. Nettie said he's exceptionally good. She worked with him before the attacks."

Williams has mentioned this a few times. The orthopedist can't do x-rays or any of the former diagnostic stuff, but Williams thought he'd be able to give a good idea of how well Leo is healing. He talked about sending Leo shortly after the fall but decided against it, not wanting Leo to travel and risk jarring the bones more.

Even though the hospital is in Rapid, it's on the other side of town, about five miles from us. Five miles was nothing in the old world, but with Leo needing to ride there in a handcart or wagon, it's more of a trip than he needs with both broken arms.

"A good plan." The deputy nods. "Now about the pups. You keeping them all?"

"I'm keeping Gerry." I rub the head of the pup sleeping on my lap. I can practically feel Leo scowl. He doesn't want to keep any of them. "We're rehoming the other three."

"When will they be ready?"

Leo leans forward on the couch. "Won't be long. They're still eating soft food, but only three times a day now. Probably be two times a day soon. Be easier to tend to them—unless someone's home most of the day." The last part of his sentence was laced with disgust. "Only good thing about falling off the horse is being here for the dogs. Of course . . . "

"Yeah. Sad situation." The deputy agrees with a nod. He gives Tank another rub on the head. "This guy spoken for?"

"None are yet. We've had a little interest, but nothing concrete. They'll probably get pretty big. We think the mom was a Rottweiler. The dad was maybe a husky mix. We aren't really sure. Both parents were big."

I look down at Gerry again as I try to force the memory of that awful day aside. Both parents *were* big. And they were only trying to care for their little family.

"We've been talking about adding a few more dogs to the department. This one just might be a contender."

In Bakerville, one of my parents' friends had a K-9 dog, and he was one of the best-behaved dogs I'd ever met. Tank is . . . well, he'd need a lot of training. He's the orneriest of our litter. He's also the most independent and has the most energy.

"He'd, uh . . . he'd be my companion too. He'd live with me and my wife. Not kept locked up in a box or anything." The deputy makes squishy faces at Tank, telling him what a good boy he is, before setting him on the ground. "Mind if I ask my sergeant?"

"Not at all." Leo's answer is quick—too quick.

I don't look up at Leo when I say, "He needs a good home. I think he's going to need lots of exercise too. He'd probably get that?"

"No doubt. So . . . I'll go ahead and ask?"

"Please do," Leo responds.

There are a few more minutes of small talk about the dogs, Leo's healing, the state of the world, and the rumors of World War III and what it means for South Dakota.

Before the two men leave, Lieutenant Paul reminds us we'll soon be a part of the National Guard. I don't correct the assumption on the Guard, but with each passing day, I'm less and less convinced joining the Guard is the correct path for us. Or for me, at least.

Truly, I'm kind of surprised Leo is willing to take on another eight years. If he wasn't willing to do a full eight years active as a Marine, why is he willing now?

After they leave, I go to the kitchen. "Did you eat?"

"Of course. At a normal hour since I was here when I was supposed to be."

Great. I'd hoped the time we spent with the deputy and lieutenant would've tempered Leo's anger toward me. I bite back an angry response. What has happened to us?

I glance at Leo from the breakfast bar that divides the kitchen from the living room. There's chunks of meat and cheese, along with a partial loaf of bread and home-canned tomatoes from our weekly rations.

Ration chips or tokens are given out based on name. We get our chips on Tuesdays. Nettie gets hers on Fridays. It's better than having one day for everyone to pick up, definitely a little less crazy. As a married couple with no children and only moderately active jobs, we're given what is the equivalent of about four thousand calories a day between the two of us.

Each district is responsible for sourcing their own food. Part of sourcing includes trading among the district organizers. The deer, fish, foraged foods, and other things brought back from the recent hunts in our district were used mainly for our residents, but they likely traded part of them for other goods too.

Another hunting crew from our district went out to a different area, returning a few days ago with more fresh and dried venison and even an elk. Elk isn't as common in the Black Hills as it was in the Absaroka-Beartooth Wilderness bordering Bakerville, but there are a few small herds.

I was hoping we'd get some of the elk meat in this week's allowance, but we only received venison and fish, along with a little beef from one of the local ranchers. Maybe even our new friend Opal Maher's ranch. She's checked in on us several times since Leo's accident.

I'm not complaining about what we do get, I know how blessed we are to even have food, but something different would be nice. Not that there's a lot of meat. We're only given enough for four meals plus a few bones to make broth. Everyone's given a certain amount of already cooked foods, but most of the rations are raw and need preparation.

We get a loaf of bread each week, along with a couple cups of wheat or field corn. Dent corn, wheat, and other cereal crops, which grow on the high plains, were focus crops this year. The goal was to grow enough to sustain not only the Rapid City and Black Hills area, but also to share with all of South Dakota and even neighboring states.

I don't bother making bread. Instead, we cook the cereal grains and enjoy them as porridge. A wave of sadness washes over me. It's not like I don't know how to make bread. My mom taught me years ago. And we made plenty of bread in Bakerville after the EMP, thanks to smart planning on my mom and Jake's part.

I glance at the woodstove. Using a dutch oven, I can cook the bread on top of the stove. Yeast isn't an issue; there're many people who keep sourdough starters. Plus, the market where we trade our ration chips for food has a grinder to mill the whole grains into flour. I could make bread for us.

Maybe a little extra home cooking, along with our indoor garden, which is finally perking up, will provide us with a new variety of food this winter. Even my tomato plants look a little less scraggly.

"Were you going to tell me about what happened?" Leo's leaning against the wall. I swear, if his arms weren't in casts, they'd be crossed and he'd be tapping a foot at me. "It was embarrassing hearing something involving *my* wife from other people."

I stare at the food. "Pretty sure I tried." The cheese is a soft variety, probably made from cow's milk since it doesn't have a strong aroma to it like goat cheese does. I use it as a spread on the bread. A fresh tomato would be a perfect addition here.

"There's a time when you would've come straight home and talked to me about what was bothering you instead of— "

I slam the butter knife on the counter. "There's a time when you would've *wanted* me to talk to you. Now you have almost zero interest in my day, or me!"

He gives me a very un-Leo-like snort. "Not wanting to hear you drone on and on about who you saw and spoke with, how you felt like you were needed, isn't the same thing as being willing to hear about something awful."

"Drone on and on? Is that what I do? Look. Just . . . I've had a rotten day. And now to find out Newsome is dead— "

"Right. You hated him."

"Hated? I got tired of him being awful to me. I hate what he did before coming here and what he said we should do with the puppies." My words are tumbling out so fast and furious, there's a squeak to my voice.

I take a deep breath. "I'm sorry I didn't come right home. I'm sorry you didn't know about what happened before the deputy and lieutenant told you. I did try and tell you. You didn't want to listen."

He snorts again. "I'm going to bed. You can take the dogs out. Make sure you wash up before coming into the bedroom. You stink."

After he leaves the room, I lift my arm and give myself a sniff. He's not wrong. I drop my head and let the tears flow. I'm mad but also hurt. The things Leo said, the *way* he said them . . . what is happening to us?

I allow myself a few minutes of quiet blubbering before going back to fixing my sandwich. I'm sure the food is fine, but it's dry and sawdust-like in my mouth. I force myself to finish the entire thing and wash it down with several glasses of water. When I'm done, I take the dogs out the backdoor to our fenced yard.

I move over to the heavy wooden picnic table that belonged to the people who used to live here. Crystal Harrington said they were gone on vacation when the attacks started, on a cruise to Alaska. I'm mildly surprised the picnic table is still here; the rest of the house was stripped of anything usable. I'd think the table would've been taken for firewood.

I lean back on the built-in bench, rest my back against the table, and gaze at the night sky. There's no moon tonight but plenty of stars.

The best thing about the lack of electricity is the amazing night sky. Leo and I used to sit outside together, looking at the constellations as he tried to tell me which was which. I still don't know.

He said knowing the night sky is easier to navigate than with a compass. I'd always be able to find my way if I got lost. Maybe that's something I should try and learn . . . along with a multitude of other things. Living in this new world has us relying on ways of old. Leo did teach me Morse code, which has come in handy on numerous occasions. We've even practiced using it on each other's arms as a way to communicate silently.

We haven't practiced Morse for months, even before he broke his arms. I tap out a few letters on the table. His name. My name. The always popular SOS. I run through the alphabet, taking my time as I struggle with some of the letters.

Leaving Bakerville wasn't easy on me. When I agreed to do it, I'm not sure I was even fully in my right mind. My mom had died only weeks before. I was hurting. Grieving. I needed an escape. I tap out *Mom* in Morse.

Joining the Volunteer Unit provided an escape. Being in the unit was odd, to say the least. Our homemade uniforms and attempts at playing soldier almost make me laugh. During that time, Leo and I were still running drills together when we could, practicing the combat skills we'd learned and working on our Morse code.

Now my time is consumed with the hospital. Learning how to care for people has been a challenge, especially since we're also short on supplies. Captain Williams and Nettie may know modern-day medicine, but they have also had to learn new doctoring and healing methods from history, new treatments using herbs, and more . . . there's so much. Too much.

Now, on top of all I need to learn and know, my marriage seems to be falling apart. I tap out a few more words. *Help me, Lord. Help my husband. Help us.*

Chapter 18

Tightening the string on the hood of my jacket, I lean back. I'd asked Leo if he wanted to walk with me, but he said he was waiting for Lieutenant Paul. They had plans for Leo to get a tour of Camp Rapid. I'd done my best to put on a happy face but couldn't help being hurt. They planned it for a day I have off, but I'm not invited. Leo could've gone with Paul while I was working. We could've spent the day together.

To avoid sitting around the house moping, I take the pups on a nice long walk. Or at least we're supposed to be walking. Right now, I'm sitting on one of the benches conveniently located along a walkway.

With Rapid Creek nearby, I can imagine this was a well-used area, popular for walkers, bicyclists, and joggers alike. Now I only see the occasional person scurry by on their way to wherever they're going, giving my dogs and me furtive glances as they keep their distance.

Leash training the pups hasn't been easy. And walking all four of them at one time is certainly a challenge. Captain Williams helped us find collars, harnesses, and leashes, which aren't something I've seen as part of our rations. I assumed we may need a special allotment.

He said he knew someone and brought them over the next day. The collars are still too large for the dogs, but the harnesses fit fine, plus Williams said it'd be better to start them on harnesses anyway. Two of the leashes are the regular fixed-length style, one in orange and the other blue. The third is a double leash with a single handle and a few feet of leash, then a ring coupler followed by several more feet going to individual snaps to attach to the collar.

The system works pretty well, as long as Tank gets his own leash. Otherwise, he's pulling the other poor pup along in his bid to outrace her. I usually give Gerry his own leash, too, putting the two little girls—who we call Ali and Ari—on the double leash.

Today is our longest training walk yet. Usually, we stick close to the house, but I needed more today. Not only because of my issues with Leo, but also because the death of Dr. Newsome has had a larger effect on me than I'd thought possible.

Deputy Shaw decided I wasn't involved, but I swear the rest of the hospital staff has been giving me the side eye—not Nettie or Captain Williams, not even Jesse Talbot. But there's been plenty of whispering from those who weren't there the day Elizabeth and her baby died.

At first, I thought it was about Elizabeth, how I'd made such a huge mistake and cost the life of her and her child. Later, I overheard the new medic talking with one of the nurses at shift change, and it was Newsome's name they said when looking at me. Do they genuinely believe I had something to do with his death? His murder?

The *clop-clop* of approaching horse hooves catches my attention. The puppies hear the sound too. They all move to their feet, tails wagging. When the pair of horses pulling a wagon round the nearest corner and come into view, Tank lets out a whimper, which gets Ari and Ali wound up too. Gerry sets back on his haunches and scratches his ear. I guess the horses aren't as exciting to him as they are to his littermates.

Captain Williams said he heard about Deputy Shaw wanting Tank. He thinks it's a good idea and Shaw will give the dog a good home and a purpose. I'm not entirely sure Tank has it in him to be a police dog, but I agree about Shaw being good for the rambunctious pup.

Oscar Harrington asked about taking either Ari or Ali. His mom will be discharged from the hospital soon, and he thinks a dog in the house might be a good idea. Crystal disagreed, though, insisting taking care of a dog full time isn't something she's interested in. She did ask if it'd be possible for her grandson to continue to play with Gerry and maybe help out with him once in a while.

Besides, it's unlikely they'd be burglarized again, at least we haven't heard about the robbers striking the same place twice.

Oscar said the county sheriff is setting up a special group to get to the bottom of the break-ins, which aren't only affecting our district but the Black Hills as a whole. The gang of thieves have everyone on edge, especially knowing they're willing to kill to take what they want.

Crystal is physically well enough to go home, but she will still have a long road of recovery. Not only is she grieving the death of her husband, but she's also exhibiting signs of traumatic brain injury.

She's especially having trouble caring for herself—she forgets what comes next when dressing. Or she'll forget what something is used for, such as her hairbrush. She knows it's a brush, but she doesn't know what to do with it. Needing so much care when she gets home, I agree with her a puppy isn't a good idea. As it is, her daughter-in-law is being tasked as her caregiver and provided a leave from her current work crew.

A wagon approaches, and one of the people on the bench waves. I squint my eyes slightly to try and make out who it is. I can't help but smile and wave. It's Opal Maher and her son Shawn. As the rig comes to a stop, she leans in to say something to Shawn before climbing down with the agility of a woman half her age. As soon as she's down, Shawn gets the horses moving again with a hearty, "Ayup."

Likely from old habits, Opal looks both ways before crossing the street. I stand and get a tighter grip on the pups, all wagging and writhing, assuming Opal is here to see them.

"Opal! Nice to see you."

"And you, my dear." She leans in for a hug, which quickly becomes awkward as the dogs do their best to tangle us with the leashes.

She lets out a hearty laugh. "Spirited, aren't they?"

"Dangerous, it seems."

As we untangle them, Opal squats to pet each of the pups. With her close to his level, Tank whips out his tongue to lick her chin. "Yes, yes. You're a sweetheart. They're bigger every time I see them. What's it been? 'Bout a month and a half?"

"Almost. September sixteenth is when Leo fell. What's today? October twenty-fourth?"

She gives a nod. "Trainin' them on a leash, huh? Got homes for 'em?"

"I'm keeping Gerry—the littlest one. There's some interest in the others, but we're taking it slow."

"Probably smart. And how's your husband faring?"

I give her a fake smile. When I open my mouth, everything falls apart. I pull my lips tight and shake my head as the tears begin to fall. So much for being a strong woman of the apocalypse.

"Ah, Katie." Opal gently guides me to sit on the bench. She wraps an arm around me and lets me cry. Gerry lets out a whimper and plops himself on my foot. It's many minutes before my sobs turn to hiccups.

"There, there. Do you have water?"

I give a weary nod and dig a water bottle from the outside pocket of my daypack. "I'm sorry. I don't know what came over me."

"Drink, then we'll talk."

I pull Gerry onto my lap, then sip my water. Opal pets the other three while giving me time to collect myself.

When our gazes meet, I lift my shoulder. "What are you doing over here?" My voice is still squeaky from crying.

"Deliveries. We help supply the distribution center with meat."

"For our district?"

"Sure. Yours and a few others. We all try and work together as best we can, like how people from both our districts went on the hunts. It's not a competition, ya know."

"Sometimes it feels like it. Dr. Newsome used to say we were always getting the leftovers from the Downtown or Monument Districts. Of course, he may have been a little bitter since he thought he'd work at the main hospital and ended up with us."

"Maybe so. The Monument District, though . . . the hospital there gets busy. They're better staffed than y'all, though, so that helps. And they have a full-time dentist too. Something I surely wish was an option here."

I give a nod. We share a dentist with three other districts. He arrives every third week on Monday afternoon and stays until Friday around lunchtime. Since our hospital used to be a large dentist office and surgery center, we've kept one of the rooms intact for his needs. "We're still waiting for a replacement for Dr. Newsome."

"Sad business, that. He wasn't my favorite person, but to be murdered . . . " She shakes her head. "And I hear they have little idea who did it."

"Did you hear I was questioned?"

"I'd suspect all of you working with him were questioned. Plenty of bad blood there, huh?"

"I guess, but I don't think there was enough that any of us would kill him. I mean, doctors and nurses save lives. Why would we . . . " I shake my head. "I don't know who it was, but I know it wasn't anyone at the hospital."

"Were you there? I heard there was a death—mama and baby— shortly before he was killed."

I drop my gaze and rub Gerry under the chin. My voice is barely a whisper. "I was there."

"I'm sorry for you, Katie. Must've been awful."

"Did you hear we couldn't find him?"

"Newsome? I heard. Heard when he did show up, he was drunk as a skunk."

"He didn't seem drunk. He was the same as always, but others smelled it on him."

"You?"

"No. I didn't get near him."

She snorts out a laugh. "Probably smart." She quickly sobers. "Still, I'm not sure how long they'll keep looking for the culprit. Doesn't seem to be much concern over Newsome dying, other than Bruce Blake. He was upset about it. Said he wanted to find justice for his late wife's brother."

"Did you hear he moved into Newsome's house? Captain Williams isn't too happy. With its location, it should be reserved for hospital workers."

She furrows her brow. "Just moved on in? Without talking to anyone 'bout it?"

I bob my head. "The captain decided to let it be. He says Blake is still grieving over the death of his wife, and now with Newsome . . . they were pretty close. Williams thinks he may be going through a lot. Wanting revenge for Newsome's death doesn't surprise me."

"See that no one repays anyone evil for evil, but always seek to do good to one another and to everyone."

I tilt my head. "Is that a Bible verse?"

"God had plenty to say about us seeking our own justice." She dips her chin to her chest. "Likely, someone after revenge is exactly how Eugene Newsome and Bruce Blake ended up in the Guard District anyway—after their town of Black Canyon was destroyed."

Chapter 19

"Did you know them before? Newsome and Blake, I mean." I rub Gerry's head as I make eye contact with Opal.

"Nah. Hadn't even heard of 'em until the rumors of the pet annihilation happened." Her barely there accent adds several extra syllables to *annihilation*.

"When did Blake's wife die?"

"Before the attacks. Not long before, but before."

I stare down the street where a couple is walking, holding hands. "Sometimes I wonder if it's easier?"

"Meanin'?"

"How we separate things. It happened before the attacks or before the EMP—before the apocalypse. Almost like, if someone died before, we don't grieve as much."

"Hmm. I don't know about that. But I see your point. Before all this happened— " She gives me a knowing look and raises her eyebrows. "See? The time before and the time after."

Opal leans back on the bench with a sigh. "When newspapers were still a thing, I read an article on an epidemic in another country, something they thought could spread worldwide. The focus of the article was how people seemed to grieve harder for those lost to the sickness than for those who died of other causes." She shakes her head.

"People in the affected area would even ask things like 'Oh, did they die of the disease? I'm so sorry if they did.' But when the response was, 'No, it was a heart attack,' or car accident or whatever, people seemed to lose interest in offering sympathy. Strange thing for sure."

"It's the same now, in some ways."

"How do you mean?"

"When Leo and I were on our way here, we realized how sheltered we'd been from the worst of it. Our community had banded together, much like the communities here. We knew terrible things had happened in other places. We'd seen some of it in the town nearby where we lived. That town had someone take things over, and he . . . " I clear my throat. "The things he did were as bad, worse maybe, than what Newsome did in his town."

Opal tightens her arm around my shoulder. "The wages of sin. We're all suffering them."

"The things in Prospect, the town we lived near, were terrible. What we didn't know was similar things were happening in other places. We only traveled across Wyoming to get here, but the stories we heard, the people we saw, the starving children . . . it was terrible. But in some ways, people were wearing it like a badge of honor."

She scrunches up her face and shakes her head. "Not sure I follow what you're saying."

"I . . . " I let out a breath. "I don't know. Not really. What you said about the newspaper article reminded me. We were camped near a town that was little more than a smoldering mess. The people there were trying to rebuild before winter. We ended up leaving many people from our Volunteer Unit there to help them."

"That's right fine. I thought the Units were for policing?"

"Officially, I guess. The town was happy to have them, even if they'd be acting as security while the town was rebuilding. I wanted to be part of the group staying behind, but we weren't chosen. Anyway, I was talking with a girl who was staying. A young girl, barely eighteen, who'd joined our unit in Powell, Wyoming. Her parents and siblings had been visiting family in Bismarck, North Dakota, when the attacks started. She'd stayed home, had a summer job at McDonald's, and since it was her last summer before her senior year— "

I let out a bitter laugh. "Not the year she expected to have. Her folks never made it home. She said she barely survived the winter. When the opportunity to join the Volunteers came up—and the prospect of having food and shelter—she took it. She was still heavily grieving the loss of her family.

"I told her I understood, having lost my mom only a few weeks prior. She asked if my mom was killed in an attack. When I told her my mom was injured during a firefight but actually died of what we suspected to be cancer, she waved me off. Then she told me how lucky I was to lose my mom in such a normal manner."

"Did that make you angry?"

"At first, maybe. I certainly don't consider myself *lucky* to have lost my mom to cancer. If the world hadn't fallen apart, if we still had hospitals and things like chemotherapy, I might not have lost her at all. Or at the very least, I might've had more time with her. She could've at least been there for the birth of my niece. My niece lost both her grandmas before she was even born. Her dad's mom—my sister's husband's mom— " I look to Opal to make sure she understands.

She gives me a nod and motions me to continue.

"She died when we had a crazy guy try and take over our community."

"You were attacked?"

"No, not by outsiders. Not that time. It was people that lived with us. Ate and fellowshipped with us. Even a few we were friendly with. They didn't like the way things were being managed, the leadership, and . . . " I shrug.

"It was a mutiny?"

"Yes, a mutiny. Several people were killed before it was stopped. I don't think my brother-in-law thought his mom died a better death than my mom did since she was shot instead of succumbing to cancer. But maybe I'm wrong. Maybe he did."

Opal gives me a kind smile. "Different people handle their grief differently. Probably, the girl you met in the Volunteer Unit was, like ya said, still grieving. I'm sure she didn't mean to— "

I wave her off. "Oh, I know she didn't mean anything by it. And you're right. It's just, it still stings. I can't explain it. And she was right. I had the time with my mom. Time to say goodbye. And I know what happened. She'll never know what happened to her family. Of course, they could be fine. Holed up somewhere."

"Or they could make it home."

"True. We had that happen. A man who was working on an oil rig when everything happened, he made it back to Bakerville."

Opal scrunches up her face. "There were people stranded here last year. Stayed the winter before heading for home. 'Course, we had many people who left. People who called the Black Hills home but left at the first thaw, not wanting to brave another winter like the one we had. I'm sure many of those people made it."

"I told you about my other brother-in-law?"

"The one who was hunting with his dad and got lost in a storm?"

"We think. We don't actually know. They never came home. We never found them. It was terrible for my sister, and for my brother-in-law's mom and sister. In some ways, I hate being here. I keep wondering what's happening in Bakerville and how everyone is."

"That's the hardest part, huh? Not only being here all alone, but not having any contact. I sure do miss being able to pick up the phone and call my family or friends. Send a text or an email. We took it for granted before. 'Course, with the mail somewhat working, that's a help. You get letters from home?"

I lift my shoulders and shake my head "Not yet. I've heard sometimes there'll be mail but it doesn't get exactly where it's supposed to. I'm hoping there's an envelope in a stack somewhere with my name on it."

"Heard that too. I'll tell ya, I was sure surprised when Ritchie Kasubowski came walking up our drive saying I had mail. Mail! Almost made me think the apocalypse had come to an end."

I give her a polite smile. "I can imagine."

"It was from my oldest sister, Pearl. She wrote half a dozen pages filled with news of what they'd been going through. She painted such wonderful pictures of their life. They had some of the same troubles we've had, of course, though she tried to put a happy spin on everything. I got me the feeling things aren't quite as good as she's letting on. So, I wrote her back and told her she and her family are welcome here anytime."

"Where does she live?"

"Montana. Used to be an easy drive. Hop on I-90 and, *bam*, seven hours later we'd be sipping tea in the backyard. Now it's a slow slog, taking one of the transports or riding on horseback. And how many people are walking? I was thinking, maybe that's why I got her letter the way I did. Her town, like ours, is right on the interstate. With the military working so hard to clear Interstate 90 all the way to Idaho in the west and, what, Sioux Falls in the east?"

"Farther, I think. Someone said they want a road to Cleveland, Ohio. I-90 makes sense . . . well, until near Chicago. I don't think things are too good there."

She snorts. "No doubt. Way I hear it, Cleveland wasn't too good either. Big death toll. But they pulled it together and are leading the reconstruction efforts along with us and Billings, Montana. Even getting the electricity back on."

"And Tulsa, right?"

This time, her snort is even louder. "Tulsa! Don't know how that can be. We're from Oklahoma, ya know."

Ah. So that explains her accent. Southern but not Texas or strong south. Just enough to be a hint. My late brother-in-law Tate and his family were from Tulsa. I can hear some similarities in the way Tate's mom spoke and the way Opal speaks. "My brother-in-law lived in Tulsa."

She narrows her eyes. "Why?"

"Uh . . . I don't know. He was born there."

"The one lost while hunting?"

"Yes. His parents were still living in Tulsa but were visiting Tate and Sarah—my sister—when the planes crashed. They moved in with my family on the homestead."

"I know Tulsa's supposed to be the bee's knees now, but I heard they lost like 80 percent of their population within the first year."

I blink away the tears stinging my eyes. "I guess it didn't matter whether they were in Tulsa or Wyoming. Tate and his dad are both missing, dead probably. And Tate's mom died in January. She faded away bit by bit until she— " I shake my head. "She probably died of a broken heart. They were a family of four, and the only one left now is Tate's sister. That's 75 percent of them dead."

Opal's face falls. She rests a weathered hand on my forearm. "Your sister's holding up okay?"

"When we left, she was . . . okay, I guess. Of course, we'd just lost our mom, so . . . " I lift my shoulders. "Even in Bakerville, we had a lot of deaths. Maybe not as many as Tulsa and other cities, but enough. Even from our own family."

Opal stares off into the distance and lets out a loud sigh. "We've all seen enough death, huh? Enough to last a lifetime. Maybe the president's right and the worst days are behind us. They'll get the Wastelands cleared out, get the sick the treatment they need. The reconstruction hubs will soon be leading the country, bringing back lights and industry. Though, I'm pretty sure Tulsa, Cleveland, and Billings will pale in comparison to what we do here in the Black Hills." She gives me an exaggerated wink. "Whadda ya think?"

Chapter 20

I give a light laugh at Opal's assertion. "You may be right. The Black Hills is pretty special. Somedays, it feels like it's all working as it should."

"Yup." She leans back and scrubs her hands over her face. "Hoping I get another letter from Pearl, a letter saying she and her family are on their way. The transports won't run as much once winter hits, if at all. Maybe the stagecoach ones, but not the buses and other rigs. We could have snow any day. Surprised we haven't already. Couple of frosts, but nothing much."

"You said she's your older sister?"

Opal pushes back the brim of her wide hat. She's winterized her look since the last time I saw her, adding a knitted band around her ears. "That's right. A dozen years older than me. There's another girl between us. Our sister Jade. Been writing her, too, but haven't heard back. She's still in Oklahoma. Didn't come north like us."

"Pearl, Jade, and Opal?"

"Ain't it a hoot? We had a baby sister, too, just younger than me. They named her Jules, but she only lived a few days. Jade doesn't live right on an interstate, though she's not far from I-44. Maybe that's why she hasn't written back. But Pearl . . . I'm expecting to hear from her soon. We could use the help. She's got two sons, ya know. They're in their forties but still fit, at least last time I saw them. But they've got younger wives. 'Course Pearl being in her seventies . . . still, we could use the help."

"I thought you had a work crew assigned to your ranch?"

"Humph. Such as it is. There're people who show up, but work is a four-letter word to some of them. I guess I can't entirely blame 'em. We get the folks who were vacationing here when it all went down. City folk mostly. Don't know nothing about a cattle ranch or how to work on one." Opal shakes her head.

"They're assigned to us until they can work out a new deal for something better. Why, we've had probably a hundred *workers* in the last three months. Oh, there's a few who give it their all, really try. We've got a couple of women helping with the small dairy herd.

They're working out fine. A few men trying to be cowboys. You saw 'em when you and your husband were getting your horse-riding lessons?"

"Maybe? But, truthfully, um, I wouldn't know a good cowboy from a bad one. I can barely ride a horse and, well, we know how the horse riding worked out for Leo."

"Ain't that the truth, dearie?" She gives me a kind look. "Do you want to talk about it?"

My eyes well again. "He's doing— " I bite my lip and drop my head.

"There now." She gives me another squeeze. "Ah, now. Not going so good, huh?"

I make a sound, something between a laugh and a cry. "Not too well. We . . . he's . . . unhappy. Tired of not being able to do anything."

"Yup. Men can be that way. And I reckon your man's used to doing what needs doing."

"He is. Exactly. He's always been a hard worker. Too hard sometimes."

"I heard they're holding his spot on the Guard. Yours too. Must be a relief."

I kick my toe into the dirt as I shrug. "He's with Lieutenant Paul today, on some kind of tour."

"And you're not with them?"

"I wasn't invited. I don't— " I shake my head.

"Feeling you made a mistake? You wanting to go home?"

My nod is so slight I'm not sure she sees it.

"Can't, though, right? You either have to find a Volunteer Unit or join the National Guard?"

"The thing is, our commitment to the Volunteer Unit is only one year. The Guard is eight."

"Mm-hmm. Didn't you know that going in?"

"I didn't."

"Ya didn't?"

"No. Leo said three years. And Lieutenant Paul said four years of active duty for sure, but the commitment is eight years. And we could be active the entire time if they need us."

"Ah, I see. Yup. I remember that's how it was with my daughter too. She went in the Army, like her cousin Braedon did—he's my sister Pearl's youngest boy. Made a career of it, he did. Rita thought she would, too, but it wasn't for her. She did four years and said she'd had enough. The next four years she could be called up but wasn't actually in the Army. Well, she was . . . but anyway, I understand. Eight years is a long time. And you're probably thinking you might want to have babies and— "

"Oh, no. I wasn't thinking that. Not with . . . " I shake my head much harder than needed. "Not now. Working in the hospital, I see how hard it is on people."

"You've lost hope?"

I rub the spot between Gerry's eyes. "I don't know. Maybe."

"Forgive me for asking, but do you know Jesus?"

I let out a laugh at her forwardness.

Opal laughs alongside me. "My mama always said I wasn't good at beating 'round the bush. But truly, Katie. Do you?"

"I do." I give a hesitant nod. "Um, I do, but . . . "

"Are you like the church in Laodicea?"

"Pardon?"

"You're neither hot nor cold. Just lukewarm."

"I . . . I guess." I look down at the puppies, avoiding Opal's gaze.

"You know what happens when you're lukewarm? He'll spit you out. But you can change that. He stands at the door and knocks. It's up to you to open it—again. You can be victorious and sit with the Father on the throne."

I let out a sigh. "I can't remember the last time I read my Bible. We haven't found a church to attend. We tried a few when we first moved here, but after Leo's fall, we haven't even talked about it again."

"We have our own service on the ranch. My son Shawn leads it."

My eyebrows shoot up. Shawn, who I haven't heard utter more than a dozen words, leads their church service?

Opal let's out a throaty laugh. "Doesn't seem like he'd be a preacher, huh? But my Shawn, he's on fire for the Lord."

"Your daughter, you mentioned she was in the Army. Does she live on your ranch?"

"Yup. She and her husband both. They skedaddled over from Sioux Falls when the planes went down. Left that night. They both worked from home, so figured it made sense to head for the ranch, just in case."

"Good thinking. We didn't leave Kansas until the day after the bridges went out. The cyberwar started when we were on our way. Made things like getting gas a challenge. Of course, it was easy compared to now."

"God was looking out for you. Still is. The ranch is a distance from here, but you and Leo are welcome to join us for service anytime. We meet at eleven thirty on Sundays and have lunch afterward. In fact, if you have time off, you can stay over. A few days respite might be nice."

I look at the puppies and shake my head. Opal raises a hand. "You can bring the little ones, though I do suspect you'll be finding homes for the other three soon."

"Yes, soon. It's about time, I think, but . . . "

"You'll miss them."

"I will. It's been a lot of work, especially the first few weeks when Leo was hurting so badly and they needed so much. But now . . . " I lower my voice. "They still need me."

"But Leo doesn't?"

"He doesn't seem to. We were arguing a lot. Now we don't even talk to each other. I don't know. I'm not sure what we're going to do."

"Are you praying about it?"

I shake my head.

"Let's start there." She removes her arm from around my shoulder, straightens her body, then gives my hand a squeeze. "Our Dear Heavenly Father, we come to You today asking a special blessing on Katie and Leo. Help them find their way back to You. Help them find their way back to each other.

"Your Word tells us older women should be an example to the young women. It's our duty to help 'em. I've seen the love Katie and Leo have for each other, the way they work together. Help them remember that love and companionship. It's through You and You alone all good things come. We pray these things in the holy name of Your most precious Son, Jesus, amen."

I wipe my eyes. "I hope—no, I *pray*—God can help Leo and me. Right now, it feels almost hopeless, like there's nothing we can do."

"I'll continue to pray for you. We can pray at our services, too, if'n you'll allow me to share the troubles."

"I don't suppose it's much of a secret. Everyone at work seems to know, though they don't say anything. They raise their eyebrows and make tutting noises. The lieutenant also knows."

"How'd they find out?"

I shake my head. "Not sure. Captain Williams and Nettie do house calls on Leo. When Leo and I are together, it's easy to see there's a problem. Lieutenant Paul stops by on a regular basis, too, so . . . " I lift my hands. "Thank you for praying for us, and please do continue to pray if you are willing. Are you meeting Shawn somewhere? Can I walk you?"

"He's around the corner."

I try to think what business or market is near here. "Oh?"

"I thought you and I might need a few minutes to chat, so he's waiting for me. I asked him to go out of sight so you wouldn't feel pressured to rush our talk."

"How'd you know I needed to talk to someone?"

"The way you were sitting here, looking like the weight of the world was on your shoulders. Give it to Him, Katie. God can help you with your troubles. If'n you let Him."

Chapter 21

I check my watch and bite back a sigh. The time continues to drag. I shouldn't complain about there being absolutely zero activity at the hospital. With Crystal Harrington discharged, as well as the little boy brought in for overnight observation yesterday because he passed out, it's wonderfully quiet.

We've already done about everything imaginable to pass the time. The rooms are shining and aseptic. It does genuinely surprise me how clean we're able to keep things here. We worked hard at our Bakerville clinic to keep a sterile environment there, too, especially in the room we used for surgery, but we didn't have near the supplies and cleansers as we have here.

The military has provided many items we need, and the distillery making the hand sanitizer and other alcohol-based disinfectants is a blessing.

Putting the final syringe in the appropriate bin, I mark the quantity on my inventory sheet before getting up from my squat. With the cleaning and inventory done, I guess I'll clean the bathrooms next.

The bathrooms are usually taken care of by the janitors. However, today, the janitor on duty is working outside. With the hospital empty, Captain Williams decided it would be a suitable time to add to our wood supply. Some of the other nonmedical, off-site staff are splitting and stacking wood. As October ends, there's a continual chill in the air.

This building was designed with central heating and all the modern conveniences of an electrified world, which, of course, we no longer have. When they decided this would make a suitable location for an emergency medical clinic and alternative hospital, it took some basic reconfiguring to convert it to something that would work in our new power-free world.

One excellent feature of the modern building are large windows on both sides, giving each room plenty of natural light during daylight hours. Solar panels were salvaged from a nearby building to give us a small amount of light at night in the surgical suite and the examination room.

The EMP destroyed the system, but the panels weren't affected, and some very smart people were able to cobble something together to allow us to collect power when the sun is shining and store it in big batteries. Although we're able to store power, the system isn't large enough to light the entire building. We use a variety of lanterns and lights in the overnight rooms.

Small woodstoves were added to the patient overnight rooms, the offices, and the breakroom. Because of the mess created by heating with wood, the treatment rooms didn't get stoves, but vents were added to the walls to facilitate heat traveling through the building.

The bathrooms were reworked with compost toilets, solar showers, and large thermoses for warm water, along with alcohol hand sanitizers. There's no on-site kitchen or cafeteria. Workers bring their own food, while an off-site kitchen provides food for any overnight or multiday patients. Laundry is also done off-site. It isn't a perfect setup, but it seems to work well. Thankfully, we'll soon be fully staffed again too.

We received word yesterday that Chastity Morrow will be our new doctor. With Bruce Blake living in Newsome's home, Chastity will share housing with Nettie and her roommate, a nurses' aide at one of the nearby care centers. Chastity should arrive in the next few days.

When I asked Nettie what she thought about getting another roomie, she gave me a tight smile. She said it went fine when Chastity stayed with her when she was on her visiting doc rotation.

But there was something else, a look on her face I couldn't quite decipher. Nettie seemed to want to say more but didn't. I didn't ask.

Nettie is a super private person. We've worked together several months now, and I've probably told her way more than I should about my life before the Black Hills, but I know little about her. She's from a small town in Kansas but wouldn't even give me the name of the town. She did receive a letter, and I assume it's from family, but I don't know anything about them. I guess, if she wanted to talk about it, she would.

After my visit with Opal the other day, I've been making a point of reading my Bible. I had a moment of panic when I couldn't find it, thinking I'd put it in the bottom drawer of my nightstand. It was actually under the bed, covered in dust.

Exactly how long had it been since I'd even opened it? Before the hunting trip, for sure. But even before Leo fell and our world seemed to shift, I'd gotten out of the habit of reading scripture, of praying. Well, other than a short "God please help me" petition. It used to be different. Leo and I would not only read and pray separately but together also. Now we do little as a couple, especially nothing as intimate as praying together.

"Ready for a break?" Nettie leans against the door to the treatment room. "I've about had it with straightening. How about you?"

"I thought I'd clean the bathrooms." I give a shrug. "Since everyone else is filling the woodshed."

"Yeah. Even Jesse is out there now too. They'll bring wood inside to fill up the back storage room. Makes things easier when it's storming. Let's have our lunch, then we'll see what to do next. I'm enjoying this quiet." A look passes her face as she slams her lips shut. "Yikes. I'd best not say things like that. We'll get a rush."

We've only taken a few steps toward the breakroom when the front bell dings. With wide eyes, we share a look and shake our heads. Nettie puts a hand to her forehead. "Cursed, I tell you. Cursed."

"Hey, Dr. Wolff. Private Burnett." Lieutenant Paul lifts a hand. "You've got mail."

"Me?" Nettie and I both ask at the same time.

"Yep. Both of you."

My heart accelerates as my face splits into a grin. "From home? Bakerville, Wyoming?"

He shuffles the two letters, handing one to each of us. "Looks like it."

"Thanks, Lieutenant." Nettie gives him a brilliant smile, which he returns, their eyes lingering on each other. "We're going to have our lunch break. Join us?"

"Better not. I've got a few more letters to take around."

"I didn't realize you were in charge of the mail." My gaze stays on the letter my fingers are caressing. It's from my sister Sarah. The impulse to rip it open is strong. I force myself to lift my head and focus on the lieutenant.

"I'm not usually. I saw these and a few others belonging to friends." He looks at Nettie again. "So, here I am."

Still holding his look, Nettie gives a nod. "It's nice to see you."

He lifts a hand and does something with his fingers, resulting in a truly awkward motion. He must realize he looks silly, as his hand quickly returns to his side. "Uh, yes, you also. I'll see you later?"

She nods again. His neck is red, with the color creeping up to his rather prominent ears. "Uh, mind if I go out the back? I'm heading that way next."

Nettie gives him a bright smile. "Sure. That's fine."

"Okay, then. Well, see you later." He speed walks to the back of the building.

Nettie keeps her eyes on him and is rewarded when he turns at the door and lifts a hand.

Once he's out the door, she grabs my arm. "Lunch is going to be so much better with letters from home."

"I didn't know you and Lieutenant Paul— "

"Know what?" She raises her eyebrows at me. "There's nothing— not really."

"Mm-hmm. That didn't look like nothing."

She waves a hand. "Lunch and letters. Then . . . maybe we'll discuss the lieutenant."

We scurry off to the breakroom. I make my way straight to the table, not bothering with my locker or my food. My finger is under the lip of the envelope flap, ready to rip it open, when the bell on the front door sounds. I smirk at Nettie. "Maybe he decided to join you for lunch."

"Help! We need some help here!"

Already moving toward the door, Nettie's eyes go wide. "Guess break is over before it started."

I stifle a sigh and tuck my letter in the pocket of my shirt. I'm stepping out the door when I hear Nettie exclaim, "Bowski? What happened to you?"

"I'm fine—mostly. It's Harrington. He's outside still. Where's your medic?"

Nettie turns and catches my eye. "I'll get Jesse." I nod as I sprint for the back door.

Swinging the door open, I squint at the brightness of the autumn day. My breath catches at its crispness. Scrubs aren't known for their warmth. Jesse Talbot and his group of woodcutters are easy to find, thanks to the noise from the axes and splitting mauls, along with the jocularity of the wood stackers.

I cup my hands around my mouth. "Jesse! We need you!"

The noise stops instantly. In the quiet, I yell again. It's mere seconds before Jesse hands his axe off to another worker and darts toward me. Back inside, he reaches for the hand sanitizer strategically attached to the wall near the door. "What do we have?"

"Not sure. Ritchie Kasubowski—I don't know if he's hurt—he said Harrington was outside."

"Harrington? Oscar Harrington?"

"I think so."

Jesse shakes his head. "I need a proper washing. I've got pitch on my hand from the wood."

I look over him. He also has wood shavings in his hair and on his clothes. At least he'd changed from his hospital scrubs into street clothes before going outside to work. "No time."

He gives a grim nod as we go for the gurney. When we reach the front entrance, I hold it while he goes through. Oscar Harrington is on a homemade stretcher—something like a travois or sled—the ends being held by a man who is vaguely familiar, but I can't name. The unnamed man has a large cut across his forehead.

Oscar's eyes are closed, and his left leg is wrapped in a blood-soaked bandage. A swatch of fabric is secured above the dressing, tourniquet style. Nettie's already kneeling at his side, pushing a cloth onto the leg.

I look at Bowski, who has a bloody bandanna around his right bicep. What have these men been into?

Nettie keeps up the pressure on the leg while I help Jesse get Oscar onto the stretcher. Bowski does his best to assist with his good arm. The man holding the travois keeps it steady, allowing us to have less of a distance to lift Oscar. Once he's on the gurney, Nettie orders us to move and for Bowski and the other man to follow.

As soon as we have Oscar in an exam room, Jesse declares he needs three minutes to get dressed back in his scrubs. Nettie tells him to hurry and to radio Captain Williams while he's at it. She looks over her shoulder at Bowski. "How long ago did this happen?"

Bowski looks to the other man, who shrugs. His eyes are slightly glassy and he's weaving. I point to the chair and order him to sit. He gives a slight nod, grimacing as he sinks into the chair.

Nettie sees and shakes her head. "Katie, check his vitals. Make sure he's not going to fall over and crack his head *wide* open."

"I'm not." The man leans forward and puts his head between his knees. "Take care of Harrington. I'm fine."

Nettie's brow knits. "Just sit. Bowski, you too. Katie, get your gloves on. We need to get this bleeding stopped."

Jesse returns, looking crisp and clean in his fresh scrubs. "Williams is on his way. Where do you want me?"

Nettie has him evaluate Bowski and the other man while I continue to work with her on Oscar and his leg. The bullet seems to have gone through the thigh, directly above the knee, but we can't yet tell if it hit the bone. With the amount of blood, Nettie thinks the damage might be severe. "Good tourniquet. Otherwise . . . "

Captain Williams arrives in what may be record time, already in scrubs with his lab coat over the top. Nurse Jacquie Haley is also with him but not yet changed out of street clothes. She excuses herself to redress while Nettie gives Williams the report.

After quickly checking Bowski and the other man—who Williams calls Zed—the doctor and Nettie whisk Oscar to the surgical suite. Jacquie will assist with the surgery while Jesse and I tend to Zed's forehead and Bowski's arm.

Jesse takes care of Zed while I handle Bowski. Although Williams called Bowski's wound a graze, it's deeper than what I'd expect. A good chunk of skin is missing from the outside of the arm. Half an inch more, and the bone would've been shattered.

"Nasty, huh?" Bowski's staring at it as I cut his shirtsleeve away.

"It's not pretty. How'd this happen?"

He lets out a heavy breath. "We got a tip."

"A tip? About what?"

"The thieves. About a job they were planning."

I look to Zed, now realizing how I know him. He's one of the Citizen Patrollers, like Oscar and his dead father. Zed had even been over to the Harringtons' home before; I remember waving to him and Oscar as they sat on the front porch. "You found them?"

"We did. They won't be doing any more thieving . . . or murdering."

I'm sure it's a consolation to Oscar to find the men who broke into his home and killed his dad, but at what cost? His own life? "Just the three of you?"

"Nah. Shaw and a couple of others are still on the scene. We were sent here."

I lift my chin toward the other man. "Why didn't someone not injured bring you?"

"We needed to get Oscar here. They had . . . they'll follow shortly."

He's barely finished speaking when the front doorbell sounds. My eyes meet Jesse's.

He gives a nod. "I'll check."

Shaw and another man follow Jesse into the room. Jesse jabs a thumb toward Shaw. "They want you to ID the men."

"The robbers? I don't . . . they were wearing ski masks when I saw them. At night. In the dark."

"But you did see them?" Shaw asks. "That's what you said the night Mr. Harrington was killed."

"I did, yes, but . . . " I lift my shoulders and shake my head.

"We have their bodies out front. We need you to take a quick look."

"Go ahead," Bowski whispers. "It's important."

"Let me finish here."

It takes me ten minutes to finish cleaning and bandaging Bowski's arm. Jesse's taken care of bandaging Zed's head. The two injured men follow us out to see the dead men.

The dead are in the back of a wagon with their heads at the tailgate. Shaw drops the gate and moves out of the way. "Well?"

I look over both of them. "I don't— " I shake my head. "I don't think so. These aren't the men from the Harringtons' home, the ones who killed Mr. Harrington."

Chapter 22

Shaw steps closer to me. "You're sure they aren't the ones who killed Mr. Harrington? Take another look."

"Sorry, no. Don't you remember my report? One had a red beard—neither of these men do. The other was tall. These guys don't seem very tall."

"Tall like Shaw?" Bowski points to the deputy, who's a good six inches shorter than him.

"No . . . taller. Um, I think more like Leo—like my husband. Taller even. His head was well above the fence. But maybe not as tall as you." I motion to Bowski.

Zed mutters something that sounds like, "No one is as tall as Bowski."

Shaw groans. "You're sure? I mean, it was dark, right?"

"Yes, but there was moonlight. I'm sure one of them had a red beard. These guys don't have red beards." I motion to the dead men in the wagon without looking at them again. "It's hard to tell the height of these guys for sure, but . . . how long is the wagon?"

The men look at each other before Bowski says, "I think it's eight by four. It's a replica of a Prairie Schooner. We could find a tape measurer, but I'm with Katie, these guys are both under six feet tall."

Shaw flares his nostrils. "I thought you said you had a tip?"

Bowski straightens to his full height as his eyes bore into Deputy Shaw. "I *did* have a tip. These guys are part of the gang of thieves. I'm sure of it. They may not have been the ones who broke into the Harringtons' that night, but they're part of it."

The two men stare each other down for several beats. Shaw breaks first, shaking his head. "Well, maybe losing these two will change things. But if not, we're going to keep at it and shut the whole thing down. And you— " He jabs a finger toward Bowski. "You're going to tell me what you know. Your black-market buddies are part of this, I'm sure of it."

"I've been straight with you, Shaw. I don't like what's happening any more than you do. I've known Oscar and his family a long time.

Losing his dad was bad, but if Oscar doesn't pull through . . . " He lets his sentence drop off as a hard look covers his face.

"You will not go vigilante on me." Shaw pokes at him again. "Everything goes through me. Got it?"

Bowski tilts his head. "Whatever you say."

Shaw ignores Bowski's smirk as he nods. He raises his voice to the man on the wagon bench. "Take them to Hugo. He can get started on the burial preparations. I'll have someone notify the families."

I turn back to the dead men, looking them over again. "You know who they are?"

Shaw nods. "Know them both. The one on the left used to own a muffler shop up the road. The other one's his brother-in-law."

"Were they . . . thieves before?"

Zed scoffs. "Doubtful. I'm beginning to wonder if they're even thieves now. Bowski, you sure about your information?"

"I'm sure." He says the words, but I don't hear the conviction of earlier. "These two are neck deep in it. And, Zed, you were gone a long time. Before the EMP and after. Things have changed. You've only been back a few months. Nothing is like it used to be. No one's the same as before."

"It's true." Shaw slams the gate of the wagon with a loud bang. "Lots of people aren't the same as they were before. This world—it changes folks." He smacks his hand on the wagon twice before telling the driver to head out. "I'm going to stay. I want to know about Oscar." He glances toward me. "I've sent someone to get his wife."

Back inside the hospital, Jesse and I wash up and then clean the room we were working in. The men wait in the lobby. I'm almost finished restocking when the bell on the door sounds.

Jesse and I share a look. "Might be one of them going out." He shakes his head as he strides toward the door.

I turn back to the supply cart. "Let me know."

It's less than a minute later when Jesse calls my name. I turn toward him. He's leading a man to the exam table.

My man.

Jesse's holding a cloth up to Leo's face. There's blood everywhere. Both arms are secured in makeshift slings. I recognize one of the slings as a dishtowel from our kitchen. I want to rush to his side, to hold him and cry out. But with the way things have been between us, I force a calm voice—professional, even. "What happened?"

Lieutenant Paul, who I hadn't noticed, answers, "Found him sitting on a curb."

"I'm okay." Leo doesn't sound okay. His voice is nasally as he talks through his nose, and he definitely doesn't look okay. "I just . . . tripped over one of the dogs."

My eyes go wide as I look toward the door, hoping to see my dogs.

Paul raises a hand. "They're fine. I took them back to your house. Put them in your laundry room before I brought Burnett here."

I swallow hard. "Thank you." I give Paul a nod before looking at Jesse. "His arms?"

"They're fine," Leo mutters. "My face is the problem."

"Figured we'd better take precautions," Paul says. "Leo says they're fine. Still seemed smart to immobilize them."

I purse my lips and bob my head. "Yes. Good. Is he still bleeding?"

Jesse moves the cloth away from Leo's face. His nose is obviously misshapen, and his lip is cut. "Some. The lieutenant helped him apply pressure, so it's pretty slow."

"I'll get him cleaned up." I look at Leo. "We had an emergency. It may be a bit before Nettie or Captain Williams can see you."

Jesse sets the bloody cloth, which I now recognize as also coming from my kitchen, on the counter. He gives me a nod as he steps toward the door. "I'll check on the doctors." He shoots Lieutenant Paul a look. "You want to wait out with the others?"

Alone in the exam room with Leo, I get a tray of supplies and then clean off the blood from the uninjured parts of his face. The lip is still spotting blood, but the nose isn't bleeding. There's also a small cut below his eye. He winces when I touch it.

"Sorry."

"It's okay. I guess I see now why Williams didn't want me getting out much."

"He didn't want you walking the dogs either." There's more snap to my voice than I intend. "You were only supposed to take them to the backyard. Let them do their— " I let out a sigh and shake my head.

"I know." Leo's voice is small, young sounding. "I just, I thought it'd be okay. I held all the leashes in my right hand, and we were fine. An instant later, Tank saw a squirrel. He went berserk. I tripped and couldn't catch myself—other than with my face." He attempts a smile, which ends in a painfilled grimace.

"Hold still. And don't talk. You'll make your lip bleed again."

He gives a stoic nod.

I set my jaw, biting back angry words. How could he be so careless?

With his face cleaned, I step back and look him over. The knee of his pants is ripped. I move it slightly and tend to a gravel-filled scrape. I roll up the material so the doctors can check his knee, then do the same on the other leg, which looks fine.

I gently remove his right hand from the sling. I check the circulation, motion, and sensation of his hand and then clean up the scrapes. I move to the fingers of his left hand and repeat the process. The wrist cast has its own layer of blood on it, but wiping it removes the worst.

His lip's bleeding again, so I get clean gauze and press it to it. Leo's staring at me, but I avoid his eyes.

"I'm sorry, Katie," he mutters around the pressure of the gauze.

"Don't talk."

I feel his knee press against my leg. Certain it's an accident, I choose to ignore it. When the pressure lightens and then happens again, I realize it's intentional. My mouth tightens into an angry line as my eyes narrow.

I shouldn't be mad he's touching me. Until recently, it would've been the norm—*expected*. But now . . . we barely even look at each other, let alone have physical contact. His knee touching my leg is almost an insult. "Don't, Leo." My voice breaks on his name.

"I'm sorry, Katie. I wasn't . . . I wasn't thinking."

Moving my leg away from him, I accidentally apply more pressure than necessary to the spot on his lip, causing him to take in a sharp breath and pull his head back. "Sorry. You need to hold still. And don't talk."

It's only a few more minutes before Jesse returns to the exam room. "Williams and Nettie are finishing. I told them about Leo. Someone will be in shortly."

"Oscar?" Leo asks.

Jesse gives a single dip of his head along with a slight smile in response. While still respecting patient privacy, Jesse gives enough for us to know he's still alive, possibly even doing well. Good news . . . for now at least. A gunshot wound—any type of severe injury—in today's world can seem fine one minute and turn deadly the next.

Even Leo tripping and using his face to break his fall could've resulted in injuries too severe for our current technology and supplies. Stella and her herbs, along with her knowledge of using them, combined with the military keeping us stocked, has saved countless lives. But until production returns in mass quantity, we have nothing in surplus. Using supplies for Leo can mean someone else won't have them when they need them.

Jesse gives Leo a quick look up and down. "Need anything?"

"The lip keeps bleeding. It'll need a few stitches. Other than that . . . " I lift my shoulders. "A couple of teeth seem loose. His nose is cut."

Captain Williams strides into the room. "Well, Burnett, what do you have to say for yourself? Heard you were quite the mess when you arrived. Looks like Katie did a fine job cleaning you up."

"She did, sir." Leo's words slur around the gauze.

I step aside, taking the gauze pad with me, as Williams begins his exam. "Get me fresh packing, please." The doctor nods toward another package of gauze. "Looks like the lip will need a couple stitches. And maybe one above the brow."

When I have the fresh gauze, he gives a nod. "Dab when you notice it oozing. I'll get your husband checked over, then you can stitch him up."

My stomach turns watery. I've done countless stitches on various body parts, but facial stitches are something else. The skin on the face is thinner than other areas and may leave a deeper scar after stitching. Do I have the skills needed to not leave my husband looking like a scarred freak?

Williams spends many minutes on Leo's face before moving to his legs, leaving the arms for last. "Well, son, you're going to look rather rough for a few days. Your nose is definitely broken. At least the bleeding stopped. The cut across the bridge needs a steri-strip—skin's too thin there for stitching. Katie can take care of it. After you're not bleeding all over the place, we're going to put a splint on the front teeth to hold them steady while they heal."

I scrunch up my face and try to envision the procedure. This building was well equipped with dentistry supplies, which have been stowed for use by the traveling dentist.

Captain Williams was the one who suggested using this former dental office as the district medical center. His brother's wife is a dentist and was one of the owners before everything fell apart. The offices had been closed the week of the first attacks, with most of the staff volunteering as part of a medical and dental mission in East Africa.

When planes were grounded, they were stuck there. With the escalation of attacks . . . he hasn't heard from them since the cyberwar took out the phones. Not only did William's sister-in-law go on the mission, but so did his brother and nephews. He said he was actually glad they were gone, since as far as we know, there wasn't an EMP or ground nukes detonated in Africa.

Of course, we don't truly know. We've all heard the rumors of wars and skirmishes throughout the world. Some even call it World War III. But there's nothing official. Not from the president, state, or even local government.

"You're going to splint after I stitch?"

"I think that's best. I don't want to deal with oozing blood." He gives me a goofy, very undoctor-like look followed by an exaggerated fake shudder. "Too bad this isn't Pat's week. This is more his forte, but I'm familiar with the procedure." He dips his head as he refers to the traveling dentist before turning back to Leo. "The good news is I don't see any obvious damage or new injuries to your arms."

My eyes find my husband's. There's something in his gaze. A kindness—*love*—I haven't seen since before he fell.

Captain Williams snaps his glove as he slips it off and into the wash bin. It'll be my responsibility to check and carefully wash the latex gloves used today. What once was disposable is now reused as much as possible.

If the glove has a hole or is otherwise unsuitable for our use, it's put aside to be picked up by someone from the salvage crew. The gloves will be used for other cleaning or similar tasks or even cut apart and repurposed. I have several hair ties made from old latex or vinyl kitchen gloves. They aren't exactly stylish, but they do the job.

"How's your pain?" Williams asks.

"It isn't too bad."

Williams gives a nod. "Let me know if it changes. Call me when the stitches are in. Nettie is with Oscar in recovery. I'll be in my office."

Jesse follows Williams out of the room.

I turn away from Leo to set up my suture tray. Captain Williams could've easily done the stitches on his own. Him giving me this responsibility should fill me with pride instead of fear of flubbing it up. My sutures will be too large, and I'll leave my husband with an ugly scar. He'll certainly have a scar either way, but good stitching can lessen it.

"You'll do fine, honey."

I blink a few times before looking at him. "You think?"

"I know. Don't bother with the lidocaine above the brow." He gives me a smile, which puts me at ease.

Our eyes linger, making my heart give a funny little beat. It's several seconds before I turn away to finish my prep.

Chapter 23

By the time Captain Williams gets Leo's teeth splinted and it's decided he's well enough to go home, my shift's been over for half an hour. Before Lieutenant Paul left, he asked if I'd be available to walk Leo home or if he should send someone over as an escort. It was weird. Leo must have said something to him about our troubles.

I know there was a huff to my voice when I answered, telling him I could handle it. He'd given me a single dip of his chin before turning to Leo. "I'm praying for you, Burnett." He gave me a smile and said he'd see us soon.

It's well into sunset, with little residual light left, when we step out of the building. When Leo left the house to take the dogs for a walk this afternoon, he didn't take his well-stocked daypack, which means he's without a light. I have my headlamp, issued by the Volunteer Unit, along with my hand-crank flashlight in my pack.

I offer him my headlamp and help him get it into place. As expected, the thing immediately blinds me when he swings his head in my direction. Determined to not pick a fight tonight, I stifle a groan.

"Williams was happy with your stitches." Leo's voice is still decidedly nasal, and his words have almost a lisp to them from the splint on his teeth. Captain Williams said it'll improve once Leo's used to the extra apparatus. He'll leave the splint in place for several weeks in hopes of saving Leo's front teeth. "You did well, Katie. I'm impressed."

I smile into the darkness and slip my hand in the pocket of my jacket, caressing the envelope I received earlier today. I've yet to have a chance to read it and am almost buzzing with anticipation.

"I'm sorry about today."

I continue to look straight ahead, shining my light on the ground in front of us. "You know better than to take the dogs for a walk. We've talked about it. About how this exact thing could happen."

"I know."

I bite my lip to prevent any of the angry retorts I have in my head from being said aloud. I want to yell at him. Tell him what a dumb thing he did. Tell him how he could've rebroken one or both arms.

But he knows all this. He knows he got off easy with the injuries he has.

I take in a deep breath as I think about 1 Corinthians. When I finally picked up my Bible after so much time away from it, I knew the thirteenth chapter of 1 Corinthians was where I needed to read. A couple of years ago, when my mom and Jake had trouble in their marriage, Mom would begin each day by reading the same chapter. When some irritation would come up during the day, she'd meditate on the words she'd read, reminding herself love never fails.

Love never fails. I believe that, especially when God is in the middle of the relationship. I'm so tired of being angry with Leo, of him being angry with me. *Love is patient, love is kind. It does not dishonor others, is not easily angered, and keeps no record of wrongs. Love does not delight in evil but rejoices in the truth. It always protects, always trusts, always hopes, always perseveres.*

Always . . .

What happened to us? Even in the treatment room, I was so angry with Leo. When he touched me and tried to make a connection, I rebuffed him. I was easily angered, and I was certainly keeping a record of wrongs.

Things have been so difficult between us for the past several weeks, and I'm scared to let my guard down. Scared that, as soon as I think we're working our way back to each other, he'll get angry and I'll end up hurt again.

Love always trusts. I wish that were true. I wish I could trust we're going to be okay, trust I'm not going to get hurt again. I want to believe in us, to believe God is here, helping us through this difficult time.

"I mean it, Katie. I truly am sorry. And— " he swallows loudly " —not only about today. I'm sorry for the last several weeks. I, um . . . I found your Bible. Saw you've been reading it again. And what you've been reading."

My spine stiffens. His words are soft, *kind*, but I prepare for the next sentence. Shortly after I returned to work, when he was well enough to stay alone, I'd suggested we go back to reading our Bible together, to finding a church to attend—things we'd been doing for our entire marriage until we found ourselves stranded in Rapid City when the rest of the Volunteer Unit left.

Stranded.

Why would I think of it as stranded? We chose to stay here. We chose to become a part of Camp Rapid and officially join the National Guard.

No . . . Leo chose it.

The realization hits me so hard I stop walking. Leo goes several more steps before also stopping. He quickly looks to the side to prevent the headlamp from hitting me in the eyes. "Katie? You okay?"

"Um, yes. I just . . . " I shake my head and resume walking.

When I'm parallel with him, he moves by my side. "I'm glad you're reading your Bible. I didn't realize how much I missed being in the Word until I started reading where you'd marked. We . . . " He lets out a sigh. "I'm messing things up, aren't I? You and me. We used to be *good*, but now . . . I'm sorry, Katie."

Tears sting my eyes. My throat is tight when I mumble, "I'm sorry too."

We're on our block when Leo speaks again. "Paul said you got a letter?"

My hand moves to my pocket again. "From Sarah."

"What'd she say?"

"I don't know. I didn't get a chance to read it." I clear my throat. "Maybe we could read it together?"

Even in the dark, I sense his body relax. "I'd like that."

Once inside, I help Leo remove the headlamp and take his jacket off before I release the dogs from the captivity of the laundry room. As always, they're yipping, squirming messes and fill my heart with joy. I quickly usher them to the backyard before there are any messes left on the floor.

When the five of us return inside, the puppies make a beeline for Leo and his chair, squirming around his legs. He rubs each of them with his calf, making sure to keep his arms and face away from them, while I add small pieces of wood to the fire to get it going again. There are still coals, so it should start.

"Did you hear Shaw when he popped his head in?"

I lean back on my heels and glance in Leo's direction. "About Tank?"

"You think he's ready? Grown enough to do well without his littermates?"

A snorting giggle escapes me as I add a few more limbs to the fire. "Tank? He's a tank. He'll be fine. It's Gerry I'm not so sure about. Will he be okay without Tank? Without the girls?"

"You have homes for the girls?"

"Opal found good homes." When she and I talked that day on the bench, I could've easily passed off Ari and Ali, let her take them to their new homes. Maybe if I had, Leo wouldn't have fallen. Of course, if Leo would've followed the doctor's orders he'd been given . . .

The all too familiar anger and irritation begins.

Love is patient. Love is kind. It is not easily angered. Love never fails. I swallow the irritation. I purposely set a kind expression on my face before looking at my husband. "I'm off work the day after tomorrow. I'll ride my bike to Opal's and let her know the pups are ready."

"We could send word with Lieutenant Paul or one of his men. They've been on patrol near there."

"Patrol?"

"There have been some issues in outlying areas."

"I'm surprised the lieutenant and his men weren't part of the thing Shaw and Oscar did today."

"Paul was surprised too. When we saw Shaw sitting in the hospital, there were some definite sparks when Bowski said why they were there. I didn't hear the follow-up since I was in getting fixed up when Paul went back out. Say . . . how about the letter?"

"You want to eat first? We have some vegetables I can boil and mash."

He makes a disgusted face, followed by a face of pain from contorting his stitches and nose. "In a bit. I'd like to hear from home."

I give him a nod and move to the small desk against the wall where we have a letter opener. Paper, even envelopes, is a rarity and will be reused. There's a lady in Rapid who makes paper, but it isn't the fine, smooth product we were used to. It has a distinct handcrafted quality to it with bumps, ridges, and odd colors. She makes it out of wood pulp and even recycled paper; although, recycled paper tends to be kept at homes to use for fire starter as opposed to passed on to her for paper making.

My hands shake as I slice open the envelope. I make a point of keeping it folded—trying not to peek at the words—as I make my way back to our couch.

"You want to . . . should I sit next to you?" Leo motions with his chin to the empty spot next to me.

A warmth begins in my toes and travels upward as I nod. "Would you? I'm excited to read this, but I'm a little apprehensive too."

He rises from his chair with a grunt. "I'm getting stiff and sore. I guess that's what happens when falling flat on my face."

"What hurts? Something new?"

"Nah. Williams checked me out good. Nothing to worry about. He said I'd be sore."

"We have some willow bark tincture and comfrey salve . . . plus a rice heating pad. I could put it on the stove and get it hot."

"Maybe later. Let's read the letter first." Leo sits beside me, closer than he has been in weeks, with our thighs even touching. "Ready?"

I open the letter, and the round loops of Sarah's carefully formed words fill the page. "Read it aloud? Or do you want me to hold it so you can see?"

"Aloud, please." He leans back on the couch.

I clear my throat. "There's a date on it, September 16. That was the day . . . " I tilt my head and raise my eyebrows.

"Yeah, the day you harvested a nice-looking buck." He gives me a wink.

My heart does a little flip. It *was* the day I harvested the buck. I haven't even thought of that much, about the pride I felt over doing something to help the people of Rapid City. One deer wouldn't stretch far, but it was a contribution to living here, to being a part of the community.

I send my husband a grateful smile before turning back to Sarah's letter. *"Dearest Katie and Leo, I'm sure you're surprised to hear from me so soon."*

"Have you received other letters?" Leo interrupts.

"No, nothing."

"Maybe it's been sent and hasn't made it?"

I give a nod and return to the letter. *"I didn't want to wait too long before sharing our sad news. Sad yet expected."*

My heart is pounding as I look at my husband. He gives a nod as his knee presses against mine. I clear my throat again. *"We sent out a fall hunting party. They found the remains of Tate and Keith."*

"Oh." My eyes fill with tears. "I thought maybe we missed something from the last letter she sent. She's right. It is sad, but . . . " I lift my shoulders.

"Right. Them being gone so long, and with the winter . . . " Leo's head bobs several times. "Still, I'm sure it's difficult for Sarah. Although, she and her children will now have closure. What else does she say?"

I blink several times before the words of the letter come into focus. *"Mike and Tim, along with Evan Snyder, convinced a few others to help them get their bodies out of the ravine. As near as they could tell, Tate probably slipped and fell. His left leg was broken. Keith probably went down after him, and neither were able to get back out. We don't know if something happened to Keith, maybe a heart attack or something. They're home now. We buried Keith next to Lois. Tate is next to him. Our little graveyard is getting too full.*

"We had a nice service, with many from Bakerville attending. Everyone was exceedingly kind to Karen and me. There were lots of sad eyes directed toward baby Tate, Marc, Sissy, and Andy. Even though we all expected Tate and Keith to have perished, to have confirmation brought up all the old emotions. And not only over losing my husband and father-in-law, but our moms too. Karen said she felt it, that Lois's death was also a sharp, fresh wound.

"I feel badly for me and my children, but in some ways, I feel worse for Karen. Losing both her parents and her brother leaves her almost entirely alone. Not really, of course, since she has the children and me. Baby Tate is her blood, but she treats Marc, Andy, and Sissy as her true nephews and niece also, even though they're adopted. Plus, I know she feels the same about Tony and Lily, loving them just as much.

"Jason and I talked about postponing the wedding—"

My mouth drops open and my eyes shoot to Leo.

He lets out a hoot of laughter. "I knew it. Tim and I were laughing about that before we left. I told him I figured we'd have a new brother-in-law before Christmas."

"You did? I talked to Sarah, and she said she didn't ever want to get married again."

"Yeah, well, it makes sense. With the way things are, they need each other. Plus, with all the kids—six between them—it does make sense. Want to keep reading?"

I tilt my head to the side as I use my finger to find the spot I left off. *"Jason and I talked about postponing the wedding, but we've decided to just do it. I mean, like I said, it was no surprise. I knew a year ago, when we moved up to the mountain, I was a widow.*

"Lois knew it too; she knew her husband and son were gone. She believed Keith would be waiting for her in heaven. She also took comfort in knowing Tate may have once again been walking with Christ. He'd spent many years angry with God, convinced He wasn't real. You know how he thought if God were truly God the world would be a different place.

"But in the weeks before he died, he began to see things differently. He started to understand God was God, Christ was Christ, and people were people. People were given free will and could often make terrible choices. Tate had been a believer as a child and into his early teen years. It was high school when he began to question Him. I think he was probably close to accepting Christ again before he left on his hunting trip. I'd like to believe he made the choice to follow Jesus before he died. Tate, Keith, and Lois are all rejoicing in heaven."

I lean back on the couch. "I pray Sarah's right, that Tate did accept Christ before he died."

"It sounds like he may have been— " Leo clears his throat and shakes his head. "If he was stuck in the ravine, he may have had time."

"What an awful way to die. Do you think they knew? Knew they would— " My nose begins to burn as my eyes fill again.

Leo shifts his body to move closer to me, and I rest my head on his shoulder. Gerry whines at my feet.

We remain nestled together for many minutes before I'm composed enough to finish Sarah's letter. There's not much left to it except a plea for Leo and me to write soon and to stay safe, along with passing on everyone's love to us.

Chapter 24

Three days after Lieutenant Paul dropped off the single letter from Sarah, he showed up at our house with an overstuffed manilla envelope, this one written in my stepdad Jake's handwriting. I wanted to rip the envelope open and get to reading, but Paul brought other news and issues to address.

"I had business at the Maher farm yesterday. Saw Opal and told her your pups are ready for their new homes. She'll connect with you when she brings in the pumpkins."

Leo cocks a brow. "The pumpkins?"

"Pumpkins, acorn squash, and butternut squash. Some of their crops. They did well this year. They'll keep some for themselves and their livestock—I had no idea cows and horses eat pumpkins. They've got beets and turnips, too, but Opal said they're waiting for a frost before harvesting so they'll be sweeter. Sure is different this year than last year. We already had six inches of snow on the ground by this time. Harvest was done in a rush."

"It was the same in Bakerville." I glance at my envelope. Did Jake write about the harvest they're having? About the weather? About how he's doing after losing my mom? Did he send this fat envelope before the one Sarah sent?

"Right." Paul bobs his head several times. "Pretty much everywhere, I guess. At least maybe we're back to a normal weather pattern this year. Anyway, she's got homes for the girl dogs, and Deputy Shaw still wants the big one. You're going to keep the small one?"

I glance to Leo. He lifts his chin. "We are. Katie's fond of him, and I kind of like him too."

"All right, then. That's good."

"Leo said there's been some troubles out near Opal's ranch?" I lean forward in my chair.

Paul lifts a shoulder. "The pumpkins. Someone was in the field, and a few went missing. We know who it was—a family camping nearby. Opal and Shawn went with me when we talked with them. She offered them lodging and work."

My eyes go wide. "Were they strangers?"

"Yep. Moved in from North Dakota. They were trying to make it farther south before winter, but their young 'un got sick. I told her we could bring them to one of the shelters in town, but . . . well, you know Opal."

I do know Opal. And I worry Opal's good heart may bring danger to her home. "How many children?"

"Three. The oldest is only six or so. Mom, dad, and another woman—a sister of one of the parents. Anyway, we'll be able to lighten the patrols there. I'm glad it turned out the way it did. Could have gone bad. In many ways."

I wrinkle my brow. "What do you mean *in many ways*?"

He waves a hand. "Opal's got a good heart, you're right about that. It's her neighbor next door—the ranch that borders the Maher's place. He, uh . . . he runs a tight ship."

Leo clicks his tongue. "Probably a smart thing in today's world."

"Sure." Paul bobs his head. "He's protecting what's his and does contribute to the reconstruction efforts. I'm just saying I'm glad his dogs didn't find the family before we did."

I look to Leo who gives a shake of his head. "What do you mean?"

"He's using his dogs as part of his patrol. He's trained them to . . . well, they're pretty brutal."

My mouth forms an *O* as the implications of the dog finding the young family becomes clear. They'd have a fight for their lives, like Leo and I did with the feral dogs. "Ali and Ari—that's not the home Opal found for them, right?"

"No, no." Paul shakes his head so hard his entire body moves. "Opal understands the need to use the dogs, she uses her own as an alert system—most people do. But she doesn't train hers to kill. Your dogs aren't going there."

I let out a sigh of relief. "I'm glad. I don't think . . . " I glance to the puppies sitting together. "I wouldn't want them to have to learn those things."

"Thanks for making the arrangements with Opal for the dogs. We appreciate it." Leo's voice still has a nasally quality to it, but not nearly as bad as it was a few days ago. With the swelling going down on his nose, it even looks somewhat normal.

Williams stopped by yesterday and agreed it's healing well enough. He checked Leo's arms, asking him to keep them slinged until he sees the orthopedist at Monument Hospital. Williams is confident Leo is healing fine but said a second opinion is a good idea. Dr. Bollinger, the ortho, will remove the casts and do a full check. Ideally, Williams wants us to wait until the middle of November to allow additional healing time.

Leo's less than enthused about remaining in the slings and casts until then.

Like Leo, I'm more than ready for his casts to come off—for him to return to a normal life, for *both of us* to have a normal life. That'll also put us closer to joining the National Guard. When Leo is given clearance to exercise and other things, it'll only be a short time until we take the oath and begin our enlistment obligation.

My finger rubs along the envelope from home. *Eight years.* Can I commit to staying here, being away from my family, for such a long time? I'll miss so much. My brother will become a man. My niece and nephews will be teens by then. And I'll miss all the babies going from infants to children. Is this really what I want?

Covertly glancing at my husband, I notice the slight happiness showing on his face. The last few days have been better between us. Not like they were before he fell, but not as bad as they'd become.

We're still stiff and awkward, and I'm careful what I say around him. No way can I tell him about my concerns over joining the Guard. I think I'm beginning to understand why Leo needs this. When he was in the Marines, he loved the camaraderie. He was hoping he'd find something similar with the Volunteer Unit, but he told me many times it wasn't the same.

He also told me how he was a fool to not stay in the Marines. How getting out and going to college was a dumb move—he should've stayed active and went for his twenty. I tried not to take it personally since, had he stayed in the Marines, we wouldn't have met.

"Shaw received another tip."

I jerk my head in Paul's direction. "Tip about what?"

"The killers—the robbers. Your red-headed man."

I narrow my eyes. He's not *my* red-headed man.

Paul waves a hand. "You know what I mean."

Leo leans forward in his chair. "What I don't understand is how no one knows this guy. A red beard—red hair isn't terribly common."

"Believe me, we know. Shaw put out bulletins to all the districts. We've talked with lots of people, interviewed every redhead we can."

"And the tall guy? He was about— " The image of the men fills my head. The tall man. Could it have been Bowski? At the time, I didn't think so, but now . . .

"Yes?" Paul moves to the edge of his seat. "Do you remember something?"

I look over to the puppies, lying quietly on a blanket. "I don't know. My mind might be playing tricks on me."

"What are you thinking?" Leo's voice is soft, encouraging.

"You know how I said the other one was taller than you but shorter than Bowski? I'm wondering . . . well, maybe he wasn't shorter than Bowski." I shift my gaze from the dogs to my husband. My voice is almost a whisper. "Could it have been Bowski?"

Lieutenant Paul lets out a noisy breath. "It wasn't him."

I shake my head. "I didn't think so either. But now I'm not so sure. The man was tall. And Bowski was part of the group who brought in the wrong guy, remember? What if he had them kill the wrong guys on purpose?"

Leo looks from me to Paul. "She has a point."

Paul rubs a hand across the back of his neck. "It wasn't Bowski."

"I don't want it to be him either, but how can you be sure?" I end my question with a shrug.

"Shaw already questioned him. His alibi is solid. Besides, he and Oscar Harrington have been friends since kindergarten. Oscar would've recognized him—ski mask or no ski mask."

Leo leans back. "Well, that's probably true. So, we're back to . . . how hard can it be to find an overly tall man and a man with a red beard?"

"We're thinking the beard may have been a disguise. Maybe both beards."

I can't help but laugh. Somehow, the idea of disguising their beards during the apocalypse is so ridiculous it's funny.

Paul lifts his hands. "I know, I know. It sounds unlikely. But something Kirstie said makes us think it's possible."

"What'd she say?"

"The beard was long, to the middle of his chest, and seemed to have an odd texture to it. She said it reminded her of a Santa beard but the wrong color."

I lean back in my seat and look up at the ceiling, trying to remember that night. It was dark, but there was enough moonlight for me to see the men. I could easily see the red beard—not a dark auburn red but an orangey ginger red—as it hung down to the middle of his chest.

I think about the shape of it. Kirstie may be right. Where most long beards are more on the wild side, this had a perfect angle to it, ending in a point on either side. It could've been fake.

I shake my head. "I don't know. It was dark."

Paul gives several bobs of his head. "For Kirstie too. Like you, she's not entirely sure. Just an impression she got when a flashlight was swung in his direction. So, we don't really know."

"If it was a fake red beard, one of the men killed in the shootout could've been him."

"True. We don't know. The tall guy, though, height can't be disguised. We're focused on him. We've talked with just about everyone six-foot or taller since you said his head was over the top of the fence. The few we thought looked good all have alibis."

Leo exhales loudly. "Any updates on Newsome's death?"

"Another dead end. His brother-in-law, Bruce Blake, is looking for answers. So far, there's none to give him. The way Shaw says it, there's little in the way of clues or anything. You heard how at first glance they thought it was a suicide?"

Leo nods while I shake my head. "I hadn't heard that."

"Really? I thought it was part of the scuttlebutt going around? But, yeah. Hays was first on scene, called it over the radio as a suicide."

I tilt my head. "Who's Hays?"

Leo turns to me. "Zed Hays. The guy who came in with Bowski and Oscar. You fixed up his head."

"Oh, sure. I only got his first name. Jesse worked on him while I took care of Bowski. He's Citizen Patrol?"

Leo looks to Paul for confirmation, who responds with a nod. "He's new—*newer*, anyway. Moved here recently from— " He looks to Paul again, who shakes his head this time.

"Don't know for sure. He used to live in the area. Had family here but had moved before the attacks. Made it back late summer. Anyway, I'd best be going." His gaze travels to Leo. "You still look like a mess."

"Yep. But I'm doing okay. Looking forward to being fully healed so I can join you in the Guard."

Paul gives a wide smile and a dip of his head. "Same. You'll be a good fit." He glances toward me. "You too. I know you have some concerns about the duration of service, and I get that. Especially with you not being from here and with mail being so spotty. We all pray things will return to normal sooner than we think, and travel will become easier. Then it won't be such a burden to be away from your family."

Does he genuinely believe that? Or is he just saying what he thinks I want to hear? I strive for a neutral expression. "Maybe."

There's a few more minutes of small talk, along with him petting each of the dogs, before he leaves. Leo turns to me and waggles his eyebrows. "Let's see what Jake has to say."

My heart is pounding in anticipation of news from home. Letters may be all I'll have of my family for the next eight years. My eyes fill with tears as I carefully slit the large envelope.

Chapter 25

Jake's letter is one of seven in the well-stuffed envelope. There's also a letter from each of my three sisters, my friends and mentors Belinda Bosco and Kelley Hudson, and our neighbor Doris Snyder. Since we'd received the letter from Sarah with the news of finding Tate's and Keith's remains, we decide to start with her letter, believing it was written before the other.

The letter from Sarah is dated September 10, six days prior to the one we received, and is full of joy as she shares about the children and her anticipated Christmas Eve wedding to Jason Hatch. She says, at first, she and Jason were simply friends, helping each other with the children and both grieving the loss of their spouses, along with Sarah still mourning our mom.

Jason lost both his parents a few years ago, and he understands the sadness. One day, something changed. Sarah can't even put her finger on what it was or exactly when it happened, but she knew they could have a future together.

Her letter has tidbits of information about other things happening in the community, including the return of Rochelle Bennet and PJ Cameron. They'd left back in March, when we were still living on the mountain, in search of Rochelle's son who was away at camp when the attacks started.

Sarah says they found him but had an incident—which she doesn't go into—on the way home. He was injured and lost an arm. He seems to be doing well. Rochelle and PJ are now married. She adds, "*No surprise there. They make an excellent couple.*"

"She's right," Leo says. "PJ and Rochelle are good together. He's a good guy. Hard worker. And with all she's been through, she still has her wits about her."

"Poor Rochelle. She has been through a lot. Too much. I'm glad she found her son, but it's sad to have him hurt so badly. Which letter do you want to read next?"

"You pick."

I rifle through, searching for Calley's letter. Her penmanship is tiny, trying to fit as many words on the single page as possible. She's even used the margins and added words at odd angles. Her letter is newsy, adding more details about Sarah and Jason—she thinks they're a good couple—along with extra info about Rochelle's return to the community.

Calley details how the incident that took Rochelle's son's arm was caused by Fred Lassiter. He was Rochelle's estranged husband. Well, that's not exactly correct. He was Rochelle's captor who forced her to marry him. Calley assures us Fred won't bother Rochelle again; she killed him.

In addition to bringing her son home, Rochelle also brought two very pregnant young teens, two younger girls, and two boys—one of which is a toddler. Calley spends a full paragraph sharing what she knows about the situation of Rochelle finding them at what she refers to as a camp full of child soldiers.

I look at Leo. "That's terrible. I can't even imagine using children as soldiers. Not here, anyway. I know it happened in other countries, but not in the US."

He scrunches his mouth and shakes his head. "It's happening in several places. Paul told me about a place he heard of where most of the adults were killed, and the kids took up arms." He looks toward the ceiling. "I can't remember where he said it was, though. Somewhere not too far away."

"Terrible. Truly terrible. I'm glad Rochelle brought those children back to Bakerville. But Calley mentioned there's others still at the camp. What about them?"

"I don't know, honey."

My stomach does a little flip over him calling me *honey*. I give him what I'm sure is a doe-eyed sappy look. Our gaze holds for several beats, my heart pounding, before he leans in and kisses me. It's light and feathery, barely brushing my lips. It's also perfect.

After he pulls back, I return to the letter. There's more info about other people we know and Calley's suspicion there may be another wedding before long—Kelley Hudson's daughter Sylvia and PJ Cameron's nephew Dax. That one makes me snort out a laugh. Talk about an unlikely couple! I like both of them, but it's terribly difficult to imagine them together. Leo chuckles along with me. "Maybe it's true, opposites actually do attract."

After finishing Calley's letter, I suggest Kelley Hudson's next so maybe we can get more of the scoop on Sylvia and Dax. Kelley's letter isn't the newsy, almost gossipy letter Calley sent. She talks about their day-to-day work and how they're preparing to go back up the mountain for winter with a goal date to begin the move October 1.

The couch squeaks when Leo leans back. "They're already there. Have been for a month now. She mention their harvest?"

"Let's see . . . " I go back to the letter and quickly read through a few lines. "Here it is. *We're once again rich in sugar beets to get us through the winter. There was also a wonderful pumpkin and potato crop this year, along with lots of field corn. We were concerned that with having to hand till and plant everything, we wouldn't get the yield we needed, but it seems God has looked out for us.*

"Of course, our numbers are much smaller now with many—like you and Leo—joining the Volunteer Unit or moving away. And of course, the number of deaths we've had in the last year weigh heavy on our hearts. I miss your mom every day, as I'm sure you do also."

My voice becomes squeaky, and my nose begins to burn as I read the last sentence. I clear my throat and cough, trying to compose myself.

Leo scoots closer to me. "Imagine I'm wrapping my arm around you right now." His voice is low and husky. "I'm hugging you and understand your sadness."

I cry harder as I lean against him, being careful of his slinged arm. Having lost both his parents when he was right out of high school, I know he does understand the sadness of losing a parent.

But no one can know the guilt I feel over my mom's death. I should've known what was happening with her. I should've been able to get her the help she needed early enough to make a difference. If there was some hope of treatment, she wouldn't have gone on the last mission. The one where she fell, paralyzing herself. She'd—

"Katie? You okay?"

I wipe my nose on my sleeve with a loud, disgusting sniff. "I guess. Sometimes it seems so . . . new. Like my mom just died and all the pain is fresh and raw."

"Do you think being here has helped? I know you were miserable in Bakerville with so many reminders of her. Is it easier being here?"

My heart starts pounding too hard, and my eyes fill again. I consider lying to him and telling him it is easier. I'm surprised when I whisper, "No."

He stiffens. I lift my head slightly so I can see his face.

His jaw tenses. He swallows. "Are you happy here?"

"I'm— " I stop and consider my response. My voice is a whisper. "I miss you."

He sighs again, this time letting the air out through his mouth. I smell a hint of garlic on his breath from our lunch—spaghetti squash with a vegetable-based sauce—as he turns in my direction. "I'm still here. I'm sorry, Katie. I know things haven't been easy. I'm . . . I'm trying."

Where his words should make me happy, instead a surge of anger courses through me. I lift my chin and stare straight ahead, not risking looking at him for fear I'll say something I shouldn't. *He's trying.*

I close my eyes and let the words from 1 Corinthians wash over me. *Love is patient. Love is kind. It does not dishonor others. It is not easily angered. It keeps no record of wrongs.* I let out a breath. *It keeps no record of wrongs.* I need to let this go and allow us to begin again. *Love never fails.*

I clear my throat. "Should I keep reading? There are a few more paragraphs from Kelley."

He nods and tells me I should. It's not until the final few sentences when Kelley talks about Sylvia and Dax. She doesn't go as far as declaring they're engaged but says she thinks they're serious.

When I finish Kelley's letter, which ends with her wishing us all of God's blessings, I notice Tank is up and roaming around. I set the package of letters on the side table. "Give me a minute to take the dogs out before we read more."

"I'll go out with you. In fact, why not bring the letters? We'll sit outside and get some air while we read the next one."

"With as cold as it is, we won't want to be out there too long. I'll get our coats."

Bundled against the November chill, we sit on the bench and lean back against the picnic table. I pull out Jake's letter first, then decide to save it for last. I'll read the one from Belinda next.

Belinda Bosco is in charge of the medical team in Bakerville. She was the one who invited me to be a part of their crew and was my main instructor. Belinda was a nurse for years before returning to school and becoming a surgical nurse practitioner.

Before our world fell apart, she worked in nearby Prospect alongside a doctor. The doctor was one of many dead when the hospital caught fire. Belinda's approach to teaching was very direct, and she used the philosophy of see one, do one, teach one. I'll admit, it worked well for me. The new training Williams keeps mentioning sounds a lot like what I learned through Belinda.

I have Belinda's letter open and am staring off at the dogs. I give a shake of my head before redirecting my attention to the letter. Belinda's letter resembles training. She talks about medical procedures they've encountered and challenges me to come up with a treatment plan in a return letter. She asks about my training here, if it's continuing or if they've relegated me to doing menial tasks. I laugh aloud.

"It's almost like she knew about Newsome," Leo says.

"Well . . . I may have mentioned him in my letter to Jake, the first one I sent."

"Have you written recently?"

"After your fall. I told them what happened. I haven't written since I've gone back to work. Since Newsome, um, died."

"Doesn't sound like they're putting as much effort into finding his killer as they are for Mr. Harrington's."

I bob my head. "I thought the same thing. Maybe it's because the robberies continue? They're trying to stop those so no one else gets hurt, and . . . well, Newsome was one person. More of an isolated event?"

"Maybe. But it sounds like Bruce Blake will keep pushing them so they don't give up on finding Newsome's killer. I wasn't a fan of the doctor— "

"At least he was nice to you."

"He wasn't nice to you. That put him on my 'not a fan' list. Even so, I'm with Blake on this. He deserves justice. I also think it's obvious whoever killed Newsome knew what they were doing, to make it look like a suicide." He motions with his elbow at the letter. "Belinda say anything else?"

We finish her letter, which has one more medical plan for me to analyze, then move on to Angela's. She talks a lot about my nephew

Gavin—her son—and the other children. Sarah's baby, Tate, is crawling and Calley's baby, Mollie, loves to laugh.

She gives details on each of Sarah's adopted children, along with Tony and Lily—Sarah's future stepchildren—and our brother Malcolm. He will be twelve in a few months. As bad as I feel for me and my sisters over losing our mom, I feel even worse for him. He's so young.

Angela claims he's looking forward to moving back to the ski resort for the winter, though he thinks it'll be strange to be there without our mom, Leo, and me. Of course, being home is strange too.

Angela says she doesn't share Malcolm's enthusiasm for moving to the mountain. She knows it's the best choice for safety and security, but she'd rather stay in Bakerville proper. She hoped, with the military coming in with new law and order, they could stay on the homestead. Maybe next year. Or maybe she'll even be able to go home to Casper sometime. She'd love to go home, but she also wants to be with the rest of the family.

There's a little more about their day to day and how she feels about all of it. In the final paragraph, she talks about Sheila Stapleton. Sheila is Calley's sister-in-law. The two were remarkably close before the attacks, but with everything that's happened, Sheila pretty much shut down. It became especially concerning when her mom was killed last January.

Belinda and Kelley essentially put Sheila on suicide watch, moving her into the small cabin we used as a medical clinic so she was never alone. During that time, she also trained for the medical team.

When Leo and I left, Sheila was doing better and no longer considered suicidal. She was still working with Belinda and doing well with her studies. Angela believes, in the last few weeks, Sheila seems to be doing better than ever. She's almost like a new person, even a pleasure to be around.

"That's . . . unusual." Leo gives me a goofy smile.

I suppress a full laugh and make a weird sound. "Indeed. Especially for Angela to say so. You know how difficult it is to enjoy being around Sheila. She's so— " I shake my head " —uptight."

After Angela's letter, we move back inside. Only Jake's letter is left. I don't know why I decided to save it for last. Maybe I'm afraid of what he's written, that he shared how much he misses my mom and I'll end up a crying, blubbering mess.

Even though he does mention my mom, the letter is decidedly upbeat. He talks about his parents and how well they're doing. Neither is looking forward to another cold winter, but they're cheerful enough about it.

When my letter arrived, it gave them hope they'd soon hear from their son Robert—Jake's brother. He lives in California, or at least he did before the attacks. With the declaration of California being uninhabitable and part of the Wastelands, it's assumed he's been moved out. Jake knows his mom and dad continue to pray for Robert, his wife, and their children.

Jake understands how they feel. When he got my letter, it was a celebration. The idea things may be returning to some semblance of normal is wonderful, and being able to stay in contact is amazing.

He finishes with, *"We pray for you and Leo daily. We know you are doing what you were called to do at this time, yet we still miss you and count the days until your commitment is over and you can return home. Please give our love to Leo."*

My voice cracks as I read the final words. Even though Jake didn't come into my life until I was almost ten, he's always been a dad to me. I know he loves me and wants the best for me. The letter he and the others are responding to was sent in the middle of August, a few days before the Volunteers were asked to leave South Dakota.

The letter I sent after Leo fell off his horse gives all the info about the Volunteers and us switching to the National Guard, along with the new commitment that will require. I can imagine Jake's disappointment over reading we'll be gone longer than the one year expected.

I just don't know if being away from my family for so many years is truly the right choice.

Chapter 26

"It's snowing. Want to see?" Chastity Morrow asks, wiggling her eyebrows as she pokes her head into the exam room. She bounces up and down a few times on the balls of her feet. "C'mon. It's beautiful."

"Really? Give me a sec. I'm almost finished."

"Hurry. This'll wait." She motions around the room and gives me a wink. "Doctor's orders. See you out front."

I laugh and shake my head. "Let me lock up the meds, and I'll be right there."

Our patient, a woman in her thirties, came in complaining of urinary tract infection symptoms. She'd tried several home remedies and visited a midwife, who mixed an herbal blend for her. After a few days, things were getting worse instead of better. She brought the herbal blend in with her, but there wasn't a label of ingredients, or even dosage.

Chastity checked the treatment book that was put together for us by our hospital herbalist, Stella, then put together a new prescription. Unlike the late Dr. Newsome, Chastity—along with Dr. Williams and Doc Nettie—is comfortable using herbal remedies in place of, or sometimes alongside, commercial pharmaceuticals. They all understand the importance of these natural medicines.

Chastity finally arrived a couple of days ago to permanently replace Dr. Newsome. Having worked here prior on a rotating basis, the transition has been almost seamless. I like her. She's not only knowledgeable on all things medicine, including alternative remedies, but she seems interested in helping our hospital thrive.

Nettie doesn't seem as excited about Chastity's arrival. In true Nettie fashion, she doesn't share anything, but there's definitely something different about her.

After locking up the meds in a designated supply cart, I join Chasity outside. Standing in the circular driveway of the medical center, I lift my face to the sky and close my eyes, letting the feathery bits of cold land on my cheeks. The first snow is always amazing. I know by the end of the month I'll be tired of it. But for tonight, I'm enjoying the sensation of the cold. I wish Leo were here with me.

My heart pounds out a crazy beat at the thought of my husband. In the days since he fell and broke his nose, we've been doing better. Not exactly like we once were, but not terrible. There's still a tenseness between us that's keeping me cautious. I'm careful of what I say—not talking much about work or my day—and careful about the things I do.

A big change is our house has become much quieter. Tank has gone to live with Deputy Shaw and his wife. We expect Opal or her son Shawn to show up any day to take Ari and Ali, at which point it'll only be Leo, Gerry, and me in our house. That'll help.

In some ways, the puppies were a blessing to us, giving us something else to focus on besides how difficult things were between us. But now it's time—time to focus on our marriage and on Leo getting fully well.

The first step to his return to health is getting his casts off. Wearing the slings full time after his fall is a setback, but a necessary precaution. As planned, Captain Williams arranged an appointment for Leo at Monument Hospital with the orthopedist. Jesse will drive us in the wagon our medical clinic has use of and bring back a batch of supplies.

I'm glad Jesse is taking us. When Williams first said he got the appointment, I thought we might need to walk. And then when he suggested taking the wagon and returning with supplies, I thought he intended me to drive it. While I probably could with a few lessons, Jesse doing it is much better.

Our appointment is the thirteenth of the month—a few days shy of two months since Leo fell off Ryder and we brought the puppies home to live with us . . . and since our marriage fell apart.

"It's lovely, isn't it?" Chastity asks, twirling around with her arms out. "But cold. Wishing I would've grabbed a jacket." She lets out a sigh. "Guess I'll go back inside. Take as long as you want out here."

"I'm ready." My entire body shivers.

She holds open the door to the medical center. "We'd best get used to it. Nothing quite like winter in South Dakota."

It's around three in the morning—three-quarters of the way through what has essentially been a quiet twelve-hour shift—and the CB base lets out a squawk. Our medic, Ryan, rushes to the base as a voice orders, "Guard Medical Center, respond."

Ryan pushes the talk button. "Go ahead."

Chastity and I move closer to the base. "We have a hostage situation. Prepare for wounded. We're sending someone for the handcart."

"Understood. Do you need a medic?"

"We have Jesse Talbot on site."

"Copy that. Standing by." Ryan shakes his head. "Wonder what's going on?"

"The handcart is in the supply shed in the back?" Chastity is already striding toward the back door. "I'm going to ask what's happening when whoever is getting the cart shows up."

"Your jacket?" I call out to her.

"Good idea." She swivels for the breakroom. "Katie, you and Ryan make sure each of the rooms are ready. Nettie and . . . " She scrunches up her face. "Which nurse is on backup?"

"Jacquie Haley," Ryan answers. "You want me to call them?"

"How far away is she?"

"Next block over."

"Wait on both until I get answers from the cart guy."

Chastity pops into the breakroom and quickly returns with her jacket, practically sprinting for the door. She hits the door hard, causing the bell to ring obnoxiously.

Ryan and I share a look and a shrug. I spin on the ball of my foot. "I'll finish room one."

"I'll take care of two."

It's only a few minutes until the back doorbell lets out a deep bong. I step out of the exam room and peer down the hall.

Chastity is standing on the rug, wiping the snow from her coat. "It's sure coming down out there. Here's the scoop. One hostage. One, um, hostage taker. Dozens of deputies, Citizen Patrol, and National Guard surrounding the home. Let's call in Nettie and Nurse, um . . . "

"Jacquie," I offer.

She dips her chin. "Right. And a medic."

Ryan lifts a shoulder. "Jesse will return with them. How about Captain Williams? Should we get him?"

"Yes, do it."

Ryan makes the radio calls before grabbing his jacket, promising he'll be right back. Since Williams isn't the doctor on call—Nettie is—he doesn't have a radio. Ryan will go to his house and wake him.

With the rooms checked to be sure they're well stocked and organized for gunshot wounds, Chastity tells me we should eat. We've just sat down with a cup of tea and our bagged lunches when the bell on the back door sounds.

I'm scooting my chair back when Ryan calls out, "It's me. Williams will be here shortly. He's going to round up a few additional people."

The front door chimes at 0530 hours. There's half an hour left of my official shift, though I know there's zero chance I'm leaving until the hostage situation is wrapped up.

Chastity lifts a shoulder and tilts her head. "Might be show time."

I follow her out of the breakroom where we've been passing the time playing Gin Rummy. Jacquie, who was sleeping in one of the lounge chairs, pops up and joins us.

Williams showed up with half a dozen people in tow, people he's picked for his new medical school training to produce additional doctors. While I know of his plans, I didn't realize he already had med school candidates in mind. The group has been in his office since they arrived, presumably beginning their training. I was surprised, and happy, to see our herbalist Stella in the group.

Ryan is already in the hall. Jesse Talbot and another man are standing by the front door.

The man is wearing a Citizen Patrol band around the sleeve of his jacket. He gives us a weary nod. "It's done. It's over. There were . . . " He shakes his head. "We won't need your services."

There's a rustling behind me as Captain Williams steps forward. "No injuries?"

The man's mouth goes into a tight line. "I was asked to let you know you can stand down. Someone will be by later with more details."

"Thank you, son," Williams says as the man spins to go. Jesse remains in place. After the Patroller is gone, the captain dismisses his trainees, telling them to get some rest and that he wants to meet with them tomorrow. "Chastity, Katie, Ryan. Why don't you go ahead and take off. The three of us— " he motions to include Jesse and Jacquie— "will begin our shift."

I feel bad for Jesse, having been at the hostage standoff for several hours and now on a twelve-hour shift. It happens, but it's still rough. I'm in the breakroom, gathering my things, when Captain Williams walks in. "Private Burnette, may I speak with you before you go?"

There's a sinking feeling in my gut as I paste on a smile. "Sure. Yes."

"In my office."

Now my heart begins to pound. In his office? He motions to Chastity, who is trying to pretend like she's not listening. "Dr. Morrow, you as well."

Chastity and I share a quick look of panic before her features smooth. She squares her shoulders. "Absolutely, Doctor."

We follow him to his office, where he instructs me to close the door. Not only is my pulse pounding in my ears, but my stomach is tight. I'm turning over the events of the night in my head, trying to figure out what I could've done wrong, what Chastity could've done wrong. Is he upset she had him called in? If so, why am I here?

"Please sit." He motions to the chairs arranged in a large circle. Instead of going behind his desk, he takes one of the metal folding chairs. Once Chastity and I are seated, he gives us a smile. "Relax. This is nothing bad. I hope you'll think it's something good. An opportunity." His gaze drifts to me. "Especially for you, Private."

My brow furrows. "Okay . . . ?"

He gives a nod. "You both know about my plans for a mini medical school. Truthfully, it's something we should've done last year, when things first went bad. But so many of us were stuck in the way things were, deciding our nurses and doctors needed schooling. Then, when you arrived . . . " He dips his chin in my direction. "I'll be honest, I was much like Newsome at first." He looks directly at me and lifts a shoulder.

"I didn't want you on our team. Especially when I heard you'd had zero medical education. You were an art major in college. I thought . . . well, I figured after a week or two, we'd transfer you to a different position. Move you to one of the care centers once I could evaluate your knowledge, make sure I wasn't passing a problem off to someone else."

My cheeks burn and my stomach gurgles. I knew Newsome didn't like me, but I had no idea Williams thought this. Did Nettie also? Were they all waiting for me to make a mistake and . . . and oust me?

"But you surprised me. All of us, even Newsome once grudgingly admitted you knew more than he expected. I'm sure he never told you that. Newsome was an excellent doctor, but we all know he had certain personality traits that were less than desirable." Williams shakes his head. "I didn't know until after his death just how cruel he was to some of the staff. Had I realized it before, I would have put a stop to it." Williams looks from me to Chastity.

"He was out of control." Chastity leans forward in her chair. "At first, I thought he was just testing me—testing Katie and the others— but I'm not so sure about that. I think he was just mean."

Williams tugs at his beard. "Perhaps. Rest assured, I'll ensure that our future staff treats people as they should." The captain looks back toward me. "You've impressed me, Katie."

The heat in my cheeks increases, this time from the compliment and from him using my first name, which is a rarity. "Thank you." My voice cracks, so I clear my throat. "Thank you, sir."

He waves a hand. "And that is why you're here. I'd like you, Dr. Morrow, and Doc Nettie to help with my school. It's going to be . . . well, I'm asking a lot because you'll do it in addition to your regular shifts."

I can't help the grin now covering my face. "Thank you. I'm not sure what exactly I can do for your . . . um, your medical school. Like you said, I'm not educated."

"That's exactly why I need you. Of the six in our first class, only one has any official medical training. Plus, Stella—as you know, she's well versed in alternative medicine and herbs. She's going to be a huge asset. They'll be starting new, just like you did. You'll be their example of what to do and, in some cases, what not to do."

Exactly what does he mean?

Williams waves his hand again. "Not to worry. I promise, you'll be an asset to our school as you help with the teaching and training. Both of you. I like this team we've built. I'm proud of having Doc Nettie, who was a medical student; Private Burnett, who had zero medical training before the collapse; and you a physician associate. You've all proven yourselves and proven you can do more than expected." He looks at both of us with a knowing smile.

"Here's the exciting thing. We're the test case. If what we do works out, it'll be expanded to other districts or— " his smile grows wider " —we'll be in charge of training for the entire area. After all, we have the space for it."

I glance around his office, but Williams shakes his head. "Not here. The office building across the parking lot. We're going to use it for the school. It'll be perfect."

Chastity leans forward in her chair. "Pardon me for asking, and I know you somewhat touched on this, but it does seem odd this isn't something already happening. I mean, Katie lived in a tiny little place, and they saw the need for training laypeople. What's the holdup here?"

"Egos, mainly. A few of us kicked the idea around, but no one genuinely believed it could work. Burnett's an example of how it can. Now, we don't expect everyone to be a Katie Burnett. Of the six people we're training, probably only half—at the most—will make the final cut to work in the hospital, to be a full-fledged physician of the apocalypse. But the others will still have valuable knowledge we can utilize."

Mimicking Chastity's posture, I also lean forward. "I appreciate your confidence in me, but I'm not sure I'm the right person for you. Well, maybe I am for the *what not to do* part. I know I make plenty of mistakes."

"But you keep at it. As hard as Newsome was on you, you've stuck with it. I heard you're still blaming yourself for your mom's death too. You thought you could have—*should have*—done more."

I chew on my lip and wonder who he's heard this from. It had to have been Leo. I haven't discussed it with anyone else.

"We've all been there," he continues. "We all have regrets and times we think we should've caught something and we didn't. Your story is important. You'll be fine. Now go on home and get some rest. I'll be adding a second schedule with the teaching assignments. I'm going to ask Leo to help with the school also. He's healing well enough it should be no problem for him to teach. Provided we can convince him to walk safely." Williams winks. "Seriously, it'll be perfect. It'll be just what he needs to get his head back on straight."

My heart fills as tears sting my eyes. "Thank you, sir. It is what he needs."

"And he's what we need. We'll use his injury for good."

Chapter 27

I have my hand on the doorknob to leave Captain Williams office when there's a knock from the other side. I look to Williams, who gives me a nod. I'm only mildly surprised to see Deputy Shaw on the other side.

He, however, does seem surprised to see me. "Sorry to interrupt."

"You're not." Williams motions with his arm. "We're finished. Everything taken care of?"

The deputy lets out a sigh. "I guess so. Sorry we had everyone called in. Thought it could be worse than it was."

Chastity leans against the nearest wall. "What happened?"

Shaw removes his stocking cap and runs a hand through his stringy blond locks. "Mind if I sit down?"

Williams and Chastity each gesture toward the circle of chairs. I'm not sure if I'm supposed to continue out the door or join them. Chastity helps me decide by raising her eyebrows and tilting her head toward the chairs.

Okay . . . I guess I'm staying.

Deputy Shaw plods slowly toward his chair, dropping heavily. He leans back and stretches his long legs out. I notice there's a smear of something on the toe of one of his boots. My eyes focus on the stain. Is it blood? I'm almost certain it is. Is it fresh? It must be.

I clear my throat. "Um, excuse me. Your boot— " I point toward it.

All eyes in the room focus on my finger, following it to the smudge on his boot. He sits up and pulls his feet in. "Sorry. I . . . I didn't realize."

I get to my feet. "I'll grab something to clean it."

After I return to the room with a couple of washcloths, disinfectant spray, and a reusable biohazard bag, Shaw cleans his boot and carefully checks the other one. When I left the room, I checked the hallway for any sign of other blood he may have brought in.

On the same wavelength as me, Chastity asked him which door he used and excuses herself to trace his path. While it's unlikely a smudge of blood will become an infectious or pathogenic issue, we take precautions with all blood and bodily fluids. Even dried blood can be dangerous. We have enough troubles these days; we don't need to add something more.

Chastity returns quickly, saying Jesse swapped out the rug as a precaution, but the floor was fine.

With Shaw's boots cleaned and his hands also scrubbed, he settles back in his chair. "I didn't even think. I should've paid better attention."

"What happened?" Williams asks.

"You know it was a hostage standoff?"

"We heard." Chastity nods.

"Did you hear who it was?"

The three of us shake our heads in unison.

"Yeah. We've tried to keep it quiet. 'Course, we all know about the Black Hills grapevine. It'll all be public knowledge soon enough." He puffs out a breath before rushing on. "Zed Hays took Bruce Blake hostage. Zed killed Bruce and then himself."

I'm sure my mouth drops open. Bruce Blake? Dr. Newsome's brother-in-law has been killed?

"Who are they?" Chastity asks.

Williams tells her about Blake and Newsome's relationship, then about how Zed was part of the Citizen Patrol team and was injured during an attempt to capture the people involved in the robbery ring.

Shaw gives a sad, weary nod. "Turns out Zed also killed Eugene Newsome. He told us everything—before killing himself."

My mouth forms an *O* as Williams shakes his head. "He told you why?"

A combination grunt and scoff escapes from Shaw. "Boy did he. And I feel like an idiot for not putting it together earlier. You all know Newsome and Blake moved here from Black Canyon? You know about the troubles they had back there?"

"You mean with the town being attacked and nearly destroyed?" Chastity asks. "Or the rumors Newsome led a campaign to slaughter all of the town pets?"

"Yeah, both. Did you hear about the man who refused to kill his dog? He kept the dog in hiding until his neighbor turned him in."

She scrunches her face. "Maybe. Sounds vaguely familiar."

I know I'd heard about it, and from the way Captain Williams is bobbing his head up and down, he definitely knows of it.

"A man was publicly executed under Dr. Newsome's orders, with Bruce Blake pulling the trigger. The man's name was Douglas Hays. Zed is his son."

I shake my head and lean back in my chair. Opal said she wouldn't be at all surprised if Newsome was killed out of revenge. He'd made plenty of enemies since the EMP, and even in the years before. He wasn't a well-liked man. Plus, I remember Bowski mentioning Zed had recently moved back to the area.

Shaw spends a few more minutes talking about the hostage situation and how everything happened, how Zed said he'd finished what he needed to finish. Turns out, the first person Zed went looking for after he made it back to the area and learned what happened to his dad was the former neighbor who turned him in. When Black Canyon was destroyed, the man had relocated outside of Sturgis. Zed found him and staged his death to look like a break-in to be blamed on the gang of thieves.

Captain Williams makes a clicking sound with his tongue. "Was Hays connected to the robbery ring?"

Shaw shakes his head. "He made a point of assuring us he wasn't. Just used their misdeeds as a cover for murder. The burglars are still out there."

Placing his stocking hat back into position, he lifts himself from his chair. "Well, that's about it. I'm heading back to Blake's house. I'll make sure the others do a better job of not tracking blood out. I think we need a refresher on dealing with bodily fluids." He directs his gaze to Williams. "You have time to give us a class?"

"I think I'll have one of my new lead instructors handle it." Williams turns to me. "Private, I'd like you to take this on."

My back straightens, and my head lifts a little higher. "I . . . uh, yes, sir. Maybe . . . could Leo help me?"

"Absolutely. Sounds like the perfect plan." He dips his chin and then redirects his attention to Shaw. "They'll coordinate with you directly to schedule it. Let's do it sooner rather than later. Our med school officially begins November 16. Once that's up and running, the Burnetts will both be plenty busy. Plus, the sergeant has an appointment a few days prior with the orthopedist at Monument. Yes, definitely sooner rather than later."

"I'll talk with Leo when I get home." I'm beaming, unable to contain my excitement at the prospect of these exciting, new things. Teaching Shaw's men is an honor. Being a part of Williams's school is amazing. And it's exactly what my husband needs. *What I need.* "I'm sure we'll be ready within a day or two."

"Good enough," Shaw says. "By the way, Tank's doing great. You all sure named him right. He's a big rolling ball of energy."

"He is at that." I let out a low chuckle. "I'm glad he's doing well."

There's only a light skiff of snow on the ground for my walk home. It's cold but not brutally so, and I suspect, if it warms only a few degrees, the snow will be gone. Definitely a much different November this year than last. This time last year, living at the higher elevation of the ski lodge outside of Bakerville, we had almost two feet of snow on the ground.

I wonder what it's like for them this year? Did they have the lovely October we had, or the cold and snow of last year? I sent off letters yesterday, sending one back to everyone who wrote, packaging them all together as Jake did. He'll make sure they get delivered properly. Each letter was crafted to respond to the individual but also contained generic information. In case they hadn't received the letter I sent after Leo fell, I shared the story again.

I told Jake about the National Guard and how we were accepted to join them, but the new time commitment is eight years. In the letter, I mentioned how Lieutenant Paul said that with Leo being a college graduate and me having so many college credits, we'd be officers if things wouldn't have fallen apart. I told him I don't know if being an officer would make any difference in how I feel about needing to serve eight years, but I do like the sound of Lieutenant Burnett much better than Private Burnett.

When I open my front door, Leo's standing by the coat rack. "Long night?"

"Very. There was . . . a situation." I plop onto the chair by the door and remove my boots.

"I've already heard about it."

I scoff out a laugh. "Of course you did. Paul stopped by? Kind of early, isn't it?"

He raises his eyebrows. "You know that man never sleeps. He'd already been to Oscar's too. Wanted to let him know about Zed. They were friends, had known each other since before Zed moved away. I'm glad he did. I was starting to worry about you." He gives me a smile.

"We went on alert, and Chastity called in just about everyone, but there was no need. It's a sad thing. You heard the whole story?"

"Think so. We can . . . um, we can talk about it if you want."

My heart does a little pitter-patter. It's been too long since he wanted to talk about something that might be bothering me. "Let me get out of these clothes and into something comfortable. I have a shift tonight, so I'll need some sleep, but I do want to talk . . . if you do."

When I return from the bedroom, dressed in yoga pants and a heavy hooded sweatshirt, the teakettle is whistling. Irritation bubbles in my stomach. Leo's under strict orders to keep his arms slinged and to avoid any lifting.

He can take the right arm out to eat, but that's it. He's not supposed to lift anything heavier than a fork or glass of water. Williams made a slight allowance and is allowing him to put in small pieces of wood to keep the fire burning when I'm at work or sleeping. But the teakettle wasn't included in the concession of allowable duties.

"Before you say anything— " he turns from the woodstove " —I asked Lieutenant Paul to fill it before he left. All I did was scoot it to the hotter part of the woodstove top. I thought you may appreciate a cup of tea."

My heart gives its crazy little pitter-patter again. "I would. Thanks."

"Chamomile?"

"The sleepy mix maybe?"

He scrunches his forehead. "Which one? Chamomile and lemon balm?"

"And lavender." I start toward the kitchen.

"I'll get it. Have a seat."

A few minutes later, we're sitting on the couch with tea and slices of bread with a smear of homemade soft cheese. I've already told Leo what Shaw told us about Zed Hays and Bruce Blake. He said it matched what he heard from Paul.

I'm bubbling over with excitement about the teaching and can't wait to tell him, but I'm a little worried about how he'll react. Will he be excited about the opportunity, or will he think Williams is taking pity on him?

I take a bite of my bread and follow with a sip of tea. "You know how I said Captain Williams brought in his new students so they'd be there to observe and act as runners or whatever we may need?"

"Yeah. Probably smart. Things could've gone very badly. You all could've been overrun with injured."

"Yes, exactly."

"Well, after it was over and he sent them home, he asked Chastity and me to join him in his office. At first, I thought I was in trouble for something, but . . . " I take a deep breath. "He kind of offered me a new job. Well, an additional job." An involuntary giggle escapes me. "Both of us."

Leo's brows furrow. "You and Chastity?"

"Uh, yeah. Her too. But I meant you and me." I give him a hopeful smile as I send up a quick prayer that Leo will see the opportunity in this and not react in anger. "He'd like us—you and me—to help teach at his new medical school."

Chapter 28

"You certainly sound happy."

"What's that?" I turn from the never-ending duty of inventorying and organizing the supplies to see Doc Nettie smirking at me, one hand on her hip and the other pressed against the doorjamb.

"I said, you sound happy. You're humming. *Loudly.*" Her smirk expands and her nose twitches.

"Was I?" My own face cracks into a grin. "Sorry, I didn't realize."

"Captain Williams said Leo was also happy yesterday when he stopped by to check how he's healing. He had a pile of books on the coffee table, planning the bloodborne pathogens class."

My smile widens. Leo started researching his class materials and borrowing books from Williams shortly after I told him about the captain's plans. "I'm glad Williams is having him teach it—having *us* teach it. It's given Leo more purpose than he's had in weeks."

"That's what Williams said. He's also kicking himself for not thinking of this sooner. We both saw Leo spiraling. We should've— " She stops midsentence when she notices I'm no longer smiling.

"Sorry. I know we should've done things differently. We thought it was enough with David . . . um, Lieutenant Paul going over as much as he could and the captain and me making house calls. And of course, you. It wasn't until he fell when we realized how bad things were." She steps fully in the room and gently closes the door. "I'm sorry, Katie. I wish you would've told me."

I pinch my face to keep the tears at bay. "Tell you about my marriage troubles?" I shake my head. "I wouldn't—I *couldn't.*"

She looks hurt. "I'm sorry we're not close enough you felt you could confide in me. I mean, I know with your mom dying so recently and moving here with Leo, it's been just the two of you. I remember when you two first got here. David said it was almost like you were one person. You were both so in sync."

"Lieutenant Paul said that?"

"He did. I think the way you two worked so well together was one of the big reasons the committee voted to take the Volunteers who wanted to join the Guard. You two were the big sell. The rest . . . well, they're important additions, too, and I understand all are doing well with their training. But Captain Williams needed you and Leo for the hospital. He and David convinced the general it was a smart idea."

"And now? Do they still think it's a good idea?" My heart beats a little faster. Leo and I *were* like a well-oiled machine. We've lost that, but maybe—just maybe—we can get it back. Maybe we can be even better than we were before.

I know I'm different than I used to be; losing my mom changed me. The guilt I felt over her death . . . I'm now beginning to realize it wasn't anything I did or didn't do. I miss her and wish things were different, but I also rejoice in knowing she's in heaven pain-free and is able to walk again.

Leo's fall also took a huge toll on us. His depression and anger sent us into a free fall and has apparently not gone unnoticed.

Nettie must see my concern. "Relax." She waves her hand. "Everyone understands what's been going on. This is a new opportunity with Williams and his school. Even if Dr. Bollinger— " A strange look covers her face at the mention of the orthopedist Leo will be seeing. She quickly recovers and shakes her head. "That's who he's seeing right? Bollinger?"

"Uh, right. He and Captain Williams are friends."

"He's the best." She practically glows as she says this. "Even without the technology we used to have, he'll give an excellent exam and will know how Leo's healing. We expect a good report. Even so, Leo still has several weeks of healing, and he'll need some physical therapy exercises to get his strength back. It'll be the first of the year before he's ready to join the Guard or is able to work in the hospital like he was."

I nod several times. "Right. We expect that. Well, I do. I know Leo's hoping Bollinger will say all is well and allow him to resume his previous duties. Deep down, he knows it's unrealistic, but he still has hope it'll be sooner than the new year."

Nettie gives me a polite smile. "And maybe it will be. I hope it is. But in the meantime, he'll be busy helping with the school. As my grandma would've said, he'll be busier than a one-armed paper hanger. I guess we will be too. And Chastity. It'll be worth it to have more people trained to work here."

I place the pile of towels I've been holding back on the shelf. "I'm confused about something with the school. Is he training medics, nurses, or doctors?"

Her laugh is hearty. "We're all confused. Williams too. I think, ultimately, he's hoping we'll have more doctors. Not necessarily from these students, but . . . well, I don't really know. But I'd certainly be in favor of another doctor or ten." She waggles her eyebrows. "I'll let you finish up in here."

She turns to leave. With her hand on the knob, she stops and half turns back to me. "Oh, and it's snowing again. My guess is we'll either continue to have a quiet day—the quietest clinic day we've had in forever—or it's all going to fall apart with people slipping and falling in the weather."

The snow from the night of the hostage standoff had melted away by midday. But that night, when the temps dropped, we had another batch of flurries along with a cold front that seems to be sticking around. My walk to work today was through about an inch of snow in places, with ice beneath.

I'm glad I wore my boots with special ice cleats added to them. The ice cleats are nothing more than tiny screws added to the bottom of the boot to give a little traction.

Last year, when we lived at the ski lodge, we mainly got around on snowshoes during the heaviest part of winter. But as spring began, people were wearing cleats on their boots to give more mobility and avoid the snowshoe awkwardness. There were a few pair of cleats in the supply store, found when unoccupied houses of our neighbors were cleared out and their goods put to community use. But there weren't enough for everyone.

Someone came up with the idea of adding screws or nails to their shoes, sort of like runner's cleats for track. They work well, and both Leo and I made sure to bring screws with us so we could turn boots into cleats for winter.

Nettie gives me a final smile before slipping out the door. She leaves it wide open, ensuring I'll hear the front doorbell. As I continue my work, the humming returns. I let out a giggle when I realize I'm doing it.

Things truly are better. Not only is Leo excited about teaching, but he's also attending a men's Bible study and prayer group—the same group who was so helpful to us in the early days after Leo's injury. Seems Lieutenant David Paul has been asking him to join the group for weeks, but Leo wouldn't go. He went to his first one last night and said it was great.

We're also planning to go to church this weekend. We'll need to go to a Saturday service since I'll be working day shift on Sunday. I'm excited about this too. It's been so long since we've gone to an actual church service, since we've worshipped with others.

I'm not back to work more than five minutes when the loud bell sounds off. I'm almost to the storge room door when I hear Nettie's greeting. "Mrs. Maher? Can I help you?"

"Hello, Doc Nettie," Opal chirps as I step out into the hallway. She raises her voice. "You too, Katie. I was hoping you'd be on shift today." She glances back to Nettie. "Both of you. That's why we came to your clinic instead of the one in our district." She gives us a smile before her gaze travels behind us. "Oh, hello, Jesse. Good to see you too."

"Miss Opal." He gives her a nod. "Dr. Nettie, you'll call me if you need me?"

"Absolutely." Nettie gives him a wave as he steps into the breakroom.

With Opal is an older woman leaning heavily on her cane and a younger woman with sunken cheekbones and dark circles under her eyes. When the younger woman's gaze travels toward me, she lifts her chin and seems to stand taller.

"This is my sister Pearl." Opal moves a hand to the older woman's arm.

"Your sister!" I step toward them. "How wonderful."

"It truly is." Opal bobs her head. "And her daughter-in-law Merissa. They arrived from Montana the day before yesterday. I allowed 'em a day to rest but believe they both need a checkup."

"Pshaw." The older woman shakes her head. "I told Opal I'm fine, but she's a stubborn one." Pearl shares Opal's barely there light-southern cadence, but her voice is decidedly lower, almost gravely. "Now Merissa, though, she definitely needs a checking out. She's been tired and sick. Got woozy a few days back an' pert near passed out."

The younger woman gives a slight roll of her eyes. "I'm fine, Mother Pearl. Tired from the traveling. I've told you."

"Mm-hmm. Ya did."

Doc Nettie turns to me. "Would you take Mrs. — " She turns back to Pearl. "I'm sorry. I didn't catch your last name."

"Weaver." The older lady waves the hand not on the cane. "Pearl Weaver."

Nettie gives a smile and a dip of her head. "Please take Mrs. Weaver to exam room two, and— " She looks to Merissa.

"Merissa is fine."

"And take Merissa to exam room three."

Merissa stands at the doorway of exam room two as I usher Pearl and Opal inside. "Have a seat. I'll be back shortly to take your vitals and ask you a few questions."

Opal looks me up and down. "Good to see you, Katie. You look . . . happy. Things are going well?"

I can't control the lift of my lips. "Much better. Thank you."

With Opal staying in the room with Pearl, I close the door and turn to Merissa. "We're just over here." I point to the smaller exam room across the hall, and she gives me a silent nod.

Inside the room, I repeat the instructions I gave Opal, telling her it'll be several minutes before I return and to make herself comfortable.

Merissa lifts her hand in a stop motion. "There's nothing wrong with me. Not really. I'm not . . . sick." She lets out a loud sigh, then whispers, "I'm pregnant. I haven't told Mother Pearl. She'll get her hopes up, and . . . " She lifts a shoulder.

The memory of Elizabeth's bloody arrival, along with her death and the death of her baby girl, rushes over me. I blink a few times. "All the more reason for a complete exam. Let's make sure you and your baby are doing well."

Sighing again, she gives a minuscule nod. "Fine. But I'm still not ready for her to know. She—my husband died recently, along with his brother. They were her only children." Her eyes fill with tears.

"I'm sorry," I say quickly as my own throat becomes scratchy. "I'm so sorry for your loss."

She purses her lips. "Mother Pearl will want this baby." Merissa looks down toward her toes. "She'll want this baby as much as I do, and if things . . . if they don't work out, I don't want her to be hurt any more than she already is." She lifts her gaze to meet my eyes. There's a toughness there I didn't notice before.

"You choosing to share is between you and her. Even in the apocalypse, we still value patient privacy." I give her a wobbly smile, then excuse myself and remind her I'll be back soon.

I've finished getting Pearl Weaver's vitals and a brief history when Nettie steps into the room. Pearl's main complaint is her ankle, which still hurts from a fall six months earlier. That along with the grief she's experiencing from losing both of her sons and her home in an attack a few weeks ago.

They were all living in Livingston, Montana. They'd been doing okay before that, though Pearl admits the winter and lack of food was difficult on everyone.

"Poor Merissa." The woman shakes her head. "The girl never could put on weight. She had a hearty appetite before. She needed it, being such a hard worker and all. She tell you she was a firefighter? Wildlands with the Forest Service. Ran the whole crew, she did. Then, with her running and riding horses— "

"Remember me telling you and Leo about my relatives who were mounted archers?" Opal interrupts, directing her question toward me.

I shake my head. "I wasn't there, but Leo mentioned it. That's pretty amazing. I have a hard enough time shooting a bow from the ground."

Opal motions from her chair toward her sister. "Katie was part of the hunting crew Shawn'n me went up to the mountains with back in September. Her husband is the one I was telling you about who fell off the horse and broke both his arms."

Pearl makes a face. "Both arms, huh? Bet that's been some fun for the both of you."

The way she says it causes me to chuff out a laugh. "Well, that's one way to put it, I guess."

"I don't blame you a bit for thinking mounted archery's a challenge. I've tried it and didn't have the knack for it. But Merissa, she's good. My other daughter-in-law, Courtney, she was getting good at it too. Our horses should be here any day." A flicker of worry crosses the woman's face.

I look to Nettie, who raises her brows. "What do you mean?"

Opal leans back in her chair, causing it to creak. "The rest of their party is bringing the horses. Pearl and Merissa arrived on the transport bus. You want to tell 'em, Pearl?"

"Not much to tell. We take the buses, or whatever vehicle the transit company has figured out how to get running, to the last stop on the company's line. Once we'd get there, we'd find a place to stay while waiting for Mr. Cox and the rest to show up. When they do, we go the next distance. Merissa and I had it pretty easy, but there were a few times poor Mr. Cox and the others narrowly escaped danger."

Opal tsks a few times. "What about— "

Pearl lifts a hand. "That was nothing." She gives her sister a pointed look. "We were fine." She glances back to Nettie and me, giving us a soft smile. "There was even one company running from Buffalo, Wyoming, to Gillette, which was pretty much a stagecoach. We were all able to stay together for that section of the trip.

"In Gillette, we found out their bus service wasn't running. They were too worried about the weather. But there was another guy with a horse and wagon who we all rode with. I'll tell you, the wagon seat was less than comfortable. He was only going as far as Beulah, which is on the Wyoming and South Dakota state line—well, not even that far.

"He went a little out of his way to get us there, since he knew there was a guy who might be willing to get us as far as Spearfish. It cost a pretty penny, but it worked out. Found another bus running from Spearfish to here. Our friends will be along with the horses shortly. Might even be at the ranch when we get back." She gives a satisfied nod.

"Is your other daughter-in-law with the horses?" Nettie asks.

"No. Just some friends. Courtney—she went west to be with her family. I can't blame her. It's good to be with family." Pearl sends Opal a pointed look as well as a crisp nod.

"I know I'm certainly looking forward to meeting Walt Cox, Pearl's new friend," Opal says with a twinkle in her eye and a flicker of her brows.

Chapter 29

Nettie and I both go to Merissa's exam room. I work on vitals while Nettie takes her history. "Your mother-in-law said you had quite the adventure getting here."

Merissa lifts a shoulder. "Could've been worse. At least we were able to find rides and Mother Pearl didn't need to walk or be on the horses. I know she'll be relieved when Walt Cox gets here."

"Have you seen a doctor for this pregnancy?"

"A nurse. We had a small medical clinic—really just a house. A nurse and her veterinarian husband ran it, and a few of us helped them out. There was a hospital in Livingston too. I'd planned to see one of the doctors there, but everything, um . . . happened."

My ears perk up at her mention of a few of them who helped out. Does Merissa have medical training?

Nettie gives her a kind smile. "I understand. Did she give you a due date?"

"We think probably April. Maybe May. I hadn't been menstruating properly, so . . . " She lifts her shoulders.

Nettie nods. "With the food rations and weight loss, many women have abnormal cycles."

When Nettie finishes examining Merissa, she scoots the rolling stool over near the exam table. "Your uterus is a little larger than I'd expect with your anticipated due date."

"I wondered. Thought maybe because I've lost so much weight it was bumping more than it should."

"Maybe. We'll keep monitoring it. Have you and your mother-in-law signed up for ration chips?"

"We did that before coming here."

"Did you tell them you were pregnant?"

Merissa gives a slow shake of her head. "Opal and Pearl were with me."

"You'll need to amend your rations. They'll give you extra and a slightly different variety. Do you plan to follow up with the clinic closer to you? Or will you continue coming here?"

"I have no idea. Opal said the local clinic is by appointment only. We came here because she was concerned about us after traveling so far. Especially with Pearl's limp."

"You're welcome to continue coming here. We have clinic every Tuesday, but any day is fine. If there's an emergency, you may need to come back. But with the weather changing, the drive may be a burden. You'll need regular appointments, so . . . " Nettie tilts her head.

"So, I'll need to tell Mother Pearl." Her pretty features change with concern. "I was hoping to wait until . . . to make sure the pregnancy is viable."

"I understand." Nettie nods.

"Excuse me." I take a step closer to the exam table. "Did you say you used to work at the clinic where you lived?"

"Some, yes. Just helping out when someone extra was needed. I had emergency medical training in the Coast Guard and as part of the wildland fire crew."

"Really?" Nettie's eyebrows shoot up. "How much training?"

"Um . . . some. Enough to know things can go wrong with my pregnancy. Especially with the way things are now."

After the three women leave, I turn to Nettie. "Do you think Captain Williams would want her in his program?"

"He might. She has more experience than some of the others. Or maybe she knows enough to work with us now. But with the pregnancy . . . " Nettie shrugs.

"You think that'll be an issue?"

"I don't know. I doubt it, but maybe. I'll tell him about her and see what he thinks. Of course, she may not be interested. Living on the ranch might be enough for her. Opal and her family can certainly use the help."

When our shift finally ends, Jesse walks Nettie and me home. With the short days, it's dark when I go to work and dark when I get off, no matter if I'm on day shift or night shift. Jesse walking me home is slightly out of his way, but I appreciate the company. The three of us are on day shift again tomorrow, and he tells me he'll be waiting at the corner for me at 0540 hours to walk the rest of the way together. We'll pick up Nettie on the way.

Leo and Gerry greet me at the door. "Hey." My husband gives me a bright smile and a peck on the cheek, while my dog squirms about my legs. "Good day?"

"Good. With good news. Opal's sister is here."

"Her sister? From Idaho, or somewhere?"

"Montana. Yes."

"The one who has a son that rides horses and shoots archery?"

"Yes, except . . . " I crinkle my lips. "He died. Both her sons but not their wives. One of the daughters-in-law is with her. The other one didn't come to South Dakota but went home to her family."

"Ah . . . that's sad."

As I'd told Merissa, we still value patient privacy, so I don't mention anything about her pregnancy or Pearl Weaver's medical complaints. My gaze travels to the coffee table, piled high with books. "Still at it?"

Next to the pile of medical tomes is an open Bible. Leo's Bible. My heart gives an extra beat. I love that he's reading his Bible again. I love we're inviting God back into our life—our marriage.

"I've got some good notes. Captain Williams was right about notetaking being good exercise. Too bad I can't read most of what I've written. Wish I would've learned to write with both hands growing up." He chuckles.

"Want me to help?" I hang my coat up on the hook and slide onto the bench. "Just let me get my boots off."

"I almost forgot. Captain Williams's wife sent over a couple of pumpkins and winter squash. She said their backyard garden produced an abundance. She bakes hers on top of the woodstove."

"Really? That's great. I've heard we should expect more pumpkins with next week's rations. Seems Opal and many other farmers have all had bumper crops. I'll put one in the dutch oven now. It should be finished before bed. And it's nice and soft. Perfect for you right now."

He shows his teeth. "Williams thinks the dental splint is working. We'll leave it on a few more weeks, but I should be fine. Maybe after Dr. Bollinger sees me, he'll put me in arm braces or splints—some kind of soft cast on my wrist and humerus. I'll be almost good as new."

"Williams say anything about your mobility?"

"He watched me write. Other than agreeing the penmanship is terrible, he seemed pleased with it. No concern about nerve damage."

Leo gives me a wink. "You did good with the precautionary measures to avoid nerve damage of my radius."

My face breaks into a grin. "You talked me through it all." My smile falters as I remember the bark that rubbed his shoulder raw. It's finally beginning to heal, thanks to an herbal treatment Stella recommended, but we're still caring for it regularly and keeping an eye on it.

He drops his gaze to his left hand, the one with the broken wrist. "Williams said we'll have some answers about the wrist when I see Bollinger. Best to let it be for now. He's right, I'm sure."

I spend a few minutes cutting two of the small pumpkins. I don't know much about pumpkin but think these may be a sweet pie variety instead of the stringy kind used for carving. Removing the seeds, I set them aside to clean and roast on top of the stove.

My mom used to do that with us when I was young. Although my heart aches, I smile at the memory. It's getting easier to remember her, to remember all the good things, without being overwhelmed by guilt. I saw what my mom wanted me to see.

She may have suspected she was sick but knew there wasn't anything that could be done for her—not in the apocalyptic world we were living in. She kept it to herself so we wouldn't worry, so we wouldn't treat her like she was sick. My not noticing her illness isn't a reflection of my medical abilities. Her good friends Kelley Hudson and Belinda Bosco—my mentors—didn't notice anything either, and they'd been practicing medicine for years.

I let out a soft sigh as a vision of my mom fills not only my head but my heart. One of the last things I drew was a sketch of her. I'd worked off a digital photo of her from my brother's tablet, which had been stowed in a Faraday cage and protected from the EMP.

Could I recreate her likeness from my memories? Do I have it in me to draw again? Maybe even do some work with oils? Artwork is such a reminder of my mom. So many times over the years, I'd finish a project and enthusiastically show it to her. Even after going away to college, I'd take photos or videos of my latest work to share with her. She was always my biggest fan.

Can I do these things again with her gone? I think . . . maybe I can. Maybe the hurt is lessening enough I can at least try.

I also need to send another letter home to let everyone know about the new opportunity we've been given to help Williams with his medical school. Maybe I'll start the letter and add to it over the next several days. It does make sense to wait before I send off the letter. Maybe Leo can even add a short note of his own.

"You okay?" Leo asks from the couch.

"Sure. Fine. Almost finished getting the pumpkin ready to go on the woodstove. I wish we had some cinnamon or something to add to it."

"We have dried basil. How would that be with pumpkin?"

I make a face. "I'm not sure I want to cook the basil with it. But maybe we can turn the pumpkin into a soup by using basil and bone broth?"

"Good idea. Sounds like the perfect food for tomorrow. You're on day shift again?"

"Yep. Last one. The next day we teach the pathogen class. The day after is our trip to Monument Hospital and your examination by the orthopedist."

A flitter of worry crosses his face before his features smooth. "Right. Monday you're on shift, and I'm teaching at the medical school. We've suddenly got a busy schedule."

I give a nod as I move the dutch oven to the woodstove. "Boy, do we!" With the heavy cast iron on the hot spot in the center, I add more wood to build up the heat. I want to get it hot quickly, then let it simmer until the pumpkin's soft. Hopefully, it'll be ready before we go to bed, but if not, I can set it on the stove overnight.

It's not cold enough yet for us to need to keep the fire going all night, so I restart the fire when I get up for work. Leo carefully—to avoid injuring his arms—keeps it burning during the day.

With the pumpkin cooking, I move to the couch. As I lower myself next to Leo, I let out a long breath. I'm tired. While I appreciate the opportunity to be part of the medical school, I truly wonder how I'll be able to keep up.

We've been truly fortunate—*blessed*—to have so many people helping us with food, wood, and water while Leo's been injured. But soon, he'll be cast-free and begin building up his strength, so we'll have to gather water, firewood, and do all the other necessities of our day-to-day life. He'll go back to work, and he'll also be teaching. How will we do it all?

"I forgot to tell you about Opal's niece, um, niece-in-law . . . Merissa. She mentioned she used to work in the medical clinic where she lived. She's a firefighter or something, so she has emergency medical training."

Leo's eyes widen as his brows shoot up. "Really? Did you tell Williams?"

"Nettie said she would. Maybe Merissa will be a candidate for the school. Or maybe she already knows enough she can be one of our medics or nurses." I purposely don't mention her pregnancy and my concern it could be an issue.

"Definitely needed." He leans back on the couch, and his right hand reaches for my left. A shiver of happiness runs through me as our flesh connects. "Katie, I'm so sorry for everything."

With my heart pounding, I scoot closer to him. Sensing my movement, Gerry whines at my feet and lifts a paw to my leg. I let out a giggle. "Feeling left out, little guy?"

"He likes to be the center of attention." Leo's voice is low and raspy. "But for now, he's going to have to wait." Leo leans toward me. "I want to spend some quality time with my wife. Time I should've been . . . " He swallows. "I've been awful. Terrible. I was so . . . lost in myself. I couldn't see how bad it was becoming between us. I'm reading 1 Corinthians 13, just like you were."

He leans closer to me, his lips near mine. "Love never fails. We're going to make sure of it."

As our lips connect, I know he's right. I may not have all the answers for our future today, but we're going to get through this together. Eight years living in Rapid City with my husband, while we fulfill our commitment to the Guard, is something I need to look at as a blessing.

Love always protects, always trusts, always hopes, always perseveres. Love never fails.

The adventure continues in Deadly Mayhem: Dakota Destruction Book 2.

Deadly Mayhem: Dakota Destruction Book 2

Coming here may have been a mistake…but going home isn't easy when the world has ended.

Living in apocalyptic South Dakota has been nothing but trouble for Katie and Leo Burnett. Not only have there been physical challenges, but their marriage has also suffered.

As winter rapidly approaches, can they come together and not only survive but thrive? Or will new challenges tear them apart?

New Rapid City resident Merissa Weaver arrives with her own troubles. Grieving the recent loss of her husband, she's just trying to get by. But she's keeping a big secret from the only family she has left…

What will happen when her secret is revealed?

Go to MillieCopper.com/Deadly to grab your book today!

Thank you for spending your time on our new South Dakota adventure.

If you have five minutes, you'd make this writer very happy if you could write a short review on Amazon, Goodreads, Bookbub, or your favorite review site.

I appreciate you!

Join my reader's club!
As part of my reader's club, you'll be the first to know about new releases and specials. I also share info on books I'm reading, preparedness tips, and more.

Please sign up on my website:
MillieCopper.com

Also by Millie Copper

The Havoc in Wyoming Series

When a series of coordinated attacks devastate the United States, the people of Bakerville, Wyoming, must come together to survive. Unfortunately, not everyone has the town's best interest at heart. Some are striving for personal gain during the apocalypse.

The Montana Mayhem Series

A group from Bakerville, Wyoming strikes out on their own while searching for the desires of their heart. Unfortunately, the road will not be easy, and sometimes the heart is hardened and deceitful. When things don't work out as they hoped, will they become stranded in the wilderness? Or will each be able to find their way home?

The Dakota Destruction Series

After a series of coordinated attacks devastate the United States, Katie and Leo sacrifice everything to help their country. But some things aren't as they seem. Is it time to go home and start fresh, or can something good come out of this terrible situation?

Nonfiction Books

Millie has penned seven nonfiction, traditional food focused books, sharing how, with a little creativity, anyone can transition to a real foods diet without overwhelming their food budget. Many of her books also include preparedness and food storage tips.

Find these titles at:
MillieCopper.com

Acknowledgments

Thanks to:

Ameryn Tucker, my editor, beta reader, and daughter wrapped in one. I had a story I wanted to tell, and Ameryn encouraged me and helped me bring it to life.

Dee from Dauntless Cover Design.

My husband, who gave me the time and space I needed to complete this dream and was very patient as I'd tell him the same plot ideas over and over and over.

Three more adult daughters and a young son, who willingly listen to me drone on and on about storylines and ideas while encouraging me to "keep going."

My amazing Beta Readers! Thanks to Barbara, Becky, Glen, Ilona, Judy, Linda, Tammy, and Tracy for your help in creating the final story. Your insights and abilities to see the things I miss are very much appreciated!

A special thank you to Kristy who gave me a peek inside the world of the Coast Guard and Forest Service. And also a special thank you to Tim, a specialist in all things that go boom, for always answering my questions and pointing out things I wouldn't even think about.

And to you, my readers, for spending your time on our new South Dakota adventure. If you have five minutes, you'd make this writer very happy if you could leave a review. I appreciate you!

About the Author

Millie Copper, writer of Cozy Apocalyptic Fiction and preparedness mentor, was born in Nebraska but never lived there. Her parents fully embraced wanderlust and moved regularly, giving her an advantage of being from nowhere and everywhere.

Millie Copper lives in the wilds of Wyoming with her husband and young son, tending chickens and attempting a food forest on their small homestead. After living off the grid for several years, they've recently gone back on the grid. Four adult daughters, three sons-in-law, and five grandchildren round out the family.

Since 2009, Millie has authored articles on traditional foods, alternative health, homesteading, and preparedness-many times all within the same piece. Millie has penned seven nonfiction, traditional food focused books, sharing how, with a little creativity, anyone can transition to a real foods diet without overwhelming their food budget.

The twelve-installment *Havoc in Wyoming* and six-installment *Montana Mayhem* Christian Post-Apocalyptic fiction series use her homesteading, off-the-grid, and preparedness lifestyle as a guide. The adventures continue with the *Dakota Destruction* series.

Find Millie at www.MillieCopper.com
Facebook: www.facebook.com/MillieCopperAuthor/
Amazon: www.amazon.com/author/milliecopper
BookBub: https://www.bookbub.com/authors/millie-copper